Sword of Kallairion

Sword of Kallairion

ALYSIA S. KNIGHT

SWEETWATER BOOKS
An imprint of Cedar Fort, Inc.
Springville, Utah

This is a work of fiction. The characters, names, incidents, places, and dialogue are products of the author's imagination and are not to be construed as real. The opinions and views expressed herein belong solely to the author and do not necessarily represent the opinions or views of Cedar Fort, Inc. Permission for the use of sources, graphics, and photos is also solely the responsibility of the author.

ISBN 13: 978-1-4621-4150-0

Published by Sweetwater Books, an imprint of Cedar Fort, Inc.
2373 W. 700 S., Springville, UT 84663
Distributed by Cedar Fort, Inc., www.cedarfort.com

Library of Congress Control Number: 2021949024

Cover design by Shawnda T. Craig
Cover design © 2022 Cedar Fort, Inc.
Edited by Valene Wood and Rachel Hathcock
Typeset by Valene Wood

Printed in the United States of America

10 9 8 7 6 5 4 3 2 1

Printed on acid-free paper

In loving memory of my husband—
Sword of Kallairion was his favorite of my books.
Thank you for all the love, support, and adventures.

Chapter One

"Krista!"

The call broke through the mellow tones coming from her flute. The instrument slipped from Krista's fingers, completely forgotten, as she scrambled to her feet. Her stomach knotted as she ran for the cottage. By the urgency in Joanna's voice she knew what was about to happen—her father was dying.

Krista bit down on her lip to keep in the sob that threatened to escape. She'd known the end was coming, but it didn't make it any easier. Her heart thundered with every footfall that took her closer to her father's side and her destiny.

Krista slowed as she reached the doorway, quietly moving past the gray-haired woman to the chair beside her father's bed. Fighting the fear that washed over her, she lifted the frail hand of the man who had once been a mighty guardian against evil. "Father." She brushed her lips over his knuckles.

Vallon looked at her with weary eyes. "I am afraid it is time." He took several labored breaths. "Kallairion will be yours." The words sounded like they were forced through thin, brittle reeds.

"I am ready," she whispered, straightening in the chair. *No!* her inner voice screamed. She was not ready for him to die or to take his place as guardian.

Her father made a slight nod to Joanna, and the woman stepped forward. Joanna paused to press a kiss on her cheek, then with her fingers she brushed back Krista's long, brown hair and began to cut it away.

Krista fought to hold back tears as lock after lock fell to the floor. Joanna finished and Krista stood, her head held high, but her chin trembled slightly. "I will be back shortly." Krista turned, going to her room to change.

"What have I put upon her?" Her father's words followed her down the hall.

Sorrow threatened to force Krista to her knees, but she pushed it back. No matter how much she wished otherwise, she knew this was what was to be. Removing her dress, she tossed it on the bed, afraid to look back at the feminine garment. That part of her life would be gone. She did not even pause to let herself wonder if it would be possible for her to return to being a woman one day. Her future was far too uncertain.

Tears slipped free, trickling down her face as she wrapped her bust flat, and then dressed in the worn breeches and large linen shirt. Krista took a deep breath and brushed the tears away. They had no place in her life. Swallowing the lump in her throat, she forced herself to return to her father's room.

Darm, the old warrior who was her instructor, guard, and friend, stood just outside the doorway. His weathered face showed concern. As she approached, he stepped back and let her enter. He followed her into the room to stand by Joanna, his wife, while this time Krista settled on the edge of her father's bed.

Vallon raised a shaky hand to her cheek. "You are still far too pretty for a boy, but Kallairion will help with the illusion." His voice broke as harsh coughs ripped away at his strength. When they subsided, he fought for breath. "Give me . . . your hand."

Krista reached out to him.

He caught her fingers, squeezing weakly. "I wish . . ." He stopped, moving her hand to the large, beautiful sword that hung on the wall above his head. "Sword of Kallairion, I give you your . . . new master. Serve her, protect her, as she upholds . . . thy honor."

Krista closed her fingers around the hilt. The sword began to glow and shimmer. To her surprise, a peculiar warmth flowed through her, followed by excitement, as if she had just met an old, dear friend.

Vallon allowed her to gaze at the sword a moment before he spoke again.

"You are master now," he gasped. "Kallairion will . . . heed your commands. It can change . . . according to your needs."

Krista leaned closer as his voice grew weaker.

"Just think of the sword and what . . . you want. A small sword, dag . . . ger," he forced the words out, "broadsword. It . . . help guide you . . . listen in . . ." he gulped a breath, "your heart . . . trust. It pro . . . tect you. Use it . . . with honor."

"I will," Krista vowed. A lone tear slid down her cheek.

"Keep who . . . secret. You are . . . only hope." His hand came up to brush at the tear. "So lovely . . ." His hand fell to the bed and the words died with him. The tear glistened on his fingertips.

Krista dropped her head and cried openly as did Joanna behind her. Even a few tears escaped from Darm, etching their way down the old warrior's weathered face.

After a few minutes, Krista straightened, brushed the moisture away with the back of her hand and stood. Taking ahold of Kallairion, she lifted the heavy sword from its hooks. "Kallairion, change," she said the words aloud.

The sword shimmered. In place of the large, ornate sword, Krista held a small, lighter one, more like the one she normally practiced with. It was exceedingly fine but in a plain, simple way. It suited her nicely, but Krista did not stop to admire it. She was in no mood. Solemnly, she slid Kallairion into her belt and turned.

"Darm." She looked to the man, keeping her shoulder stiff. "Will you dig the grave, please? As soon as my father is buried, I would like to leave."

"You are not going to wait for morning?" Joanna's voice trembled with compassion.

Krista shook her head. "I still have half a day to travel."

Krista could tell Joanna could see her pain and wanted to object, but with the simple tilt of her head, Joanna acquiesced, understanding this was her way of handling her grief.

Stepping forward, Joanna placed a kiss on her cheek before moving back.

Darm took Joanna's place, studying her. "I will see to it," the burly man said, then turned and walked out.

Krista waited until they were both gone before she dared step from her father's bedside. Her knees shook, but by the time she made it back to her room, they were a bit steadier. Still, the longing to cry ate at her. She wanted to scream. *I am not ready.*

How am I supposed to face a fallen-god when so many before me have failed? It did not help that she had known of her fate for years. She buried her face in her hands and tried to draw air into her lungs. Several minutes passed before she managed to shove down the weight of having her entire life turned upside down by what was expected of her.

Krista forced herself to take time packing her meager belongings, instead of just cramming them in her bag as she is longed to do. Nothing in her life was neat and orderly, why should her belongings be? Drawing on the methods she'd learned from her father and Darm to calm her mind, she finished packing and went out to saddle her horse, Shea. Krista ran her hands over the young chestnut mare, following the long, lean muscles, letting the familiar motion of tending the horse soothe her further. Unfortunately, the effect did not last long.

At her father's grave, a few simple words were said, and Krista stepped forward to lay a single flower on her father's wrapped body. Tears tried again to break free, but this time she held them back.

Joanna broke the silence. "Are you certain you would not rather wait until morning?"

"No. It is truly better that I face it now." Krista smiled encouragingly. "Do not worry, I will be fine."

"You have the letter of introduction?" Darm asked, referring to a letter a friend of her father's had written some years prior, ensuring that Krista would be accepted for training. Krista nodded. The man reached out and pressed the small flute she had dropped earlier into her hand.

Words caught in her throat. Reaching up, she wrapped her arms around the man's thick neck, giving him a hug. "You have taught me well. I will remember."

"Remember to conceal some of your skill. It would look suspicious if you knew too much," he counseled, patting her back awkwardly.

Settling back down, she took a deep breath. "I understand."

Darm tried to hold to the gruff manner he used in teaching. "Practice your skills. I will not be there to check on you."

"On my honor." Krista forced a smile then turned to Joanna.

The woman reached out and ran her fingers through Krista's now short hair. Tears clouded the older woman's eyes. "It is hard to send you off. It will not be easy for you."

Krista hugged her. "I love you, too," Krista whispered in her ear. She turned abruptly and in a fluid motion swung onto Shea's back. She didn't look back until she was too far away to see the cottage and the only two people she had left in the world that she considered family, then she paused.

Back there was the life of Krista. She turned to face northeast. Her new life, the life of Kris, the Champion of Kallairion, waited there. One last time, she glanced back before nudging Shea with her foot. The horse moved forward.

After three days of travel, Krista was relieved that she would reach the castle of Arlanda before nightfall. Her mind still clung to the loss of the life left behind, and the fear of being recognized as a woman. If discovered, she would be sent away and all her efforts would have been in vain.

A tingle of alertness had Krista jerking upright in her saddle. The sound of thundering hooves barely reached her before two horses with riders rounded the bend, headed straight at her. Only the hours she'd spent training on Shea's back with Darm attempting to knock her off, saved Krista from being thrown when Shea reared.

Both riders swerved. One held to the road, his horse rearing away. The rider managing to remain in the saddle. The other horse stumbled as it halted, and the rider flew over its head into the stream running alongside the road.

As Krista fought to settle Shea, the man who had remained on his horse broke into laughter at the other man. Around the bend, a third man appeared, traveling at a slower pace. He brought his horse to a stop, viewed the scene, and joined in the laughter.

"I would judge Garion the winner," the last to arrive declared. "To win a race, you have to stay on your horse. Roud will have to give you more riding lessons, Brock. Everyone should be here to see this."

Krista eyed the men. They were all only slightly older than she was. The two men who were still on their horses were fair-haired, lean and strong in appearance. A glint of quick wit and intelligence sparkled in their eyes.

The man in the water stood and shook out his wet, dark hair. He was of a heavier build and his face was red with rage. "It is not I who needs a lesson in riding, but this clod. He should not be on a horse until he is old enough to handle it."

"He is still on his horse. That is more than you can say," the same one who spoke before answered.

"Not for long." The man in the water charged up the bank. Immediately, Krista dropped her hand to Kallairion.

"Leave the boy alone, Brock. It is not his fault. We were the ones racing, and you lost," the other spoke up.

"I would have beaten you if he had not gotten in the way." Brock ground the words out.

"You have not beaten me, yet," the winner, Garion, countered.

The angry man glared, then continued up the bank toward Shea. Krista flexed her fingers on the hilt of her sword. Never had she imagined this would be the way she would first draw Kallairion. As the dark-haired man reached out and caught Shea's reins, Krista kicked out, catching him in the shoulder. Surprised, he let go, stumbling back.

"Why you . . ." Brock started forward again but was stopped as Garion brought his horse between them.

"That is enough," Garion ordered.

"I will not let him get away with that," Brock countered.

"You deserved it," Garion answered.

"I cannot let dirt like this go around kicking his betters. He needs to learn respect," Brock snapped, arrogance heavy in his tone.

With that, Krista finally spoke. "It seems to me that you are the one who needs the lesson in respect. But I have no time for this, nor am I in the mood. Just apologize and I will be on my way." Krista couldn't believe the anger she felt. All the emotions she had built up over the last couple of days seemed to boil up inside her and flow out.

The man, Garion, still between them, lifted his eyebrow in obvious amusement.

"You think you could teach me a lesson?" Brock challenged, trying to get around Garion's horse.

"You may learn a few things," Krista answered firmly.

"Stop! Brock, on your horse. That is an order," Garion declared before he turned to Krista. "You should not accept challenges from someone so much bigger than you."

"Size does not matter to the point of a sword, and I will not claim fault just to soothe the ego of one like that when I have done no wrong."

Chapter Two

The young sandy-haired man didn't hide his smile, but Krista had no time to react to the tilt of his lips.

"I will teach . . ." Brock started forward.

Garion cut him off, moving in front of him again.

"Cam, get him out of here. I will catch up with you." Garion spoke with an authority that stated clearly there would be no further objection. He watched the wet man, still cursing under his breath, mount his horse, and waited for the two men to ride off in the direction they had come before turning back to her. "Brock is not the kindest person," Garion said.

"You do not have to convince me of that."

He smiled. "Yes, well, the best thing is to avoid someone like that or, at least, try to put up with them."

Krista nodded. "I did not wish to fight him. I do not look for trouble. In fact, I would rather avoid it. But, I will not run from it either."

"No, I can see that. I apologize for Brock's behavior." Reaching down, he stroked his horse's neck.

Krista bowed her head. "I, too, must apologize." She lifted her chin. "I am usually not so easy to anger. He just caught me at a bad time. I am sorry for the trouble."

Krista now studied the man called Garion closer. At first glance, she judged him to be about her age, maybe slightly older. He was good looking. Though, being kept away from other people most of her life, she had little to compare him with, but she found his looks to be appealing. His eyes were a bright blue. His features were strong, well aligned, but they softened as he smiled. His smile pulled at her.

"Well, I am glad there are no hard feelings. I must take my leave now. Good-bye."

"Good-bye." Krista lowered her head in acknowledgement.

In an easy movement, he spun his horse around and galloped away.

Krista continued to watch after he disappeared around the bend. She let out a puff of air. "What is wrong with me?" she said aloud. "Staring after a man I will never see again. Almost getting in a fight."

She shook her head. At least, she realized, they had not guessed she was a woman, but that was the only positive thing about the situation. She had not handled herself well at all. It was not her lot to be getting into fights with headstrong, insolent, young men. That was not what her training was for.

With a gentle touch to Shea's sides, the horse moved forward. Krista's thoughts drifted to her life as it had been. She had been raised in a cottage in the middle of nowhere, hidden away and protected. Joanna and Darm were the only people she really knew, other than her father, and he had only been around the last few years.

Joanna had raised her and loved her as a mother. Darm had been her guardian since she was a baby. He'd taught her swordsmanship, hand-to-hand fighting skills, and how to ride. He also made sure she learned blacksmithing, surviving on the land, and how to play the flute, telling her that even warriors needed beauty in their lives. Besides, it would keep her fingers limber. He mixed in strategy games, forcing her to be quick and clever. *Darm had taught her everything, just not what to do around loutish blusterers,* she thought with a grimace.

Funny, she had never regretted not being raised around other people. With her training she had not had time to be lonely. Now, she realized, that one of her greatest challenges would be having masses of people around. Well, she would have to learn. She was the Champion of Kallairion, though no one else would know it. She had her duty, a duty she had been born to, like her father and his father before him.

She swallowed hard as she remembered the day when her father returned to stay. He was no longer the same robust man who had dotted her childhood memories. In his younger days, he had been as one would picture the Champion of the Sword of Kallairion—tall, strong, and full of honor—but his last battle had taken a heavy toll on his body. He had lost the movement of his left arm and walked with a pronounced limp.

She could still hear his words in her mind from that hot autumn day when they had gone for a walk. Dry leaves crunched under their feet. They had not gone far when her father settled down on a boulder, having to catch his breath.

On the slope above them, Darm stood guard, making sure no one was around to overhear. Her father had started by asking her if she had heard of the Sword of Kallairion. When she nodded, he continued.

"Then you know how it was given by the Mighty Ones when one of their own fell in greed, desiring to dominate the people of Arlanda. You know that the Mighty Ones picked a human champion, your great-grandfather, Lord Vallon. It was decreed that his bloodline would be the Champion of the Sword. The protectors of the royal family until the fallen, Kuel, was either destroyed or he destroyed the royal family, winning his rule over the people of Arlanda. Since that time, the sword has been passed three times from father to son and four from brother to brother."

His voice faltered with emotion as he described their stories with such vividness that she could have sworn she had seen them herself. She knew most had died from their battles with Kuel. Her grandfather and uncle had both died at the hands of the fallen-god.

Her father continued, pulling her thoughts from her ancestors. "And with my death, you, Krista, will be the only one left with the blood line of Vallon to command the sword. I had hoped it would never have to fall to you, but there is not likely to be enough years for you to bear a son and raise him to be the next champion. At least, my last confrontation with Kuel weakened him as much as it did me. It will be years before he has strength enough to return. That will give us time for you to grow and prepare.

"You will have at least one advantage. He does not know you are alive. Kuel is vain. It is one of his weaknesses. You can use that against him. Also, he likes to play mind games with us humans. He does this by appearing in different forms. Knowing this can help you prepare for him, to be able to see signs of his coming."

Her father paused and drew in a breath, then turned to her, taking her hand. "Krista, you are not without choice in this. No one would think less of you should you choose not to take the sword. In fact, no one would ever have to know that you still exist."

Pain filled her father's eyes. He did not want her to face Kuel. She could tell he almost wanted her to refuse, and though the thought terrified her, she also knew she had no choice. Someone would have to stand against Kuel, or all would suffer. Even at age eleven, she knew she could not live with that on her conscience.

"I will face Kuel." She held her head high, her back straight. "I will work hard and learn. And I will face him."

So she had prepared for her responsibility with her father overseeing her training. Mornings, she worked with Darm on swordsmanship, hand-to-hand, horsemanship, and whatever else he saw fit. Midday, she and Joanna studied reading, figures, and etiquette. In the evenings, she worked with Darm again before she was allowed to drop wearily into her bed. Over time she grew stronger.

Breaking through the trees, Krista's thoughts were pulled from her memories. Before her stretched a large valley, and across it, the most incredible structure she had ever seen. The castle of Arlanda was far larger than she had imagined possible. It sat on the hillside towering over the valley with the village that stretched out around the base. Its high walls glistened white in the sun. Intricately patterned gardens spread out around it on three sides until they disappeared into the forest. On one side, a gleaming pond sat nestled below the hill.

Fear gripped her. She was no longer in her protected world. She knew no one. Would she be accepted? Could she pull off the charade of being a boy?

Krista took a deep breath and steeled herself. This was her destiny. She would face it. She could do it. Leaning forward, she hugged Shea's neck and then urged the horse forward.

Chapter Three

Wide-eyed, Krista rode through the village. People scurried about, taking care of their duties without paying any attention to her. The guards also paid her little heed as she passed through the gates of the large castle wall. The yard was huge. The distinctive ring of the smith's hammer echoed on the side next to the stables. Across the yard, several men were gathered, practicing fighting skills. There were more buildings than she could imagine.

The spectacular castle towered ahead, built not for protection, but for beauty and size. Six massive rows of windows stretched across the front. The building extended back on both sides for an incredible distance. Krista couldn't help but stop and stare.

"On your way." A gravelly voice pulled her attention back.

She turned to a portly man. "Can you tell me how to find Sir Herald?"

"Second door, that side," he answered dismissively with the wave of his hand.

"Thank you." She looked ahead to where he indicated.

Krista tied her horse next to several others. She paused to brush off the dust the best she could. "I can do this," she muttered to herself, mounting the steps.

The door stood open. She stopped and peered in before entering. Her heart thundered in her chest. She rubbed a damp palm over her pant leg.

Several people moved around inside. At the far end of the hall, a group of young men exited a room, talking. One jerked his head toward her and said something to the other boys, who glanced in her direction before continuing down the hall.

It was almost enough to send her back outside. She would never be able to pass herself off as a man. Her hand brushed against Kallairion. She caught the hilt and locked on. A rush of calm washed over her, soothing away the anxiety.

Drawing in a deep breath, she forced herself forward, cautiously approaching a cleaning woman. "Excuse me." She cleared her voice. "Can you tell me where to find Sir Herald, please?"

"Open door on the right." The woman motioned down the hall.

"Thank you." Krista straightened her shoulders and continued to walk down the hall. Her boots made a hollow sound on the stone floor that echoed how she felt inside, but her resolve was back in place. She paused, then knocked.

"Enter," directed the man at the desk, his head down, studying the papers on the desk. She stepped in, studying the room and the man. He was lean-built, and she could see that his graying hair had once been black. He lifted his head. "What may I do for you?" He looked her up and down.

"Are you Sir Herald?"

The man nodded.

Krista stepped forward, handing him the letter. "I was instructed to give you this when I arrived."

Krista forced herself to stand still while he read the paper. After a minute, he raised his head and reappraised her. "It seems that we are to make you into a man. You will be taught fighting skills and book learning. After that, what you make of your life will depend on you. While you are here, you will work hard. There are rules you will be expected to follow. Breaking them will result in severe punishment. You will be instructed in all that later. For now, let's get you settled. Come with me."

As the man stood, she saw that he was much taller than she had anticipated. She nearly had to break out of a walk to keep up with his pace as they moved down the hall. She fought to concentrate on the path. Up two floors, around a couple of turns, then she counted eight doors in.

"This will be your room until you are advanced. Then you will be moved to a different floor. Or, if you are fortunate enough to be chosen as a companion to serve someone in particular, you will be roomed near them. Your advancement will depend on your skills. Any questions for now?"

"Yes, sir. Where do I keep my horse?"

"They will assign you a stall in the stables. You will be responsible for your own animal's care. Now get settled, then meet me in my room and I will explain everything else you need to know."

"Yes, sir," Krista answered as he left.

She opened the door. The room was extremely small, just enough space for the bed, a small box which served to put her belongings in, and a writing table. There was a candle sitting on the table, a blanket on the bed, and a tiny window that gave light to the room.

Krista let out a sigh of relief, leaning back against the door. She didn't care that it was small. It was private. She'd been terrified that she would be sharing a room, or worse, sleeping in a large dormitory room. That idea had scared her to death. Not only would it have made keeping her secret more difficult, but even more worrisome, she didn't know how she'd handle being around when the other boys changed.

Deciding she'd better get settled, she headed back the same way she'd come. In the stable, she was just finishing brushing down Shea when behind her she heard several other people enter. She didn't bother to look up, intent on finishing her job. Then one of them spoke.

"Whoa, Brock, when you go swimming you are supposed to take off your clothes."

"He was not swimming. It rained on him." Another voice rang out.

"What is the story? Come on, Cam," the first speaker spoke again.

"Quite simple, Brock thought he could beat Garion in a race and ended up all wet." It was a voice Krista recognized from earlier. A wave of laughter followed his words.

Brock pulled his horse into a stall next to Krista. Undoing his saddle, he shoved it off. The stirrup hit the pole next to Shea, startling the horse. It was when Krista moved to calm Shea that Brock noticed her. His anger, multiplied by the laughter he had received, exploded at the sight of her. He vaulted the divide and charged.

Krista sidestepped and stumbled back out of the stall, away from Shea's hooves. The open area gave her room to maneuver. She crouched close to the ground as Brock dove at her again. This time she came under him and lifted.

Brock's own momentum sent him sprawling into the stall behind her. He rose, shaking his head.

Krista set herself as he started to advance again, and then a form moved between them, Garion, the same man who had broken up the fight earlier. He was joined by the other man from earlier, forming a barrier between her and Brock.

"Enough, Brock," Garion ordered firmly.

"I owe him." Brock strained forward.

"What happened earlier was that you lost. You cannot blame him for that or for going into the water. It is over. Shake hands." When Brock didn't say anything, Garion added, "Now!"

Krista remained on guard the whole time. Now she relaxed, stepping forward to extend her hand.

Brock's shake was more like a slap, but it was all he offered. "You cannot expect me to apologize to this unintelligent oaf, can you?" he scoffed at the look Garion gave him. "He does not even know who you are. Bow to your prince, boy."

Krista looked to the other young man. "Prince," the word burst from her, barely over a whisper, but he smiled reassuringly. Without thinking, she dropped to one knee. "Your highness, I pledge my life to protect you."

The prince looked taken aback.

Brock's laugh rocked the stables. "That is not worth much."

Still on her knee, Krista cast a glare at the antagonist. Her head held high, shoulders straight, she met his look with firmness.

"On the contrary, it shows great worth," countered an authoritative voice coming through the door. "And who have we here?"

Krista looked toward the large man making his way through the other young men who had been watching at the door. Several scars showed through the gray stubble on his face. One long scar etched its way above one eye. His large body promised great strength, and his smooth stride left no doubt he knew how to use that strength. He was well over middle age, but his years hadn't decreased his formidable appearance.

With a quick look at the prince, Krista scrambled to her feet. She tilted her head to the older man in respect. "Kris, sir."

"You will come to call me Roud. I take it you just arrived in Arlanda."

"Yes, sir." She felt humble in front of him.

"And you have already been involved in a fight. That, in itself, does not speak favorably, but it seems you did not start it," the man continued in a low voice, sending a quick glance toward Brock. "You will learn that fighting is not permitted but, if it seems fit that one does have to take place, you are to come to me so that I can oversee it to make sure that it is a fair fight, and that no one is seriously injured, understand?"

"Yes, sir." She lowered her eyes to the ground.

"Brock, you know that, though it is known you do not always adhere to it. Now, you should attend to your horse. And you, Kris, should get settled." The man stepped back, indicating for her to leave.

Krista grabbed her belongings, bowed quickly to the prince, and headed out. Behind her, she heard Roud informing Brock he was to meet him in his room later. Then he commended the prince and Cam for their efforts to stop the fight.

It didn't take Krista long to settle into her room. She guessed right away, when she met again with Lord Herald, that he had been told what happened in the stable. He stressed thoroughly the point of not fighting. Next, he went over duties to be assigned weekly and then asked her a number of questions.

She took care with her answers, not letting him know all that she had studied and to what extent. Few boys of her status and pretended age, two years younger than her real age, would have had such training. Krista knew it would raise difficult questions, so she admitted to knowing only a little reading and figuring. After only a few minutes, Lord Herald seemed to be satisfied.

It ended that, in the mornings, she would be taught reading, writing, and figures on a basic level, and in the afternoon, she would have lessons in horsemanship and fighting. At the end of the day would be time for studying, completing other duties, and possibly, free time. More free time would be awarded when it had been earned.

Finally, Sir Herald called in one of the young men to show her around. Marcus was about her height with a bulky build and reddish hair. Krista found herself liking him immediately. He was quick-witted and enjoyed making people laugh. One of the first things he told her as they walked down the hall was that his parents were wrong to send him here for training. They should have sent him to be a jester.

Most of Kris's assignments would be with Marcus for the first week until she learned her way, which, as he was showing her around, Krista realized would take some time.

Marcus chatted as they walked. "The prince is 'Garion.' That is how he likes to be addressed. You will probably like him. He is nice to everyone and is always willing to help. Garion tries to take special interest in the younger boys and help them along. Cam is the prince's best friend and cousin on their mothers' side. He is also a good man."

"What about Brock?" Krista asked.

"So you have heard about him. Well, most of us who are younger or smaller try to avoid him. He can be mean. You will see him cozying up to the 'higher placed people'. He tries to be around Garion, but Garion does not seem to like him much. I do not blame him. Besides being mean, Brock is always bragging that he is the best in everything. It is pretty annoying."

Krista understood that.

A chime sounded in the distance. "Come on, it is time to eat. After dinner, I have some studies to catch up on. You are lucky, you get the evening free," Marcus informed her as they hurried down the hall.

"I need it. I am dead tired after my ride here," Krista commented.

"How long was it?" Marcus looked at her.

"Three days. Normally, I think it is done in at least four. I just did not want to waste time getting here."

"You came by yourself? That is quite a ways. Where are your parents?"

"They died when I was little. Another couple raised me. We lived in a cottage not far from a small village. It was good there, but I am excited that my guardian could arrange for me to come here. I have never seen anything like this castle and all the people." Krista knew that by morning her story would be all through the castle, so she went on to tell just what she wanted everyone to know.

After dinner, she returned to her room, ready for sleep. As she lay back, she went over her day. It had gone pretty well. She'd made it to the castle. Her letter had been accepted without question. No one seemed to guess she was a woman. She'd even met the prince, the main person she was there to protect.

The only bad thing was the fight with Brock. That was something she really didn't need, but she'd take Marcus's advice and try to avoid him. With as many people as there were, it ought to be easy.

Morning seemed to come early to Krista as her nervousness didn't allow her much sleep. Her thoughts vacillated between the possibility that she could get away with pretending to be a boy, to the absurdity of her ever battling a god. The latter she tried to keep from her mind. It did her no good to deal on it, all she could do was accept the fact and prepare.

So, Krista dressed with care, then picked up Kallairion. Marcus had said they were not allowed to take their own swords to class. Taking a deep breath, Krista pictured a dagger in her mind.

"Kallairion, change," she whispered softly.

In an instant, the sword was gone, and a small dagger rested in her palm. Krista could hardly believe what she saw. There was no way to explain how something so large and heavy, could shift into something so small and light. It was kind of like when she looked at herself in the mirror. She was still Krista, but yet she wasn't. She seemed more like a boy. It was confusing and comforting at the same time.

She strapped Kallairion to her leg inside her boot, finishing just as Marcus knocked on the door.

Breakfast was a hurried affair, then they headed to the study hall.

Light filled the hall through windows that ran from floor to ceiling on one side. At the back of the room, shelves held more books than Krista thought could possibly exist in one place. Around the room, young men gathered in small groups to talk. Krista immediately recognized the prince sitting on the edge of one of the long tables. Cam was one of the four men talking with him. Alone by the window, Krista noticed Brock. Fortunately, he didn't seem to see her.

Marcus leaned over. "I heard that you and Brock were in a fight at the stables. I also heard about the horse race and what happened. They say you stood up to Brock. Let me give you a warning. Do not pit yourself against him."

Krista could see his concern, but she really didn't want to talk about it. "Just a misunderstanding," she said.

"Yeah, well, I would not want to get into any misunderstanding with him."

"Believe me, I will try to keep that in mind," Krista said dryly.

"I am serious. We had a boy who left here. I am sure it was because of Brock, though he never would say." Marcus was about to say more when an extremely tall man entered the hall. Abruptly, everyone moved to their seats. Marcus pushed Krista into a chair next to him as she tried not to gape.

Lord Cowley walked to the front of the room as Krista studied him. He was sharp-featured and oddly thin. He kind of reminded her of an egret. With jerky movements he turned, surveying the room until his eyes halted on Krista. She fought not to shift under his gaze.

"So you are the new student. Rise, please."

Krista stood under his scrutiny. He was so intent she couldn't help but worry that he would see past her disguise. Her only comfort was how she had felt that morning, looking in the mirror. She had seen herself as Kris. Though her features truly didn't change much, she was different. It was a strange illusion that she didn't quite understand.

"What is your name?"

"Kris, sir," she kept her eyes focused straight ahead.

"You have had a little learning?" he questioned.

She swallowed, "Yes, sir."

The man raised his eyebrow. "Good, I hope you can keep up. I cannot slow down to nursemaid you through. Anything you have missed, you will have to ask one of the other boys to teach you." He moved on before Krista could even nod.

A few moments later, Krista realized that Sir Cowley was an interesting instructor. She also realized he was not as gruff as he had first sounded. He took time on each point, making sure everyone understood before continuing on.

Sir Cowley taught lessons on three levels at once. Krista had been assigned to the middle level. It made it extremely easy for her to keep up and gave her quite a bit of time to listen to the advanced group's lecture. Some of the things she had learned before, but others were new and fascinating. After the lectures, Sir Cowley wandered around the room helping the boys.

Several times, he paused beside her to watch her work until satisfied, then moved on. Krista took her time with her work though most of her concentration remained focused on what he taught the advanced students, which she found far more interesting. Krista had to admit she was rather bored with the work that she was doing, but it was best to play the role that had been set for her.

She was truly relieved when it was time for lunch. The best part was just to stand. After sitting on a horse for three days, then in a chair all morning, she wanted nothing more than to move.

Marcus groaned beside her. "I still did not finish. I like the figures, but the poetry is going to get the best of me. I will never get a girl if I have to impress her with flowery flattery."

Krista couldn't help but laugh. "That is not all that girls want, you know. They like sincerity and humor."

"Humor, I may have a chance at but wait until you see me dance." Marcus made a very ungraceful move that, if Krista had to describe it, she would say looked like a crane losing its balance.

Behind them came a cold remark. "You two fit quite well together. Two oafs." Brock stepped from behind the corner.

Marcus blanched as he looked at Brock, but Krista turned, tilting up her chin to meet his look straight on.

"Brock, I do not want to fight with you," Krista tried.

"No, I doubt you do," Brock answered coldly. He looked around before continuing in a low voice. "But I would not count on this being over." He rammed his shoulder into Krista as he moved past.

Krista reached up to rub the area, making a slight grimace. Her attention followed the seething young man as he walked way. Something told her it was not going to be the last bruise she would receive from Brock.

A hand came down on her shoulder. Turning back, she found herself looking up at the prince's blue eyes.

"Do not let Brock bother you." He smiled down encouragingly. "He likes to pick on anyone younger and smaller than he is. You fit both those qualifications. If he gets too rough, let me know. We will have a talk with him. I have had about all I can take of him. If it was not for the fact that he was Lord Wallum's son, he would have been sent home long ago." Then he winked at Marcus, "Let's go eat."

Krista could not find the words to answer, so she just bowed.

The prince gave a sour smile. "Has Marcus not told you? When we are studying, relaxing, or in the yard, unless it is a formal occasion, you do not have to bow to me and you can just call me Garion."

Krista found herself being led out in the hall with six other young men.

Throughout lunch, she became lost in the conversations that flowed around her. Seated next to Marcus, across the table from the prince and Cam who sat at his right, several times she found the prince staring at her with an odd expression.

When a distant bell sounded, they all pushed back and stood. As they left, Marcus whispered, "Strategy and sword practice. Compared to this, I am excellent at studies."

A few minutes later, Krista found herself sitting on a crude bench with the impressive man who had broken up the fight the day before, speaking to them as he paced back and forth. After some instruction, they were paired up and donned large, padded breastplates. With crude, wooden swords in hand, they faced off, practicing and executing the assigned moves. Krista, still partnered with Marcus, could see that he was not exaggerating his lack of skill. He was truly awkward with a sword in hand.

Roud walked up behind her. "You have a nice hold on the sword, lad. Light on your feet, that is good."

"Those are words he will never tell me," Marcus commented, making Roud smile.

"That may be true Marcus, but unless Kris grows quite a bit more, he will never be able to lift the heavy broadsword that I am sure some day you, my boy, will."

A slight beam of pleasure crossed Marcus's face.

If Krista hadn't had reason to respect the man before, she did now.

They spent the afternoon on several more moves, drilling over and over again. Finally, they stood in the circle as Roud again chose pairs, this time to go out and demonstrate. Several took their turns. Then, as the last pair, Krista and Chad were chosen to face off. Chad was sixteen, slightly taller and stockier but was closer to her size than most of the others.

At the signal, Chad moved in quickly, but Krista met him with a block. She struggled to remember the moves they had just practiced. Chad's recovery and moves came quickly, but Krista held her own. It was different from fighting Darm all the time. She had gotten so she could almost predict his moves. Chad, though, didn't have the smooth skill of Darm. It was his awkwardness that took her by surprise. When mixed with keeping moves simple, it made her work harder and have to pay more attention to her own moves than she usually did.

Chad advanced.

Krista stepped back. At the same time she raised her sword to deflect the blow, her foot came down on a rock. The stone rolled, pitching her forward right into Chad's wooden sword. Krista crashed against him. Both went down, his sword scraping her side, tearing the pad away. Her body hit the ground hard, knocking the air out of her.

The next thing Krista was aware of was hands rolling her over and a booming voice, commanding, "Give him some room." Then she felt someone loosening the padding. "Let's get this off and see how bad he is hurt."

Recognizing it as Roud's voice, she comprehended the intent behind the words. Krista forced her eyes open and grimaced as she tried to take a breath. Anxious faces collected above her. Roud and

Chad knelt beside her. Roud had lifted the pad aside and was about to reach for the bottom of her tunic to raise it.

Grasping his hand, she halted him. “I—m fine,” she gasped.

He tried to push her hand away as she fought to take several deep breaths. “Just lay still while we have a look.” The man pushed back on her shoulder as she fought to rise.

“No, truly . . . just had . . . the wind . . . knocked out of me,” she gasped again, wrapping her arm tight around her stomach as she leaned over, resting on the other arm.

Roud nodded reluctantly.

She knew he was assuming it was her pride showing through. So be it. It worked to her advantage.

“Everyone go on. We are done for the day,” Roud told the others. Several young men hung around asking if she was all right until Roud motioned them off.

Krista was relieved as they moved away. Taking a couple deep breaths, she probed her side at the bottom of her rib cage. Pain flared, but she quickly decided that nothing was broken. She was most likely scraped up and maybe had a sliver or two.

Marcus approached her. “That was some fall. You sure you are all right?”

Krista nodded.

“I thought I was awkward, but that beats anything I have ever done.”

“That makes me feel better.” Krista gave him a weak smile.

“I would say you had some help.” The voice pulled Krista’s attention to Cam, who had come up with Garion. He tossed the rock up in the air, catching it.

“What is that?” Roud asked, coming over from where he’d been watching.

“I saw it roll across the ground and he slipped on it, sir,” Cam answered, tossing Roud the fist-sized rock.

Roud eyed it. “This should not have been on the field. It is to be kept free of objects to reduce accidents in training. Well, I will have to be more careful in inspecting the field next time. You sure you are all right? Maybe you should see a healer?” His concern showed.

“That will not be necessary,” Krista answered quickly, starting to get up.

When the prince's offered hand appeared in front of her face, she caught it, letting him pull her the rest of the way up. She struggled for a second to steady herself. Marcus reached down, picked up her sword and pad, and together the group walked off the practice area. They waited for Marcus to put away her gear before heading toward the castle.

"You know, I do not think it was an accident," Cam spoke up.

"What do you mean?" Krista suddenly became alert.

"Roud is always very careful to check the field before we start. He does not want anyone hurt in needless accidents," Garion answered, with a nod of agreement from Cam.

"I would bet my supper Brock was behind it," Cam added.

"That does not make sense. He could not have been sure I would step on it. Chad could have fallen just as easily." Krista tried to shrug it off, but silently wondered if he was right.

She didn't like being so suspicious, but maybe she should be more careful. *Kuel could return in anybody's form. Could he be Brock? Could he know who she was already? Now she was being paranoid.*

Once inside, Krista had an opportunity to return to her room to check her side. A large bruise was already forming and, as she had guessed, the area was scraped, but the bleeding had already stopped. It stung as she tended it, but it would heal fast and, hopefully, not even leave a scar.

She was thankful it was not more serious. She had never thought about what she would do if she was ever badly injured. There would be no hiding her identity then. She would have to be a lot more careful from now on.

Later that night, Krista found out at supper that, though Garion took his midday meal and quite often his breakfast with his friends, most of the time he ate supper with his parents in the main hall. She also learned that, at times, he was allowed to choose someone to dine with him there, and at other times the young men would be stationed on duty in the dining hall.

After Krista finished her duties, she made her way down to the stables to care for Shea. Brushing the horse gave her time to reflect on what she had learned. Life at the castle was not as difficult as she had pictured it. It was not by any means lax either, but she decided she liked it. She liked the feeling of having friends around. Everyone, except Brock, had accepted her and made her feel welcome.

Heading back to the castle, she decided to take time to explore. She made it a quarter of the way around the castle when she came upon a side entrance to the incredible gardens. Drawn in, she moved around quietly in awe of the beautiful flowers and bushes pruned into intricate shapes. On the small pond, a couple of wild ducks swam, uninterested in her presence.

Krista had never seen anything like it in her life. The array of color and manicured perfection was breathtaking. She remembered her father describing it to her once, but she had never pictured anything this immense and fabulous. She couldn't help but press farther in, wanting to see it all.

Across the garden, Krista noticed several older ladies walking, and she realized she had not asked permission to enter. Unsure if it was allowed, she turned to hurry out.

"You do not have to go." The voice startled her.

Captivated by her surroundings, she had not seen Garion sitting under a nearby tree. Krista realized he must have been watching her for some time.

She bowed. "I am sorry. I did not mean to disturb you." She took a nervous swallow. "It is so incredible. I just wanted to see."

"You are not bothering me," he assured her.

"I did not ask permission to enter." She looked down.

"Permission's not needed. The gardens are for everyone. How is your side?"

"Fine, just a small bruise and scrape," she answered.

"Just a small one?" He cocked an eyebrow in doubt. "Why don't you join me?"

Krista looked hesitant. "I would not want to be a bother, Your Highness."

"You are not, and please, it is not necessary to address me as 'Your Highness.' 'Garion' is quite all right," he stressed, and smiled again. "It is a lot easier to become friends when you are not bowing to me."

Krista couldn't help but break into a smile at the look and the wink he gave her. Moving tentatively forward, she settled on the grass by him.

"Are you done with your studies?" he asked.

"I finished in class."

"I wish I could say that." He frowned. "I'm afraid I am not quite grasping what we have been learning of late. I missed the class when it was introduced due to meetings with my father. You catch on fast to finish your work on your first day here."

"I already understood it, so it was not hard. Besides, I am not on the same level as you are." She tried to act modest.

"Well, I wish you understood what we talked about today, but I will wait until the others come down. Maybe one of them can help me," Garion answered back.

"Others?" Krista questioned.

"Did Marcus not tell you? We meet over there at the edge of the garden in the evenings to help each other with our assignments. I do not get to meet with them all the time, but I do when I can, especially when I have a problem like this evening."

Krista looked down at what he was working on. "What is the problem?"

"It is not coming out right, and my father expects me . . ." he let it hang, frustrated.

Krista leaned forward, yearning to help. She studied his work. It only took a minute to see the error. "Your problem is not your figuring but in how you are laying it out on your paper."

He looked up at her. "You know how to do this?"

"Well, not really, but I was watching as Lord Cowley was explaining it. Imagine that this number was the amount of grain that you had, and it had to be divided up so it lasted for this length of time," she pointed out. "Each day you had to ration it out to this many people. That part you have right, but you are not figuring in these other numbers for the seed for planting and feed for animals. That changes the amount each gets each day."

"Then you do it like this." He reworked the problem through. "I cannot believe I was trying to make it so difficult. Thanks."

"I am glad I could be of assistance."

"I was told you were here under a letter from Sir Camford. That there was a trust left for you after his death," Garion commented curiously.

Krista nodded. "I do not even remember him, but my parents died in his service, afterwards, he found a kind couple who were childless to raise me, and then set this up for me to come here for training when I came of age. He has left me a great opportunity. I hope I do not disappoint him."

"Something tells me you will not," Garion assured someone he obviously thought was a zealous young man.

Krista and Garion continued to talk until the other young men came out. It wasn't long until Garion had to excuse himself. Krista stayed helping Marcus and several of the others with their work, but she, too, left the group early to turn in.

The next day, Krista was stiff when she awoke. By practice time, she could hardly move, but Roud seemed to understand. He let her work on light exercises, mainly with Marcus. The next couple of weeks passed quickly. Krista became totally accustomed to being at Arlanda. She learned her way around, as well as her duties and responsibilities.

She kept to herself to protect her secret of being a girl and became known as a loner. Which wasn't too bad. It made it easier for her to bow out when the group went swimming at a nearby lake or down to the baths.

The bath became her greatest challenge since it was an open room under the castle with little privacy. Krista found she had to sneak down very late at night when no one was up to catch her. Then she made sure she was quick and stayed covered as much as possible in case someone walked in.

After a month, Krista thought she had the routine down, then a ball was announced. Practice in the yard ended early and everyone was freed to head for the baths to clean up.

Krista hung back, taking her time as the others rushed to put away their gear. "Come on, Kris," Marcus urged when all the other boys started to leave.

"You go ahead," she returned.

"Come on, you do not want to miss any of the ball."

"I was not planning on going. I have some studies to finish."

"You never have studies. You have to go," Marcus objected.

"Yeah, come on," another boy spoke up. "You are not scared of girls, are you?" That erupted in an onslaught of more comments by others.

A wave of uneasiness hit her as the teasing escalated. She shrugged it off, accepting it as good-natured joking as they walked back toward the castle.

"I will see you later," Krista said when they reached the turn to the pools and headed for the stairs.

She'd only taken two steps away when hands locked on her.

"You are going to the baths," Sigmon, a lanky young man with straw-colored hair, called out.

"Bath, bath, bath," became a chant picked up by the other young men as she was hoisted off her feet.

Panic washed over her with the thought of being discovered. She began to fight. Hands clawed at her, and with the odds of one against eight, Krista found herself being dragged and carried toward the baths. Her fighting to get away only seemed to add to the excitement of the group.

Krista clung to every corner and doorframe they passed, only to be pried free. No one heeded her demands for release. Once inside the bath, she was forced to the ground, and someone sat on her back, while the others tried to pull off her boots. Her face scraped against the rough floor. She knew they were not trying to hurt her but, with all the weight on her, she could hardly breathe. She was aware of one boot being ripped free, then the other.

Terror filled her with a burst of adrenaline. Bucking up, she knocked the boys off her back. She tried to roll to her feet but was still unsteady when hands locked on her again. The chant of "bath" picked up once more. It crescendoed with her being lifted over their heads and flung into the pool.

Chapter Four

Krista was still struggling when she hit the water. Her shriek was cut off as water rushed into her mouth. She came up choking, but managed to get her footing and scrambled out. Panic and fear ran from her like the water as she turned on the others.

"Do not ever." She forced the words out through her rugged breathing. The chamber fell silent before her fury. She fought to control herself before she started again. "Unless I smell," she drew the words out, "or there are things growing in my hair, just leave me alone about baths, or swimming for that matter." She turned abruptly and ran into Garion and Cam who were standing in the doorway.

The prince eyed her a moment then stepped aside so she could leave.

"What is going on?" she heard Garion ask behind her.

"We just wanted Kris to come to the ball with us," one of the boys mumbled.

"By trying to drown him," Garion stated firmly.

"We got a little excited," the speaker replied sheepishly before the voices faded away.

Krista managed to make it to her room. Leaning back against the door, she fought to control the fear, pain, and rage that stormed through her. It took time for her breathing to return to normal. She was back in control of her emotions when the boys knocked on her door to return her boots and mumble apologies. If any noticed the dagger sheathed to her calf, they didn't mention it, nor did they mention anything about her going to the ball.

The next day, Krista caught fragments of rumors that she was afraid of water. She was sure there were probably other rumors, but she chose to ignore them.

As time passed, though she remained friends with the boys and they still came to her for help in their work, a distance developed between them. Krista found them immature. She fit in better with the older group, and as the prince and Cam accepted her, the others did too. So gradually, she shifted more into that group. It wasn't long after that, that Lord Cowley moved her up a level in lessons, which further reinforced her place with them.

Krista struggled to find time on her own to practice with Kallairion. She finally located the perfect location in the corner of the garden on the far side of the pond where she could be alone after her studies. There she went over her exercises and skills routine.

As usual, late one evening, she stealthily made her way there. It'd been a hot day, and the shade of the trees felt wonderful. The summer heat was becoming unbearable, made worse by the vest she wore over her shirt, plus the bindings over her breasts. As she walked by the pond, she looked at the water longingly. She thought of how good it would feel to take a swim, but she continued on. Reaching her spot, she scanned the area, making sure it was clear before she drew Kallairion.

Krista thought the words in her mind, and Kallairion changed in her hand from the small dagger to the mid-sized sword she favored. She took her stance and started her routine. Her movements flowed with grace and ease. She implemented what she'd learned from Roud into her workout, repeating each movement over and over until they became as natural as the ones that she had learned long ago under Darm's tutelage. Finishing, she took a deep breath and relaxed.

Light caught the edge of the sword as it blurred in an arcing motion. Garion could hardly believe what he was seeing. The block and thrust actions Kris made were amazing. The fluid movements conjured the word "grace" in his mind. He smiled to himself. Kris probably would not like the term applied to him. He worked too hard to fit in. Unfortunately, there was something that set him apart.

As he studied Kris, he wondered again what was different about him but couldn't pick out a specific thing. He was definitely zealous in his education and training. He always pushed himself. Garion figured he just wanted to prove himself because of his small stature.

He thought back to the day of Kris's arrival. Another smile came at Kris's apology when he almost got into a fight with Brock by the stream. The smile disappeared as he remembered the seriousness in Kris when he had bowed and pledged his life to him. He had no doubt of the conviction behind the words. That knowledge kept him frozen in place as he watched.

He'd never seen Kris move like this in practice. Kris did well in class, but now, Kris's movements were smooth, precise. They showed a skilled routine that was long practiced.

Garion shook his head in wonder as he thought of another thing he couldn't explain. The two of them seemed to share a bond. It was strange. Even though they had only known each other a short time, something seemed to be pulling them together. Maybe they were destined to become best friends.

He would say the notion was crazy but Kris seemed to understand him, even in a way Cam didn't, and since Cam had met Celeste, they had started to grow apart. He did not fault Cam. In truth, he envied his cousin. He wished for a special lady of his own. He just had not found her yet.

Garion sighed. It was probably just as well with the threat of Kuel hanging over his head. He was not a safe prospect for marriage. Marriage to him would be dangerous, even deadly.

He knew Kris had finished when he froze then relaxed his stance.

"That was really remarkable." Garion let out the words he'd been thinking.

Kris spun to face him, the sword point rising. It lowered when Kris recognized him.

"Sorry, did not mean to startle you. I saw you walking this way and decided to follow. Where did you get the sword?" Garion questioned, drawing near enough to know it was one he didn't recognize.

"I, uh . . . brought it with me." Kris stumbled over the answer. "It has been in my family for a long time."

He reached out. "May I?"

Krista's heart pounded from being startled. She'd been so locked on her drill she hadn't seen him. *Careless*, she thought as she eyed Garion's hand stretched out to her. She hesitated a moment before handing Kallairion to him, then stepped closer, not wanting to take a chance of being outside of Kallairion's influence. She had no idea how far the effect reached, but was afraid that, without Kallairion near, Garion might see her as a maiden.

He took a couple of practice swings, testing the sword's weight. "It is nice. Has a good feel, though it is very light."

"I am not very big."

Garion laughed. "So I've noticed. You know, you should give up and get a smaller shirt. You are never going to grow into that one."

Krista tried to look hurt. "I like my shirts big. Besides, you never know. I might grow into it."

Garion laughed again. "Do you always sneak down here to practice?"

"I like the privacy."

"Well, I am impressed. You do not fight like that in class."

"I am waiting to surprise Roud when the time is right." That was the truth, she thought, but not just Roud. More like Kuel.

Garion nodded, accepting her answer. "Would you mind practicing with me some evenings? I could use the extra time."

"Of course, anytime." She felt a wave of excitement at the thought of having a real opponent again.

"Good. I do not have a sword with me now, but how about some hand-to-hand, if you're not too tired already?"

"What about your clothes?"

Garion glanced down. He was dressed in a nicer linen shirt, but he just pulled the scarf from around his neck, tossed it aside, and loosened his collar. "It is all right." He took a stance opposite her.

As they faced off, he commented. "This is not a fair fight. I have you by quite a bit on height and weight."

"Weight is not everything." She met his challenge. Krista moved over to lay Kallairion by his scarf. She then turned to eye him, watching for movement.

"So I remember you saying before." Garion sprang forward, going for her ankle.

Krista dodged away, coming around behind him. She gave him a little shove. Garion, already off balance from his miss, went down but continued the roll right back to his feet.

Facing her again, he grinned and waited for a minute for her to advance. When she didn't, he attacked. Once more she sidestepped, giving him an elbow in the side.

"I think I am glad we are pulling blows," he commented, rubbing his ribs after he lunged for her a couple more times, only to have her dodge away. "You do not ever attack, do you?"

"As you pointed out, you have me by quite a bit on weight, and on strength and reach. It would not be wise for me to get in where you could get a hand on me."

He nodded in understanding. "Let me wear myself out."

Coming in again, this time she moved under him, as she had done with Brock. She let his own momentum carry him over but Garion was ready for the trick. As he went over, he caught her arm, pulling her with him. She tried to roll away, but before she could make it to her feet, he grabbed her ankle, dragging her over on her back.

Krista tried to twist free as one arm locked around her waist. He stood, lifting her all the way into the air, and then laid her back to the ground, careful not to drop her too hard. Krista arched, trying to get her feet under for leverage, but he came down with his full weight. No matter how she squirmed, she couldn't break free. He caught one wrist and brought it up over her head, pinning her flat to the ground with his body.

"Yield, Kris?" He forced out between hard breaths.

Krista struggled a second before she relaxed. "Yield," she gave in.

The glee of victory crossed his face. Then, as he looked down at her, his look changed to confusion, as if something seemed wrong, but he could not put his finger on it. Krista became aware of his weight pressing down on her and gasped for a breath. "I can not breathe."

Garion rolled off to the side. "Sorry. Weight does win."

"I need more practice," she answered back.

"Anytime, but I need to cool off now." Standing, he brushed off his breeches.

Krista rose quickly to her feet, grabbing Kallairion as he reached for his scarf, then she followed him to the pond. Garion settled down on the bank, pulled off his boots and socks then lowered his feet into the cool water. Krista followed suit.

"That feels good," she sighed.

"No other lessons to study tonight?" He leaned back into the cool grass.

"No, he gave a light assignment. You missed a dance lesson."

"No need to worry about that. I had enough of those when I was younger. It does not look good to have the prince falling over everyone on the ballroom floor." He paused. "Actually, I like to dance."

"I did until I got partnered with Sigmon today in practice and had him stepping on my toes with those big feet of his," Krista said dryly.

Garion broke out in laughter.

"It is not funny. I would rather fight the guy than dance with him any day," Krista added.

"And I thought I had it bad having to sit in a harvest meeting with my father."

"Is there not anything exciting going on?" Krista probed.

"Actually, one of the nearby villages is having trouble with a pack of wolves killing livestock. The wolves are just going in, killing and leaving. Not eating anything. They are going to set traps for the wolves, but if that doesn't work, there will be an organized hunt. They may let some of Roud's students participate."

"You are hoping to go?"

"I will admit. I am excited."

"It could be dangerous," Krista pointed out.

"Are you on my father's side?"

This time Krista had to laugh, knowing he had already heard the lecture. Garion had told her about feeling overprotected.

"You know, it is frustrating." Garion kicked the water. "They want me to take on more responsibility, even think of getting married, but they still treat me like a child who isn't safe out of their sight and is never allowed to do anything. Being the only remaining heir to the throne makes life difficult. I wish my family had been like Cam's with a lot of children."

Krista wanted to comment, but she didn't know quite what to say.

When she remained quiet, Garion continued. "I can understand their concerns, truly I can." He paused again. "I had an older brother. He died fourteen years ago at the hands of Kuel. My mother is afraid of losing me, too. It's never talked about at the castle, but everyone knows that sooner or later Kuel will be back after me and this time there is no Champion of Kallairion here to face him. Lord Vallon hasn't been seen for nearly six years, not since his last fight. He was injured so seriously that everyone thought he would die. Then he just disappeared."

Pain flowed through her at the thought of her father. It wouldn't be much longer until Darm sent word of her father's death.

"Enough of that," Garion said, trying to break the mood that had settled over them. "What do you think of Cam's love?"

They talked about Cam's romance and several other people at the castle. As they talked, Krista realized that, for all that Garion did to make others feel comfortable around him, he still didn't feel accepted. Maybe that was the bond they shared. She too knew, underneath, that she didn't fit in.

It seemed like no time until the sun began to set. They said good night and headed in their different directions. Krista took the back way to the boys' quarters. No one was around, but that was not unusual. She walked, lost in thoughts of Garion, paying little attention to her surroundings.

Since she had met him, Garion had continued to invade her mind. Now that they had become friends, it was more so. Krista found herself feeling guilty, not letting him know she was a maiden. She also felt guilty about that with the other boys. Some of the things they said in front of her they would never say to a female.

She consoled herself that she was always honest in her comments to them. She had even been able to help several resolve their problems with young ladies, because she could see it from a lady's perspective. She tried to be extremely careful of their privacy, partly not wanting to embarrass herself. Still, she felt deceitful.

An odd feeling of danger swept over her as she came around the corner. Unfortunately, the moment she took to think about it, made it too late to react. Krista turned just enough to catch a glimpse of the object a split second before it hit her. She managed to dodge slightly, but still the blow sent her crashing into the wall. Dazed, she slid to the floor.

A shadowed hand grabbed the front of her shirt and pulled her up. She tried to strike out, but her punch was easily knocked away. Shoved back against the wall, the next blow hit her in the ribs. Pain flooded through her fogged mind. A fist to her stomach doubled her over and was followed by another, catching her in the side.

Again, Krista tried to strike back, but she had little control of her swing and connected with nothing. The momentum sent her stumbling against the wall. Using it as a shield for her back, she pulled up her arms to block the blows, but they always seemed to find an opening. Then a fist landed solidly on her cheek, and everything went black.

Krista had no idea how long she had been unconscious when she finally came to. Total blackness surrounded her. An eerie silence filled the air. The raging thunder in her head made it impossible to think. She tried to move and grasped her stomach as a wave of pain gripped it. Muscles cramped. When she tried to stretch them, she came in contact with another wall.

Using the wall for balance, she worked her way to her feet. Nausea hit her, almost sending her to her knees. Leaning against the cool stone, she tried to catch her breath and hold back the dizziness. Several minutes passed before she dared move, even clinging to the wall for balance.

She stumbled. The sound of metal striking stone echoed in the darkness. She'd forgotten about Kallairion being in sword form. Dropping her hand, Krista fingered the hilt. A sensation of relief rallied her. At least it had not been taken. That would have been disastrous.

Using the stone wall as a guide, she made her way along what she figured was a hallway. Where she was in the castle she wasn't sure until she came around a bend. Moonlight sliced through an opening revealing her location. She was in one of the observation turrets, a level up from her room.

It felt like an eternity before she came down the steps and reached her room. She met no one the whole distance, so she guessed it was quite late. Entering, she didn't bother lighting the candle. Using the light that filtered through the window to guide her, she poured what water was left from that morning into a bowl and splashed it on her face. Head in her hands, she sank to her bed with a groan. She didn't try to take off her boots or even think of who had hit her. She just gave in to the oblivion of sleep.

Morning came too soon. Krista didn't feel at all rested and didn't need a mirror to know she had a black eye, though it seemed to be the only damage to her face. Her ribs and stomach were a different matter. After several minutes of inspection, she decided that nothing was broken, but a groan escaped her as she studied the discoloration. The bandaging and heavy vest, that she had bemoaned the day before, had protected her some. She was sore, but she had been bruised often enough in her training to know she would be all right in a few days.

Her mind finally turned to who ambushed her. Due to the dark and being stunned by the first blow, she had not seen her attacker. Brock was the only person who came to mind who would do such a thing, but she could not make an accusation based on the fact he didn't like her. Krista drew a deep, painful breath and let it out slowly.

Splashing more water on her face, she pulled on her clean shirt and changed Kallairion into a dagger before heading out. She made her way to the place where she had been attacked the night before. She really did not expect to find anything and was right. There was no sign of who it might have been. Krista went back down the hall. Running into Marcus and Chad, she tried to cover the side of her head with her hand, but it was of little use.

"Whoa, what happened?" Marcus exclaimed.

"I had a little accident." Krista tried to shrug the question off.

"With whose fist?" Marcus came back.

"Just forget about it, all right," Krista urged. Marcus looked like he was ready to press it so she continued. "I do not feel much like eating. Would you mind bringing me a piece of bread from breakfast?"

Marcus hesitated before nodding. "Sure, but believe me, everyone's going to notice that when you go to lessons."

Krista grimaced holding her head. "I know."

"Are you all right?" Chad asked, the muscles around his eyes tightened as he studied her.

"Fine," she answered, not bothering to hold back the sarcasm from her voice.

As Marcus said, it did not go any better when she went to lessons. If it weren't bad enough that everyone asked what happened, the first thing Lord Cowley did when he entered the room was make her stand and question her. Krista tried to pass it off as running into something in the dark, which in part was the truth, but he did not accept the explanation. After a lecture in front of the class about not fighting, he finally went on with the assignments.

On the way to the practice field after lunch, Garion got her on her own. "You going to tell me what happened?" he pressed.

"I ran into something."

"We have all figured that out. We even figured out what you ran into. But, what I want to know is whose fist it was?"

"What makes you think it was a fist?"

"Oh, let's see . . . because it is obvious. So why not stop this and tell me who it was."

"So you can, what, beat them up for me?" she flared. "I can take care of myself."

"Kris." He held up his hands to appease her. "I know you can. You are a good fighter, but you are also smaller than a lot of the others. It is not fair for you to take abuse."

"How do you know it was someone bigger?" She couldn't stop the defensiveness from coming through.

"Because almost everyone here is bigger than you, except for a few of the youngest, and you can take any of them. I would also guess it was a cheap shot, because you can hold your own with most of the men. So, who was it?"

She drew in deep breath, tilted her head back in frustrated concession, and let out the air. "I cannot tell you."

"Kris!"

"Look. I do not know who it was." She flung out her arms, losing her patience. "I never saw who it was. It was dark, and the first hit came from the side. I do not remember much after that."

Garion bit back an oath. "Let me take a look." Unable to resist, she stood still while he examined her eye and cheek thoroughly. "It appears to be all right. Anywhere else?"

She shook her head. "Just a few bruises. I am sore, but I'll be fine in a couple days."

He sighed and nodded. "I do not like allowing whoever it was to get away with this."

"Me neither, but as I said, I do not know who it was."

"But you have an idea." It was obvious by his tone that he had the same suspicion.

"I can make a good guess but seeing as I have no proof to make an accusation, there is no use. I will just have to be more careful in the future and pay more attention to my surroundings," she assured him as they continued to the practice field.

The bruises had started to fade when the consequences hit three days later. The wolves had made another attack on the herds, and this time, they also went after a small child. Luckily, a herdsman was able to rescue the boy before he was seriously harmed. But now, it was time for action. The hunting party would leave first thing in the morning.

The young men were on the practice field when the announcement came that many of them would be allowed to attend, and then the list of names was read. Everyone fifteen and over was announced, except Kris. After practice, Roud called for her to wait. When the others had left, he turned to her.

"Why?" Krista started.

Roud cut her off with the raise of a hand. "I am sorry about you being left behind. I thought you deserved to know the reason, if you have not guessed already." The scarred face didn't hide his sympathy.

His demeanor was straightforward. "It was felt that, as a punishment for fighting, you should not be allowed."

His hand came up again, holding off her objection. "I know you may feel this is too strict, especially since you have not chosen to name who you were fighting, so he could share in your punishment, but that is how it will be."

"But please, sir. I was not fighting."

Again, he cut her off. "It is quite obvious that the black eye was from someone's fist. Do you deny that?" he questioned unwaveringly.

"No, sir, I do not, but I also do not know who hit me."

"You expect me to believe that someone stood in front of you, close enough to hit you in the eye, and you did not see him."

"Yes, sir. If you will just let me explain. I was jumped. I never saw who it was," she tried.

"Then why did you not report it immediately?" he questioned.

"It would not have done any good. I have no idea who it was. It would have just started all sorts of rumors."

"I am sorry, Kris, but the decision has been made. There will be work left for you to do," he said finally, but there was kindness in his voice.

Krista looked at him, trying to decide what else to do, but she knew the man well enough by now to know that he wouldn't change the answer, no matter what she said.

"Yes, sir," Krista answered quietly, dropping her head. She moved off to the stable to care for Shea.

She'd just begun to brush her horse when Garion entered. "I was waiting for you to come back then guessed you might be here. I'm sorry that you are not allowed to go. Did Roud say why?" He settled on a nearby rail.

"For fighting, what else?" she answered in frustration.

"Did you tell him what happened?"

"I tried but . . ." She shrugged her shoulders.

Garion paused as he watched her run the brush over the horse. "I could have it cleared." He broke the silence.

Krista froze, taken aback by the offer. She looked at him then shook her head. "No, I do not want people to think that I run to you for favors." She managed a smile.

He returned it. "Thanks."

"You ought to just wait and do that tomorrow." The voice came from the doorway, and Brock sauntered in. "You will have nothing better to do, since you are not going anywhere." His dark brows rose and his lips twitched in undisguised mockery. "In fact, you might as well groom all the horses, but then, most of them will be gone." Brock accentuated the last few words.

"What do you want, Brock?" Garion didn't bothering to hide his annoyance.

"Just making sure my horse is ready for tomorrow. It should be a good hunt. Well, I think I will head in to eat now." He smiled coyly at Krista.

After he left, Garion spoke up, "You know, I would still wager he was behind your attack."

Krista stared at where the figure had disappeared. "Same here, but as I said before, I have no proof."

"And without proof, you cannot make any accusations," Garion finished for her.

Krista nodded. "Let's head in now. Brock is right, I will have plenty of time to do a really good job tomorrow."

The next morning, Krista watched as the others rode out. It didn't take her long to finish the tasks left for her, then the day dragged by until she went for a walk in the garden. There she met Lady Adele, a middle-aged woman who had been widowed for many years. After a greeting, the lady asked if Kris would mind helping her move some furniture around, so that was how she spent the rest of the afternoon.

Krista liked Lady Adele. The woman was open and kind. She talked freely, treating her with respect rather than ordering Krista around like a few of the "ladies" did. Most ladies were kind, but few were as easy to please as Lady Adele. She made the boys and young men her concern, down to the point of counseling them on personal matters. Quite often it was to her they went to when they were injured or ill, since she was experienced at healing and more pleasant than the castle healer.

Krista hadn't had much opportunity to be around her, so she relished the afternoon hours with the kind woman. Until that moment, she hadn't realized how much she missed Joanna or having a woman's company.

The only contact Krista had with other young maidens was in her role as a boy, which was a role she could not feel comfortable playing. For the most part, she avoided the maidens and attended the balls only when assigned to serve. Some of the boys still gave her a hard time about it, but no one had tried to force her into going since the time when it had gotten out of hand.

Krista was back in the practice yard when the riders returned. All the men looked weary, and there were no signs of success. Krista moved to where Cam and Garion were dismounting.

"I would dare guess no luck," she greeted them.

"There were a few signs, but nothing. Even our best trackers could not follow them," Cam answered.

"You definitely did not miss much," Garion added. "We are going out again first thing in the morning. For now, I am starved."

"You two go in. I will take care of your horses," Krista offered, taking the reins.

"Thanks," they echoed, needing no persuasion.

That night Krista didn't sleep well, plagued with an uneasy feeling that didn't fade, even with the morning light. Breakfast held no appeal. Finally, she shoved it aside and headed to find Roud. He was already in the yard preparing for the hunt when she located him. He looked up as she strode forward.

"Good morning," Krista greeted, knowing that her anxiety showed through.

"Morning. And what may I do for you this early?" he acknowledged her.

"I came to ask permission to attend the hunt today," she asked straight out.

"Kris, I am sorry, but it has already been explained to you."

"Yes, sir, but I sincerely request to be allowed to go."

"Kris."

"Sir, it is important." She didn't realize until the words were out to what extent the feeling of necessity boiled within her.

"Kris—"

"Please, sir. I must be there." The words rushed out of her so that they almost sounded like pleading.

He looked taken aback but stayed firm. "I am sorry, but no."

Bands of unease tightened in her chest, but his look had her turning away in defeat. Unable to do anything else, a short time later she stood off to the side, watching the group ride out again.

Concentrating on her work was futile. She tried to convince herself that she was being foolish, but the anxiety burning in her stomach strengthened as the morning progressed. She wasn't sure why, but she knew that she should be there. She tried to push it away then a wave of certainty hit her so strong, it nearly doubled her over.

Garion's life was in danger.

The wooden sword she was practicing with fell forgotten to the ground as she ran for the stable. There wasn't anyone around as she saddled Shea. The second she finished, she swung up and headed out the castle gates. Krista turned Shea into the woods, riding quite a distance before she finally reined Shea to a halt, looking around her.

It was stupid, she thought. She had no idea where to find the hunters, not even the direction they had ridden. Garion was sure to be safe. He'd be surrounded by the other men, and for all she knew, they could already be headed back to the castle.

She threw back her head and pushed her hands through her hair. A sinking feeling came over her. She was going to face such a severe punishment for leaving. The urge to return to the castle was strong, only to be dashed away again by the certainty that Garion was in danger.

Krista lowered her chin, determined that she had to go on. She knew she needed help, and she had only one thing to rely on. Pulling Kallairion out of her boot, she glanced around quickly before concentrating on the blade. In a brief shimmer, it changed to sword form. "Please! Guide me to Prince Garion," she whispered under her breath.

Confidence filled her, and with Kallairion still in her hand, she urged Shea to a gallop. She wound her way through the trees, not knowing where she was going, just putting her faith on the sword and her feelings.

Krista paused to get her bearings as she broke into a clearing. The sun told her it was well past mid-afternoon. Wondering if she had missed the hunting party, she spun around to her left, searching for Garion and the other men. There was no one to be seen, but something wasn't right.

A low howl echoed through the trees. The mare tensed under her and pranced in unease. Krista had to coax Shea forward. She could clearly hear the growling and snarls now. Then, they were in front of her.

Nearly twenty wolves circled the glade with Garion standing in the center, trying to face them all at once. No other hunters were in sight, just him. Krista spurred Shea to a run, but before she could cover the distance, several wolves attacked.

Chapter Five

Garion spun, trying to drive the wolves back, but they were everywhere. While one nipped at his heels, another sprang from the side, catching hold of his wrist. Krista heard him yell as he struck the animal, forcing it away. He had no time to recover as another leapt at him. Garion went down, using his arm to protect his face as he tried to push the wolf away.

Krista drove Shea through the center of the pack, sending the wolves scattering. She jumped off her horse as Kallairion sliced through the wolf that would have torn into Garion's throat.

He looked up, shocked, as the animal fell to the side. "How . . .?"

"Can you get up?" she cut him off, extending her sword arm down for him to grip while holding Shea's reins with her other hand.

The horse pranced nervously, pulling her slightly off balance. Krista's eyes darted around as the wolves closed in. Garion made it to his feet as the first wolf charged. Krista swung around, driving it away. Behind her, another wolf made the same movement, but Garion was ready for it.

A couple wolves sprang forward to nip at Shea's heels. The horse kicked out, pulling the reins from Krista's hand as she turned to face another wolf. The spooked horse broke away and fled through the trees with several wolves in pursuit.

Back to back, Krista and Garion faced the pack. Several animals darted in. Krista struck out slicing through one, while pivoting to meet the next.

With a yelp, one wolf fell dead and then another. One more moved away wounded, but the wolves kept coming, wearing their prey down. One got through, tearing its teeth across Garion's leg but not penetrating his boot before Garion managed a killing blow.

"We cannot keep this up much longer," he gasped behind her.

"We have to kill the leader, and then maybe the others will give up. There, that one," Krista indicated a large animal with a black and gray coat, off to the side.

"What do you suggest?" Garion swung as a wolf ventured close.

Krista thought for a moment. "Kneel down, rest, but keep watching the leader out of the corner of your eye. I will keep the others back. Wait until he makes his move. Once he gets close enough, make yours."

"Right," Garion slumped into a crouch, dragging in several deep breaths. His sword rested on the ground in his hand. His other arm covered his head in case any wolves got by her.

Several wolves made their attacks. Krista sliced through two, mortally injuring one. The other she just caught with a glancing blow, but it was enough to send the wolf scampering away. Then the leader came. His attack was swift, going right for Garion's throat, teeth bared.

Garion was ready, bringing the sword up under the wolf as it charged. The wolf's own weight carried it onto the sword full force. With a final gnashing of teeth, the killer fell still.

The other wolves pulled back, pacing around the two people nervously. One sprang forward and Krista swatted it with the side of her blade. It yelped, jumped back, turned, and fled, howling. The mournful sound was picked up and rippled through the remaining wolves, then they too turned and followed.

Krista and Garion waited frozen in place for several minutes, making sure the wolves really had left. Finally, they let out a combined sigh of relief.

"They are gone." Krista felt exhausted. Behind her, she heard a low groan and turned in time to see Garion drop his sword to grab his left arm, cradling it in front of him. Sliding Kallairion into her belt, she stepped to him, taking his weight onto her. "Here, sit down." She helped him move to a nearby fallen tree.

"Let me see." She took his arm, gently lifting the torn, bloody cloth away from the skin. Grasping the sides of the material, she carefully tore the sleeve open. "It does not look too bad, but we should get it tended as soon as possible."

"My water jug is over there," he directed. As she walked to pick it up, he asked, "What are you doing here?"

"It is hard to explain. Simply, I felt you were in danger. Here, this is going to hurt," she warned, pouring the water over his wrist.

He jerked and cursed softly under his breath. "You were right. I thought I was dead. I could not have lasted much longer. Thanks."

"You are welcome. I hope you do not mind, but I need to bind your wound. Besides, your shirt's ruined anyway," she said as she cut loose a piece of cloth from the bottom, then tore off a long strip. Using it, she bandaged his arm. "That will have to do until we get back to the castle. Where is your horse?"

"It took off, but it had pulled up lame anyway."

"Well, unless Shea comes back, it looks like we are in for a long walk. Are you up to it?"

"Let me rest a minute first." He looked around at the wolves they had killed. "What a fight. I can hardly believe it, except that the evidence is there, and my arm's throbbing."

"What happened? Where is everyone else?" Krista finally asked the questions plaguing her.

"We got separated. There had been no signs all morning, and we had put a little more distance between each of us to cover more area. I was on the outside. I guess my horse stepped on something. Anyway, it came up lame. I stopped to check it. By the time I got the hoof cleaned out, the others were gone.

"The next thing I knew, my horse started acting spooked. I looked around but couldn't see anything. Just as I put my foot in the stirrup, the wolves came out of nowhere. My horse shied away, dumping me on the ground with the wolves circling around, where you found me a few minutes later," he concluded. "Shall we go?"

"They just attacked? It's odd that they would pick on a man like that. Look at them." She motioned to the dead animals. "They are well fed. It's unusual . . ." She cut off, turning the other direction. The men from the castle came galloping through the trees toward them. Garion stood as they approached.

Krista took a couple steps back at the sight of Roud. This was not a meeting she craved. He had made it very clear she was not to come.

"Your highness, are you all right?" One of the lords spoke up at the sight of the disheveled prince.

"Garion," his father's voice rung out, concerned, as he moved forward. "We thought we had lost you. What happened here?" He looked at his son, then at the dead wolves not far away.

"It is a long story, but if Kris had not come along when he did, I would have been their next meal."

"Kris?" The king looked past his son.

Krista swallowed nervously. She had only been in the presence of the king a couple of times and he had never addressed her personally. "Your Majesty," she bowed and held there.

"Rise, lad, I owe you my thanks," he addressed her, then turned back to his son. "How did you two get separated? You know you should have stayed with the group."

"My horse came up lame, then the wolves were on me. They had me on the ground when Kris showed up. I could not have lasted much longer," Garion explained.

"Why did not you alert someone when you left the group?" The king turned to address her again.

Krista cast a nervous look at Roud, who eyed at her with a slight scowl, but a hint of appreciation as well. "I was not with the group, Your Majesty." She drew in a deep breath. "I was to remain at the castle."

"Remain at the castle?" the king questioned.

"He was under a punishment," Roud offered.

"And you broke it and followed?" the king asked.

"Yes, sire. I am ready to accept any reprimand."

"One more question first. Why did you come, when you knew you would be punished? Surely you did not want to get in on killing a wolf that bad?" the king probed.

"No, sire," Krista didn't know how to answer. "That was not it at all."

Garion took over her defense when it was clear she was not going to offer any. "May I tell you what he told me when I asked him that question?

"Please," his father encouraged.

"He said he came because he knew I was in danger," Garion answered.

Several of the men looked openly shocked.

"Is that so?" the king asked directly to Krista.

"Yes, sire," she answered, her head cast down. She felt the weight of his gaze on her and fought not to shift under it.

It was Roud who spoke up, calling her attention. "This morning, when you told me that it was important that you were to come, did you know it then?"

Krista looked up at her instructor. "No, sir. At least, not truly. I was not sure what the danger was. I just felt it was important for me to be here. I am sorry, sir. I did not mean to go against your orders, but I had to come."

"Well, it seems a good thing you did, but I am afraid you will still have to face a punishment for breaking a direct order. Under the circumstances, however, I do not think it will be too severe a punishment," the king added gently.

Krista's eyes locked with Brock's, who was glaring at her from the back of the group.

"You know," Sir Herald spoke up. "If we had not come back looking for the rider of that horse, we might not have found you for some time. You would have had a long walk back." He motioned, and one of the men led Shea forward.

"Shea," Krista exclaimed, relieved. The horse tugged to come to her.

Herald continued. "As it is, you get the spoils of the hunt—seven wolf skins."

"The big black and gray one over there was their leader," Garion told them. "The others fled."

Roud nodded, "Good. It may be we will not have any more trouble out of them."

Roud selected a group to remain and help bring back the wolves, while the rest rode ahead to get Garion back so his arm could be tended properly. Since Garion's horse hadn't been found, and Kris was the lightest rider there, Garion climbed on Shea with her.

Back at the castle, the celebration was short lived. Garion had to go straight to have his arm tended and Krista was sent to her room until the final determination of punishment could be made. On the way back, Garion told the whole story in detail so, by evening, Krista was a hero.

After supper she was called into Sir Herald's office where he, Roud, and Lord Cowley were waiting. By way of punishment, she was confined to her room for the night. She was also assigned to help some of the younger boys with their studies for a month, given an extra hour of sword and archery practice and, lastly, would not be allowed to attend the ball at the end of the week.

That night, as Krista lay back in her bed, she wondered if Garion had helped choose her punishments because none were things she minded, especially not going to the ball. She already practiced an extra half hour or more with Garion every night, besides her own practice. And even helping the younger boys with studies was not all that unusual.

Picking up Kallairion, she ran her fingers over the smooth polished blade. It was Kallairion that had allowed her to save Garion. It had directed her to him. Within her, she sensed that her gratitude pleased the sword.

She'd achieved the first trial of her duty to guard Garion, though it was not Kuel they faced. A chill ran through her at that thought. Could Kuel have been behind the wolves? Was it possible he could've sent them? Could he control their reactions?

Unease spiked within her, and she decided to shift her thoughts to something more pleasant. To her surprise, her mind went to the ride back to the castle and Garion sitting behind her. She remembered every touch of her back to Garion's chest and the times his hand occasionally resting on her waist for balance. Krista felt herself flush, then pulled her thoughts around.

Now, she was being absolutely foolish. Garion meant nothing by his touches. He thought she was a boy, his friend. The guilt she felt rose again, pushing out the giddy feeling of young womanhood. There, between tumbled emotions, she finally fell asleep.

Garion walked across the yard to where Krista was waiting for her extra sword practice.

"What are you doing out here?" she greeted him as he got close.

"I came out to practice with you."

"Is that wise? You were kept from duties all day." She felt a wave of concern.

He just shook his head. "It was my mother's idea. She was afraid I was too weak from my harrowing experience for strenuous activities today. But I've been given the approval to practice with you tonight if you promise not to bloody me up." There was no missing the cynicism in his voice.

"And they figure I am too small to do much damage to you." She tried to add a hint of teasing to her voice.

"For my mother, a child would be too dangerous for me to fight, but she was assured of my safety."

"I will go gentle on you then."

"Not too gentle, I need to work some of the soreness out of my muscles." He flexed his bandaged arm.

"Are you sure it is all right?"

"Certain. I need a sparring."

So they started their workout moving slowly at first. Krista let Garion set the pace. Gradually, the movements and speed picked up. In ways, his extra half foot of height should've given him an advantage, but she was so used to fighting a taller opponent, that it made no difference to her. Though she did hold back on some of her skills, she let more than normal come through, and by the end of the practice, they were both breathing hard.

"You still do not fight like that in Roud's lesson." Garion sucked in air.

"There, I am trying to learn new moves. Besides, like I said before, I want it to be a surprise."

"Where did you learn so much?"

"There was an old warrior," she sent a mental apology to Darm at the reference of *old*, "where I was raised. I think he found it amusing to teach me." That was true, Krista thought. Darm took great pleasure in teaching her. He was hard on her but always told her she was an adept pupil. He found it immensely amusing that he could train a girl to beat any warrior.

"Garion, you will not tell anyone about how I can fight, will you?" She looked over at him.

He shook his head. "No, I will keep your secret."

"Thank you."

"What are friends for? Besides, after today, I figure I owe you my life."

Making their way back to the castle, she and Garion found a group of boys waiting for her. Settling in the grass by the castle wall, they began to tell her their problems with their studies. Krista went over the lessons with them, explaining until they understood. As they studied, the numbers grew, as was common. They had just about finished when Marcus spoke up.

"Now, if you could only help me memorize this poem," he said with frustration and disgust. "I do not see why we need to learn it anyway."

"What is it?" Krista asked.

"By the Lake of Haven," he answered.

"Actually, it is quite beautiful. You can impress the ladies with it," Krista pointed out.

"Not the way he reads it," another of the boys spoke up, causing laughter to ripple through the group.

Krista joined in then said, "Let's hear it."

Marcus frowned and started to read. The words came out awkward and rough, with no flow at all.

"Wait," Krista stopped him. "He is right. You will never impress a lady like that. It needs to flow like music, with a beat." She started to recite it, clapping her hand along with each line.

After Marcus tried it several more times, she stopped him again. "Better, but maybe it would help to do it as song."

Krista drew the small flute Darm had given her on her tenth birthday from the sleeve in the opposite boot from where she kept Kallairion. Putting the flute to her lips, she played part of a tune then recited the words following the beat of the music. After going all the way through it once, she encouraged Marcus to recite the words as she played. Several other boys joined in before they finished. The next time through, most of the boys did the words.

"I have got it!" Marcus cheered. "Do you think you could teach me to play that?" He indicated to her flute.

"Probably, it is not that hard," Krista answered.

"Are you kidding? His fingers would never fit on that tiny thing. They are too large," Sigmon kidded.

"My hands are about as big as his," Krista said defensively, holding up her hand.

"Your fingers are long, but his are fatter," Sigmon returned with a laugh.

"Well, you would be surprised how well large hands can play. The man who taught me was an old warrior with much larger, rougher hands, and he could play better than I could ever hope to." She gave Marcus an encouraging look. "I will teach you if you would like."

He smiled, satisfied. Krista put the flute to her lips and once more played the song. Ending, she slipped the flute back in its sheath. The young men broke into groups, heading to their other activities. Garion moved off with Krista.

"I never knew you played," he stated.

"I am not able to find the time much anymore and, usually, it is just when I am alone."

"Well, I like it. Maybe you should start playing for the ladies. But then, you would end up like Cam, and I would not have anyone to talk with."

"I would not worry much about that."

They were quiet for a moment, then Garion spoke up. "You should not worry so much about your size. You are not that small, and you never know, you could still grow some more."

"I doubt it. Besides, it really does not bother me. I have already resigned myself to being smaller than all the men or, at least most."

"Just do not let anyone bother you about being smaller. You are a better fighter then most of them. Sometimes your moves amaze me. I swear you learn fast. I think you could hold your own with any man here. And I would rather have you with me than any of my father's guards."

"Thanks. I had better get to bed. I have early duties in the morning." Krista left him.

The hallway looked empty when she started down it. When Brock stepped around the corner coming from the other way, she almost changed directions. She knew it was no use. There was no avoiding him, and she refused to let him have that much control over her life. Still, she could not stop her muscles from tensing though she managed to keep her stride smooth. "Good evening," she acknowledged, moving toward him.

He glared in return. "I see you got away lightly after disobeying orders. You even came out the hero."

"Brock—" Krista started but he cut her off.

"You made me look bad to Prince Garion. And now you are his friend, but do not think he will always be there to bail you out of trouble." With that, Brock stormed away.

Krista wondered what Brock was referring to. She wished she could change things between them. She had a hard time understanding him, but decided not to let it bother her, and headed to her room.

Brock headed the other direction down the hall where the visiting nobles stayed. Knocking at a door, he entered his father's chambers. Moving in front of the man seated behind the desk, he stood still while he waited for his father to acknowledge his presence.

"Brock, you said you wanted to talk with me. Now, what may I do for you?" Lord Wallum asked, looking up at his son.

A sly look crossed Brock's face. "I would like you to have Kris assigned to you. He's causing trouble for me."

His father silenced him as a knock sounded at the door.

"Enter!"

Sigmon opened the door and looked from father to son back to father.

"I am sorry to disturb you, Lord Wallum, but Sir Herald asked me to bring this to you."

"Yes, here." The Lord held out his hand for the young man to cross the room and hand over the document. The large man took it, not even acknowledging Sigmon. Instead, he directed his attention to his son as Sigmon returned to the door.

"I will see about having Kris assigned to me in the morning, if you are sure that is what you want."

As Sigmon closed the door, he heard Brock answer, "Precisely."

Chapter Six

Sigmon knew what he heard meant trouble for Kris, but wasn't sure what he could do to help. He thought of telling Kris, but there wouldn't be anything Kris could do to stop the assignment. Coming around the corner, he met Marcus and told him what he had heard.

Before he'd even finished, Marcus pushed him back down the hall the way he came, saying. "Come on, we have to talk to Garion."

Both young men were relieved when they knocked on Garion's door and he answered. The prince didn't hesitate letting them in. Before he could ask why they were there, Marcus started.

"Garion, I think there is going to be trouble for Kris. Brock has asked his father to have Kris assigned to him."

Garion raised his hand. "Wait a minute, start over."

"Sigmon was delivering some papers to Lord Wallum and heard Brock asking his father to have Kris assigned to him," Marcus repeated, while Sigmon nodded in agreement to what he said. "You know how Brock feels about Kris. It must mean no good."

Garion was silent for a second. "You are right. Just what we can do to stop it is the question. I doubt that they would let me reassign him once Lord Wallum has made a request. Our only chance is to have Kris appointed to someone else first." Garion paced the room, talking while he was thinking.

"Lord Wallum said he would see to it in the morning," Sigmon spoke up.

"Then we better do it tonight. Is Sir Herald in his office?"

"He was a short time ago," Sigmon answered.

"All right, let me talk to my father. I have an idea."

The next morning, Kris was told to meet with Sir Herald before attending to her other duties. Confused, she entered Herald's office, waiting for the man to address her.

Herald's eyes were grave when he looked up. Her heart skipped a beat when he started to talk. "You are being assigned as a special companion. You will be expected to keep up with all your other studies, plus help with anything that is requested of you."

The man paused, letting what he'd said sink in. "Your duty is a special one. It is a great privilege, and you should feel honored to be chosen. It is highly unusual for someone as young as you to be chosen, especially for the position . . ."

Krista was so intent on trying to think of a way to decline, that she almost missed what he said next, ". . . to be the companion to the prince. That Garion feels so strongly about this is the only reason it is being allowed. You will be expected to be at his side whenever needed. Do you understand your duties?"

Krista could only nod, too stunned to get a word out.

By the time she entered the morning class, the news had spread. She was greeted with congratulatory slaps on her back. Garion leaned against the window with a large grin. The only person in the room who did not share the celebration in her honor was Brock. He stayed in the back of the room, fuming at Kris's good fortune and the failure of his own scheme.

That afternoon, Krista moved her things to a room that adjoined Garion's. It had an entrance to the hall and another door that led directly into Garion's chambers. Though small compared to Garion's room, it was about three times the size of her previous room.

Over the next few days, Krista became accustomed to her duties as the prince's companion. She noticed that most things didn't change, except for the fact that she spent more time around him. She still took her meals with the other men, but it was made clear that she was to accompany Garion whenever he wished and, any time he left the palace, she was to be by his side.

She felt blessed to be so close to Garion and not need to have an excuse to be near him. She was also relieved that Garion never just barged into her room but always stopped to knock before entering her room, though there was no lock on her side.

As before, mornings were still spent with Lord Cowley, and afternoons with Roud. The only variation was the time in the yard. There was more bow and hand-to-hand practice, and occasional training on horseback just outside the castle wall.

Krista had been Garion's companion for nearly a month when one such horsemanship training occurred. They were outside the castle going through their routines. One group was trying to maneuver through a course on horseback without using their reins to guide them. Garion was with the group fighting with wooden swords on horseback. Krista was with the third group, doing target practice with the bow from horseback.

She hadn't tried to hide her talent with the bow because many of the boys were quite good. She mainly tried to cover her skills with it on horseback, though it was obvious she and Shea worked well together. Well enough, that no one noticed that when Shea went the wrong way, it was at Krista's encouragement.

Krista relaxed in the saddle, enjoying the afternoon while waiting for her next turn. The sun was not too hot and a gentle breeze was blowing. All in all, it was a beautiful day. The peace shattered so abruptly with a wave of alarm, it almost unseated her. The recognition of what she was feeling hit hard—Garion was in danger!

Spinning Shea around, she searched the field for him. Behind her, the man supervising their group shouted at her. Krista paid no attention. Her eyes scanned the field until she found Garion. She detected no threat. Still, she headed Shea across the field in a full run, ignoring the trainer's yell.

Several shadows passed overhead, but she paid no heed to them either, until one of the boys in Garion's group yelled and pointed up. She made only a quick glance up, but it was enough to fill her with horror at the flock of large scavenger birds diving directly at Garion's back.

Krista had covered only about half the distance to Garion and was still quite a ways away when she brought her bow up. Without thinking, she drew an arrow and let it go. From her full gallop, the shot flew straight, impaling the first bird just a body's width from Garion's head.

Garion turned as the bird shrieked and dropped to the ground. Startled, the next bird veered away, but the third kept coming. Garion had just enough time to throw his arm up to cover his face while he swung out with his wooden sword, striking the bird. It went down, but before he could recover, the next bird slammed into him, knocking him from his horse.

Without thinking, Krista pulled Kallairion from her boot, changing it into her sword almost before it cleared the leather. Krista was there before anyone else could react, slicing through a large mass of feathers even before she was out of the saddle.

The flock descended around Garion as he tried to beat them away, unable to rise. Swinging the sword down just inches from Garion's face, she cleaved two birds away. Behind her, a bird hit her neck. She came around slicing through it and then down across another scavenger on Garion in one motion. Squawks echoed, and then were drowned out by the other young men yelling as they ran forward to knock the birds away with their wooden swords. Flapping filled the air as the birds fled to the sky.

Krista dropped to the ground beside Garion. "Are you all right?" She searched for signs of injuries amidst splattered blood. "Garion?" Frantically, she searched for the answer as she tried to release the ties holding his protective chest pad in place.

He lay still. "I'm all right, I think. It was just . . . they were all over me." Putting his hands to his face, he wiped away some of the blood. "Augh, disgusting, but it's not mine."

Krista settled back on the ground and realized dozens of legs surrounded them. Looking up, she met faces with an array of disbelief, shock, and fear.

No one said a word as they just stared at the prince.

Roud pushed his way through the gaping group. "Prince Garion." Anxiety showed on his scarred face.

"I am fine." Garion pulled himself to a sitting position. "Just a mess."

Anger burst from the older man. "Kris, you could have killed him with that shot! From that distance! At that speed! On horseback! So close to him! What were you thinking? You could have hit the prince as much as that bird. And where did you get that sword?"

Krista was too shocked to respond, but Garion reacted, cutting him off. "Wait, he just saved my life or at least my skin."

Roud stopped, holding his breath a moment before letting it out. "You're right, I am sorry, Kris. It is just . . . what you tried takes a great amount of skill. Garion could have been in more danger from you than from the birds."

"I would never endanger Garion," Krista answered quietly. Now that the pounding of her heart eased, she felt weak and shaky. Roud's comments stung though she understood what he was saying.

Roud tried to soften the sting. "Of course you would not. I just can hardly believe what I saw. Some of the best archers I know would not have tried that shot."

"Well, he did it, and I owe him." Garion slapped Krista on the back.

She managed a weak smile.

Roud straightened himself. "True, he certainly did, and it was some nice swordsmanship. Where did you get that?"

For the first time, Krista truly noticed Kallairion on the ground by her leg. A cold sweat broke through her as she fought for an answer. Had anyone seen Kallairion change? It would have been on the opposite side of Shea, hidden from almost everyone on the field but . . . "I had it in my saddle. I was planning to practice later."

Roud extended his hand. "May I?"

Nervously, Krista stood, holding Kallairion out to him. Roud studied the blade carefully. "Very fine workmanship, very fine. It is a beautiful sword, but light."

"Kris is not very big," Garion pointed out, he too rising to his feet.

"It was made for you?" Roud asked curiously.

"Ah, no, it has been in my family for some time. I am just the first one to need such a light blade."

Roud nodded. "Well, take care of it—it is a beautiful sword," he directed with obvious appreciation, handing it back to her.

She let out an inward sigh, sliding it into her belt. "I will."

Roud's attention went back to Garion. The talons and sharp beaks had shredded the pad he wore. Most of the stuffing was hanging out. Blood covered the pad and his torn shirt. It streaked his face and matted his hair, making him quite a sight.

"You had better head in and clean up," Roud instructed. "I would suggest you do not let many people see you, especially your mother, or you may never be allowed out of the castle walls again."

Garion nodded. "Come on, Kris." The crowd that had stood there wordless the whole time split to let the two pass. Taking their horses by the reins, they slowly headed for the gate, neither choosing to mount.

"I owe you another thanks," Garion broke their silence.

Krista shrugged.

"Hey, do not let Roud upset you. He did not really mean it. It was just his over protectiveness coming through. He tends to be strict, but he really worries about us."

"I know," Krista said softly. "Just . . . I would never do anything that could harm you. I . . . I would not have shot if I had any doubt." Krista felt a little awkward.

"I know that. Now, as I said, do not worry. You saved my skin again."

"You are truly all right?" Krista's concern showed now.

Garion looked over, grinned, and nodded. "Look that bad?"

"Yeah," Krista smiled.

Garion laughed. "You had better get me out of this pad then before my parents see me or Roud will be right. They will never let me out of the castle." They stopped and Kris helped him remove it. Garion looked at it grimly. "I am glad it was the pad and not me. I think I will toss it to be burned."

Once at the stable, Krista brushed down both horses while Garion tried to clean off most of the blood with a cloth. Krista paused once to help him pour a bucket of water over his head as he tried to work the blood from his hair. Then they headed in, with Krista checking the hallways for him. Garion stayed hidden while Krista ordered water for a bath. They made it to his chambers without anybody getting a good look at him.

Closing the door behind them, Krista heard a groan behind her and turned to see Garion stretch and move his arm around.

"I came down on my shoulder." He winced.

Before Krista could say anything, he pulled off his shirt.

"Looks like I pretty much ruined it." He tossed the shirt aside.

Krista stood frozen, her eyes locked on Garion. Suddenly she felt nervous. She'd been around him and most of the others in the yard without their shirts on, but never in their rooms.

"Kris, will you rub my shoulder?" Garion sat down on the couch.

Krista didn't move.

"Kris?" Garion looked back questioningly.

"Maybe I should get someone else to look at it." Krista found the words as she fought for a way out.

"It is all right, really, just sore. If you will rub it, and after a hot bath, it will be fine."

"Maybe I should get someone to rub it for you." Even as she said it, she knew it was no good. As Garion's companion, it was her responsibility to do it.

"No, that is why I have you," he confirmed her thought.

"But I have never . . ." She broke off.

"That is not a problem. Come to think of it, I have never had anyone rub my shoulder before. You are my first companion. I have not had anyone assigned to me since my nursemaid when I was small." He stretched out on the couch, oblivious to her turmoil.

Krista forced herself to step beside him and settle down on the edge of the couch. Laying her hands on his shoulder, tentatively she began to rub the muscle as she had done on occasion for her father and Darm.

"You can rub harder. You are not going to hurt me," Garion kidded then gasped as she did. "Ohhh, that feels good." Relaxing, he let her hands work over his shoulder, massaging the muscle. "I think I have found a new duty for you."

Inside, Krista trembled. Thankfully, her attention was turned to the knock on the door.

Garion moved into his bedroom as she answered it, letting in the servants with the bath water. They moved to the door in one corner that led to the prince's private bath. It was a small room; only the tub, fire pit, a small table, and dressing rack fit inside. Light streamed in through a window, warming the room nicely without the need for a fire. With the water in the tub, the servants left. Krista closed the door behind them.

She started to cross the room, then stopped as Garion stepped out of his bedroom with just a dressing robe on. It came only to his knees. Krista stared at his bare calves and feet, then looked up. The robe hung open to his waist revealing his bare chest. Warmth flooded over Krista, heating her cheeks and leaving her flustered. She wanted to spin around and cover her eyes. Her mind raced for a way to escape.

"Garion, I . . . I would like to clean up now. Would you mind?"

"Oh, no . . . sorry I should have thought sooner. Go ahead, I will be awhile. Would you rub my shoulder again this evening?"

Krista hesitated but nodded before fleeing to her room. With the door closed behind her, Krista crumpled to the floor. Her heart beat so fast she felt like she couldn't breathe. Her face burned.

What was wrong with her? She hoped Garion hadn't noticed her reactions. Just thinking of his muscles under her fingers sent quivers through her.

Feelings of deceit swept over her. If he had known she was a woman, he would never have walked in front of her in just his robe. This was her prince and she had overstepped the bounds. It was Garion, her closest friend. She felt guilty about the feelings within her, feelings that, if she was honest with herself, seemed to be surfacing a lot more often.

No, she didn't want to think of that. She groaned, burying her face in her hands. Maybe she should find a way to have herself removed as Garion's companion. But she couldn't do that. This was the best position for her to protect him.

Protect him. Her mind locked on the thought. It was a safer subject, though no less disturbing. She'd almost allowed Kallairion to be discovered. But, even if Kallairion had been recognized, it would've been necessary. Kallairion, itself, had warned her of the danger.

For the first time, she thought how odd it was that the birds had attacked Garion. Again, she felt thankful that Kallairion was at her side to warn her, so she could protect him. She could not let anything happen to him.

In a flash Garion's image rose in her mind. She pushed it back. Going to the basin, she started to wash, splashing the cool water on her face to settle her thoughts.

At supper, stories of what had happened buzzed around the room, gaining in glory as they were retold. Krista found she sounded like a mighty warrior splitting a hair with an arrow. Finally, unable to take it any longer, she gave up on dinner and went out to practice with Kallairion.

Garion did not join her, and she was back in her room for some time before she heard a knock on the door between their rooms. She opened it. Garion looked more harried than he had after the attack.

"Would you mind rubbing my shoulder now?" He didn't wait for an answer, moving back into his chamber to a couch.

Krista followed slowly, relieved when he didn't stop to take off his shirt. She swallowed as he stretched out on his stomach but settled on the edge of the couch beside him. Placing her hands by his neck, she began to work them down over his shoulders. Several times he let out a sigh or a groan. His eyes closed and a smile of contentment crested his lips.

His muscles were tight but, under her hands, she felt the tension leave. Warmth flowed up her arms. Krista jerked back her hands.

Garion opened his eyes and rolled to the side to look up at her. "Is something wrong?"

"Oh, no." Embarrassment once more washed over her.

Garion's expression hardened. "Say it, Kris. I am surprised someone hasn't said it already. I'm sure that was what had Roud so upset."

"What?" Krista asked, honestly taken by surprise at his words.

"I know they were scavenger birds. They do not attack live prey. So why did they attack me? Why come down in a crowded field and attack me?" he burst out.

Reaching out, he grabbed her arms, giving her a shake. He released her as suddenly as he had grabbed her and ran his hands back through his hair. "Sorry."

Krista had spent her whole practice thinking about that very thing and hadn't come up with an answer. Now she wished more than anything that she had one for Garion. "It is hard to say what could have attracted them." She tried to sound reassuring.

He looked over and gave a weak smile. "Yeah," after a pause, he continued. "You know, I wish you were a woman sitting here by me."

Krista couldn't have been more shocked if he'd hit her. "Why?" she stammered out.

"I could use someone to hold and cuddle tight right now." He let out a light laugh.

Krista could tell he was teasing. "Well, I am afraid you will have to look elsewhere for that," she teased back in effort to raise his mood.

"It's all right. I cannot think of any of the young ladies I want to cuddle up to. I guess I will have to settle for you rubbing my shoulders," he said rolling back over. As Krista began to rub again, he let out a sigh. "I could always imagine that you have a nice curvy shape of a pretty young maiden."

Krista squeezed down.

"Ah," he groaned out, "but I am not sure she would be quite tha-at strong." He laughed.

Krista relaxed, working her way back down the muscles. Underneath she had to smile. What would he say if he had known how right he was?

Chapter Seven

Only a few days later word of her father's, Lord Vallon's, death arrived. Immediately, a somber mood settled over the palace. The fear and uncertainty of what would happen when Kuel returned without the Champion of the Sword to stand against him hung heavy in the air. The attack on Garion by the birds only added to the uneasiness. People whispered that Kuel had sent them, and that Kuel himself would be coming soon.

The first evening after the announcement, Garion caught up with Krista in the garden. The news of her father hit her hard even though she had been there when it had actually happened. She could hardly hold in the desire to drop to the ground and weep. She missed him, Joanna, and Darm.

Garion had stood off watching her for some time before he approached. "Is something bothering you?" he asked as he finally moved to her.

"Oh no, sorry," Krista looked up.

"You are thinking of Lord Vallon. It is all right. The whole castle is, though, no one is saying much. There is nothing to worry about. If Kuel comes, we will face it. I have known about the possibility most of my life, and I will not let it worry me now. Besides, no one would expect you to stand against him," Garion tried to assure her.

"That is not it, it is just . . ." She couldn't find the words.

"It is hard when a legend dies," Garion finished.

Krista nodded. "He was a great man." Her voice was solemn.

"He was. I remember him well. He was here until I was thirteen. Lord Vallon used to give me lessons with the sword. He continually watched over me. It was a comforting feeling to look around and see him there. He was never too busy to talk." Garion paused a minute. "His last battle, when he almost died, he was protecting me."

Krista looked to Garion stunned. Her father had never talked about it.

"I had snuck off to the village alone. Well, actually, not alone. I went with a man who I thought was a worker from the castle. He told me that my father had sent him to bring me to the village, that my father had something he had purchased for me, so I went with him."

Krista watched quietly as he continued.

"When Kuel turned on me and I figured out who it was, I panicked. I was trapped in a dead-end lane. There was no way to get away. I tried to run. Kuel knocked me to the ground just like he was swatting a fly. I still remember lying on the ground with Kuel standing over me. I had a bloody nose and was so scared. There was no one to help, and then, Lord Vallon was there."

He glanced at her, then back at the water. "The battle was awful, and all I could do was watch as Lord Vallon kept himself between me and Kuel. He was amazing to watch. I thought for a moment he was going to defeat Kuel. Kuel must have, too, because he fled. The battle was over. I went to Lord Vallon's side. That is when I realized how badly he was injured. He leaned on me until we found some help. Even then, he kept me by his side until he was put into bed. I was forced to leave while he was tended. I was covered with his blood."

Garion paused, remembering. "I missed him after he left. I wondered where he went. Was he alone? Was someone with him who cared? Now, I cannot help wonder about his sword. Do you think it is gone with him?"

Krista wasn't sure what to say, so told the truth. "I cannot tell you that." She knew Garion didn't take the statement as she meant it.

He nodded. "Come on. Let's practice to get our minds off it." The practice helped, but that night Krista lay awake thinking of her father. How would she fare when it came her turn to stand and protect Garion? She hated to think those thoughts, but she couldn't escape them and the cold sweats they brought.

A couple of weeks later, Garion entered the study hall, a large grin lighting his face. When questioned, he just answered, "It is a surprise."

A few minutes later, Roud entered with Lord Cowley. The boys fell silent waiting for what the men had to say. As Lord Cowley announced that there was going to be a weeklong trip into the mountains of Han, a ripple of excitement ran through the room.

First, they were placed in small groups as traveling companions; two older, two younger. Garion, Cam, Kris, and Marcus made up their group. Instructions were given on what to take, and they were dismissed so they could gather their belongings and make sure the horses were ready to ride at first light.

The next morning, every young man was out in the yard well before the appointed time. Roud and Sir Herald took the lead with Lord Cowley bringing up the rear. Krista had seen Lord Cowley on a horse several times now, but it was still an odd sight. Riding a horse really didn't seem to fit his manner, but it was his long legs that made him look so awkward. One had to wonder if, when he took them out of the stirrups, they would drag on the ground. During the day, Krista couldn't help but be impressed by his knowledge of the woods.

At different times the three men took turns riding up and down the group, talking with the students. They also took breaks to teach about plants, pointing out which ones were poisonous and which could be helpful. Krista, like most of the group, had been taught much of what was covered, but it was still interesting, and there were a few things that ended up being new to her.

They had covered quite a distance when Roud halted them for the night. Assignments were given. Each group constructed their own shelter. Some were to gather wood, and others prepared the food. They ate in a large group around the fire. As darkness fell, Lord Cowley told them several legends, and then it was time to turn in.

Krista had worried about this moment from the time she got back to her room after the trip was announced. Cam led the way to the shelter where their bedrolls had already been laid out. Ahead of her, Garion and Marcus stopped, pulling off their shirts before ducking to enter. Immediately, Krista froze. She was going to be sleeping by them.

"Is something wrong?" Garion asked as he sat down to pull off his boots.

"Ah, no, I will be back," Krista fought for to answer.

"Just do not step on me when you get in." He grinned.

Krista hurried a short distance into the woods. Leaning back against a tree, she tried to calm her nervousness. She'd worked and studied beside them for months. She was their friend. But, she was not sure she could go in and sleep beside them.

She was being foolish. They still had their pants on. She would remain dressed. She swallowed hard—but to lie beside them. She blinked back the tears that threatened. This time, she was really overstepping the bounds of their friendship.

Setting her jaw, she reined her thoughts in. It was pointless. There was nothing to worry about. To them she was Kris. They would never know it was a woman sleeping beside them. Nothing was going to happen. It was just one more activity she shared with them. She drew in a breath and let it out. She could do this.

She stepped away from the tree and quietly made her way back. Pausing outside their shelter, she pulled off her boots, took one more steading breath and stepped inside. Cam was already snoring. A rather loud rumbled that almost made her laugh, easing some of her tension.

Krista paused letting her eyes adjust before crawling in.

Garion stirred. "I was about to come looking for you. Thought you got lost."

"I see Cam snores," Krista said in way of an answer.

"Yeah, good luck sleeping. Think I should tell Celeste before he asks her to marry him?" Garion whispered back.

Krista gave a little laugh. "I don't think it will matter." She stretched out in her bedroll next to his, staying close to the outside. "Good night."

"Good night." His answer was followed by a yawn.

Krista laid there for some time, just listening to him breathe. As his breathing stilled and grew farther apart, she knew he was asleep. Closing her eyes, she drifted off.

Krista woke in the morning hearing Garion and Cam whispering and stirring around behind her while they dressed. Keeping her head covered with the blanket, she pretended to be asleep until they left, then quickly got up, leaving Marcus still asleep.

The next two days passed much like the first. Each night Krista waited until the others had gone to bed before going in. On the third day, the low hills gave way to rockier, higher mountains. The riding grew rougher. Several times they had to dismount and lead their horses. By late afternoon on the fourth day, they were beginning to tire of being in the saddle.

The mountain they were climbing was steep, causing them to keep their attention locked on the trail as they worked their way through the thick foliage. Then they crested the ridge and a valley opened up below with a beautiful emerald lake nestled in the bottom.

"We will make camp here tonight," Roud announced. "Once camp is set up, you all can go swimming."

A cheer went up from the young men echoing through the valley, and the pace down the slope quickened.

With their shelters up and horses tended, the young men headed for the water. Garion paused as Krista headed the other direction into the woods.

"Kris, you are not coming?"

"I told Jared I would gather the wood so he could go. I will find time to go down later."

"Would you like me to help?"

"No, go ahead. I need to feel ground under my feet for a while."

Garion hesitated a minute, then shrugged, heading for the water.

Krista made sure that she stayed well out of sight of the water and took plenty of time gathering wood so that she did not finish until all of the swimmers had enough time and were back in the camp, dressed. She had a nice-sized fire going when Roud and the hunting party returned. Once the meat was cooking, the entire group settled around on the ground.

Roud started to tell about the area. "On the morrow, we will climb some cliffs not far away." He pointed out the different landmarks. "Over the ridge that way, is the Valley of the Sisters of Laire. I do not want any of you to venture there. I will stress that—you are not to go there. The valley is to be left in peace."

Marcus spoke up. "Is there really a group of women living there?"

"You mean the Sisters, certainly," Lord Cowley answered. "The legend of the Sisters of the Valley is long and old, but very true. It is really not known how the community started or why for that matter. The women come from many places. It is said they are drawn there for one reason or another, some due to trials in their lives, others for the pursuit of knowledge and learning, and some just to worship. Men are forbidden to enter the valley. I have only met a few of the Sisters. There are not many and they do not leave the valley often. When they do, it is said to be for a very special reason. Wherever they go, they are to be treated with the highest respect."

"Why is that?" Krista voiced her curiosity.

"Not every woman who goes to the valley becomes a Sister. It is said to take a great deal of training, patience, and learning. They dedicate their lives to truth and right. We might not totally understand them and their ways, but it is for us to still respect them."

Krista nodded her acceptance.

Lord Cowley continued, "One thing known about them, which you all should find fascinating, is that every once in a great while, a group will leave the valley. Most are just escorts, but there will be one among them who is a 'Chosen', chosen by whom I don't know, just that it is for a special task, a task which only that person can perform. It is truly very mysterious, but any assistance asked for is to be given to a Chosen group."

"No one knows what the woman is to do?" one of the boys asked.

"Not before it is done and then sometimes not even after. I have never heard of it happening in my lifetime. All I do know is that the Chosen never utters a word once they leave the valley until their task is completed." The conversation went on until the meat was cooked and they started to eat.

On finishing dinner, Marcus turned to Krista. "Do you have your little flute with you? I want to show Lord Cowley how I finally memorized that poem."

Garion must have picked up the hesitancy that passed over Krista because he poked her in the ribs with his elbow. "Go ahead, we will all sing."

Krista pulled the small flute from its sleeve and began to play while the others joined in.

When they finished, Lord Cowley spoke up. "Very nice, now I see why everyone has passed that off to me. I have not heard it in song for ages. What else can you play?" Krista played several other melodies, then one to which Lord Cowley joined in with words. "That is another song I have not heard for many years."

"My instructor was an older man. I guess that was what he knew," Krista muttered evasively, not wanting to say more about Darm or her past.

Lord Cowley instructed her to play it again and proceeded to teach the group the words. "That was very good, but now, I am afraid, it is time to retire. Good night, lads." He rose and moved to his tent.

Krista slid her flute away and went straight to bed, pulling the blanket up around her. She feigned sleep when the others came in a short time later. She lay still for quite a while after the camp fell silent, then waited longer to make sure everyone was asleep before she carefully worked her way out of her blanket. Extra blanket in hand, she moved quietly, pausing to listen for any other movement before making her way toward the lake.

Krista walked along the edge of the water enjoying the quiet. Moonlight glowed across the ripples. She moved on. Around some willows, she found another opening to the water that was secluded, the perfect place for her swim.

With a final glance around, she removed Kallairion from her belt. For a moment she considered changing it to a dagger and strapping it to her leg, then decided against it. Carefully, placing Kallairion so that the rocks hid it, she removed the rest of her clothes. At the water's edge, she laid her blanket over a bush then entered the water.

The slight chill felt refreshing after three days of riding. She sank down letting it cover her and then pushed off the bank. Her strokes carried her effortlessly through the water. It'd been too long since she had been able to enjoy a swim. With regret, she knew she didn't dare stay long. After scrubbing and rinsing her hair, she made her way back to the shore coming up near the bush. The air was crisp after being in the water. She hurried to wrap the blanket around her.

Garion had been only partly asleep when he heard Kris stir beside him. It wasn't until something in his mind picked up that Kris hadn't stopped to pull on his boots, that curiosity woke him fully. Garion looked out in time to see Kris move out of the camp, heading toward the lake.

His curiosity soared. Pulling on his boots, he followed in the direction Kris had taken. Breaking through some willows, he could see his friend moving along the shore. He lost sight of Kris as he moved around the trees and bushes. Still Garion continued to follow, wondering where Kris was headed and why he was so far away from camp.

Garion had almost decided that he had lost Kris when he broke into the small opening by the shore. Looking around for which direction to take next, Garion noticed the pile of clothes to the side. It was what was on top of the pile that drew his attention.

He lifted a strip of wrappings that might be used for a bandage. Kris hadn't mentioned an injury, and the bandages were clean. Looking out over the water, he could just make out the head of his friend. Everyone, including him, thought that Kris could not swim since he would never join them, but there he was, swimming without any trouble in the middle of the night.

Garion glanced down at the wrapping in his hand. Kris had always been a little hard to figure out, different in some ways, but he felt a special bond with him. Garion himself did not understand what it was about Kris, but this time, he decided to wait and get some answers—like, why Kris would sneak off in the middle of night to bathe.

Stepping back into the bushes, his wait was not long. He heard the quiet splashing as Kris moved to shore. His friend was wrapped in a blanket when he approached his clothes and came into Garion's line of sight.

With panicked movements, Kris searched the clothes and the ground around them. Garion looked down again at the wrapping still in his hand.

"Looking for this?" Garion questioned, stepping forward. Kris spun around, startled. Moonlight gleamed off bare shoulders. Suddenly, Garion was aware of something he had never suspected. The softness of Kris's shoulder flowed down to an even softer curve hinted at under the blanket.

"Garion!" Kris's gasp was almost a whisper.

He raised his gaze to meet startled, uncertain, and frightened eyes. Her breathing became unsteady as she locked one arm around her waist, the other over her front holding the blanket tight. For a moment, neither could say anything. Garion's eyes moved up and down her as feelings of pain and betrayal filled him.

"You're a girl," he finally stammered with anger and shock in his voice.

"Garion, please." Krista trembled visibly as she stepped toward him. She fought to get words out. She blinked rapidly, but he didn't soften.

His anger flowed. "You lied to me . . . pretending to be a boy, to be my friend."

"No!" Krista tried to interrupt.

"Who are you? What is this?" Garion fought to understand what was before him.

"Garion, I'm sorry. I never wanted—"

"Why?"

"I cannot, please." A tear rolled down her cheek.

"Is it a game, a joke? Becoming my friend, my companion, is it all a game?" His voice filled with more pain and anger.

"No," Krista gasped.

"No? What is it then? The joy of being a man, fighting, talking—"

This time she cut him off. "No, I hate it. I hate deceiving you," she cried so openly that he was taken aback.

As he stared at the young woman before him, her tears washed away some of his anger. He softened. "I do not understand." He suddenly felt a longing to step forward, to comfort her, but stood his ground.

"Garion, I am sorry. I never meant to hurt you. I wish I could explain, but I cannot. I am only doing what I have to. Please trust me."

He felt his anger rise again. "Trust you? What do you mean you cannot explain? You cannot expect me to let you go on . . ." In frustration, he lost the words.

"Garion, please, it is important," she pleaded.

"Why?"

"It is my destiny."

"To be a boy," he stated doubtfully.

"No! No, to protect you!" she cried out.

He shook his head. "What makes you think you are to protect me?"

"It is my destiny. Please, I cannot tell you anymore. I have already said too much."

"On the contrary, I do not think you have begun to tell me, and until you tell me everything, you are not getting your clothes back." He stepped over them.

Krista took a step back. "Garion, please."

He shook his head, folding his arms in front of him. "Tell me everything, and I am making it a royal command."

She looked trapped, frightened, but he didn't soften. She started to speak several times but couldn't get anything out, then her shoulders drooped as she gave in.

"Garion, what I am about to tell you, you cannot tell anyone else, not even your parents. Please promise me that. One day it could mean my life."

"I will have to wait until I have heard what you have to say before I will promise that." He remained rigid.

Krista nodded, forced to accept his terms, but looked around carefully before she started. "You know of Kallairion."

"Of course, but what does this have to do with that? It disappeared with Vallon."

"Do you know anything of Vallon's family?"

"I know he had a wife and daughter, but they died when I was very little." He was becoming annoyed.

"What if I was to tell you that the baby did not die?"

"The baby was killed by Kuel. They found the body," Garion stated sharply.

"The baby they found in the cradle was not Vallon's," Krista answered getting close to tears.

"What are you saying?" Garion demanded, feeling a fissure of unease at what was coming.

"Kuel killed my mother, but . . ." Krista paused to take a shaky breath.

"Are you trying to say you are Vallon's daughter?" Garion finished for her, instantly knowing the truth in the words.

Krista nodded, pulling the blanket tighter around her.

He figured the action was more for comfort than to ward off the chill. Garion looked at the woman before him. Everything seemed so hard to believe. How could he have mistaken her for a boy? She looked so soft, so vulnerable, and so pretty. Beautiful actually. And here she was, telling him she was his protector, that she was a person believed to be dead. "No, it is impossible."

"Will you let me prove it?"

"How?"

"Just let me touch my sword. I do not even need to pick it up. Just touch it."

"All right," Garion nodded but didn't back away.

Krista pulled the blanket up and nervously stepped beside him. Squatting down, she rested her fingertips on the hilt. She looked around, up at him, and then dropped her eyes to the sword. "Kallairion change," she commanded softly. Light shimmered from the sword. The small sword that she carried expanded and shifted. When the glow subsided, the greatsword that was best known as Kallairion lay on the ground.

Garion gaped, not sure if he could believe what he'd just seen. Krista wrapped her hand around the handle and, with effort, lifted the sword with one hand, extending it out to him. Garion reached out to touch it, then pulled back in awe.

"It is all right. Kallairion will not hurt you. It is sworn to protect you. I am sworn to protect you."

"With your life," he said softly, remembering what she had said in the stable when *she* found out he was the prince. "When she," the words escaped in a hushed tone as the significance hit him. He reached out and fingered the ornate hilt. "I still do not understand. Everyone thought you were dead."

"It is a long story, but . . ." she shifted. "Friends of my mother's had stopped to visit and to show her their baby. While they were visiting, I grew fussy and would not stop crying, so my nursemaid took me for a walk. The other baby was asleep so they'd laid it in my cradle. Kuel came . . ." Tears tickled down Krista's cheek. Garion slid his hand down over hers on the sword. "He killed them all."

"When the maid returned and saw what had happened, she hid me away. The message had already reached my father of the deaths. He faced Kuel and drove him away. Afterward, the nursemaid had her husband, who was a good friend of my father's, bring him to me. My father decided that, since everyone, especially Kuel, thought I was dead, it was best to leave it that way because, if Kuel ever found out I was alive, he would come after me again just as he had before. Joanna, my nursemaid, and her husband, Darm, agreed to take me away and protect me. They raised me as their own while my father remained at Arlanda.

"My father had hoped he would be able to eventually destroy Kuel or at least live until I could bear a new Champion. When he was injured, he knew he could not stand against Kuel again, and began to have me trained. When he died, I became the Champion of Kallairion. It was decided that it was best for me to come to Arlanda as a boy so no one would guess I was Vallon's daughter." She lifted her eyes to meet his. "Garion, please, you cannot tell anyone. My advantage when I face Kuel will be surprise." Her eyes pleaded with him.

"I cannot believe you are a girl," was all he could manage to get out.

"Kallairion helps with the illusion."

He looked down at the rags in his hand. "It is a little hard to believe. Kallairion. You are my champion and a woman. I mean, I have seen you fight, and you have saved my life twice already, but . . ."

He paused, then nodded, extending the wrapping to her. "I give you my word. I will keep your secret."

Krista took a shaky breath and smiled.

Again, Garion's gaze moved over her, taking in the blanket and the curves beneath it. "I am afraid it will take me awhile to get used to the idea that a woman is my guardian."

Krista blushed. "I think I had better dress."

Garion stepped aside so she could pick up her clothes. When Krista moved behind the bushes, he turned his back.

"I will wait." His anger had drained away, leaving him overwhelmed with what he had learned. He remained quiet, thinking of her until his thoughts reached a point where they had to come out. "Kris, is that your real name?"

Behind him, he heard her move from the bushes. He turned to face her. She was dressed as Kris but still did not look like him. Her face seemed soft and fine. Her eyes were beautiful. Even in the moonlight, he could see how bright blue they were.

"It is Krista." Suddenly she looked about to cry again. Garion moved forward, tentatively touching her cheek as her chin trembled. Without thinking, he reached out, wrapping an arm around her shoulder. For a moment she stood rigid, then she buried her head into his chest. Tears came even as she fought to suppress them.

Only a minute passed before she pulled back, wiping away the tears. "I am sorry. I have not cried since my father died, since I became Champion of the Sword." She reached down, picking up Kallairion. Without a word, Kallairion shimmered in her hand, and changed into the sword she normally carried.

Garion stared. "That is amazing. How do you do it?"

"I just have to think of commanding it. It knows my thoughts."

He looked at it in amazement.

"That is how I knew you were in trouble on the wolf hunt. It warned me and then led me to you."

"It talks to you?"

"Not exactly, it is more like I get feelings. I am not really sure how it works."

"You know, a second ago, I could not believe I ever thought you were a boy. Now, you look like Kris standing before me." Puzzlement filled his voice.

She shrugged her shoulders. "Kallairion finishes the illusion."

"It is still going to take a while for me to get used to you being a woman."

Krista grabbed his arm. "Garion, you cannot think of me as a woman. You must treat me just the same as you always have. If anyone ever suspected, it could be disastrous."

"I understand. It is just . . . there are instances, like changing in front of you, swimming, you know," he said kind of embarrassed.

"I promise, I never look."

"No, you do not, do you," he observed. "That is the answer to the big mystery that has everyone baffled." He could tell Krista was blushing, even in the darkness. "We had better get back to camp before someone notices we are missing. You know, I have never slept by a woman before." He winked.

"You did last night," she teased back.

"That does not count. I did not know it then."

"Well, I suggest you do not think about it now."

"I am afraid you have given me quite a few things to think about." They walked in silence back to camp. As they worked their way quietly into their bedrolls, their eyes met. Garion gave her a grin that she couldn't help but return before laying her head down to sleep.

Chapter Eight

Krista was helping prepare breakfast when Garion crawled from the tent. His gaze went right to her. There was a tightening around his eyes and she figured he was trying to see through the illusion. She wondered what he saw.

Later as they rode, Krista caught him staring at her again. "Stop that," she hissed. She was glad that he knew, but it also put them in a hard position. He was fighting to come to grips with his knowledge, but his scrutiny was becoming disturbing, and she was afraid that someone else might notice it.

Just before noon, they arrived at cliffs set into the hillside, and Roud called for a halt. They spent the rest of the day climbing up and down the cliffs as Roud instructed them on scaling. Krista found that she did very well, being able to climb and descend the mountain faster than any of the other men.

"Kris is lighter and built closer to the ground—and being as agile as a mountain goat does not hurt," Lord Cowley commented.

A wave of laughter followed with several slaps to her back.

The climbing continued, letting them gain experience and confidence. Late in the day Krista ended up being one of the last ones to go down the most difficult climb. Once they dropped over the outcropping of rocks, they had to rely solely on the ropes and the person above to lower them for a distance until they could reach the jagged side further down the mountain. Even after that, it was a long, rough climb down to the campsite below.

Marcus took his position holding Krista's rope, bracing his feet behind a couple of rocks. Carefully, Krista moved to the edge and was about to step over.

"Snake!" The cry broke the air. One boy jumped back, and another froze just a foot from the hissing reptile.

"Do not move," Roud commanded. Everyone watched the older man draw his sword. He moved so slowly, so carefully, then in a blur the sword dropped, and the snake fell still.

Before anyone could release the breath that they were unconsciously holding, Roud spoke, "On with it now."

Krista took a second to look at the man before she started backwards over the edge of the cliff. All eyes shifted to her as she measured the placement of each foot. The rope tightened as she dropped against it. Feet spread, she cushioned the impact with the rocks. Bouncing back out, she slid down farther. Just as she swung back toward the mountain, Krista felt a violent jerk. The next instant she dropped free. The momentum smashed her into the side of the cliff. It jarred every bone in her body and knocked the breath from her.

In desperation, she clawed at the mountain, trying to catch hold of anything to stop her fall. Rocks scraped and cut her fingertips. Another jerk ripped through her body as her fall stopped. Pain filled her arm, but she didn't let go of the rock she'd managed to grab.

Krista hardly dared breathe. Above her she heard cries and shouts, while below her friends stared up in horror. Carefully, she felt around with her other hand until she found another hold. Taking a deep steadying breath, she heard Lord Cowley yelling instructions to help her find footing. His directions became the center of her focus. On the first attempt, she missed the foothold. Then, to her relief, she felt a small ledge under her feet.

Lord Cowley yelled her circumstances to those above, telling them there was no way she could climb down or up.

"Can you hear me, Kris?" Garion called down.

"Yes," she squeaked out, hardly daring to answer.

"I am coming down. Just stay still," he yelled.

Over the pounding of her heart she heard what sounded like an argument. Roud was telling Garion he couldn't go and Garion answered he was going. Then Garion commanded Cam to take hold of his rope.

Krista could hear Garion as he stepped over the edge. Shifting her eyes up, she caught a glimpse of him. As he dropped from the outcropping, a shower of dirt and pebbles rained down. Krista jerked and the footing crumbled out from under her. She felt herself slipping. Pain again shot through her arms. Once more, she clung to the rock with only her handholds.

"Garion, I cannot hold on much longer," she cried out.

"I am almost there. Just hang on." He worked his way to her, careful not to bring more rocks down.

Krista did not dare look up to see where he was, but she was comforted as the sound of his breathing came closer. With a gasp, she felt her handhold give under the strain. Her scream was cut off by the jerk on her waist.

Garion groaned from the strain on his arm. When the downward stretch of the rope halted, Krista dangled from the rope around her waist, staring at the jagged rocks and the horrified faces below. Garion's grab had came just as her hold broke free.

"I have you." Garion's voice sounded labored, but it was the most wonderful thing she'd ever heard. "Lower slowly," he yelled to the people holding the rope above. With a jerky action, the rope inched them down.

"Halt," he shouted up, swinging her close to a crevice. "See if you can catch hold and right yourself," Garion instructed her. After a couple of attempts, Krista managed to grab the rock facing, bring herself upright and get her footing.

"That's it," he calmed. Using his body, he forced her closer into the rock. "Now, grab hold of me."

The fear of releasing her handhold locked her muscles.

"Take hold of me," Garion snapped, breaking the spell over her mind.

Reaching out, she caught one arm around his neck, then the other. "Garion." His name escaped her lips.

"It is all right. I have you." He braced himself and then caught the end of her rope, securing it around his waist. "Just hold tight, we are going down now." He waited while she tightened her grip around him then yelled above. "All right, we are ready, lower away." It seemed like an eternity until their feet touched the ground.

The others crowded around as Garion untied the ropes. Krista's knees were weak. She wanted to drop. She wanted to cry but held it in. The next thing she knew Garion was guiding her to their tent.

"Let's give him some air and a chance to rest." Garion turned to Lord Cowley. "Keep everyone back for a little while." He pushed her into the tent, stopping just long enough to grab a water jug before pulling the cover closed behind him.

With the others shut out, Krista crumbled to the ground. Her hands shook violently in front of her face as she tried to fight back the sobs. Garion knelt down in front of her, wrapping his arms around her. He pulled her to him. She buried herself against him, taking his comfort as silent sobs shook her body.

He slid one hand behind her head and drew her in, tucking her under his chin. The other arm pulled her even tighter to him as he tried to calm her. She knew he was afraid that any moment someone would enter, but she couldn't stop the release of tension.

After a brief time, he took hold of her shoulders forcing her back. "You are all right." He enunciated the words, adding strength to them.

Krista nodded, taking a couple shaky breaths to calm herself.

"Kris."

She raised her eyes to meet his look, and recognized of his warning. "Yes." She closed her eyes and took several deep breaths. When she opened her eyes, her composure was back.

Dampening a corner of a blanket, he wiped the tears from her face, and cleaned where the rocks had scraped her cheek.

"Where are you hurt?" he asked, his voice maintaining a forceful tone.

"Just bruises, I think. I thought I was going to fall." Her trembling started again.

Reaching out, Garion caught her wrists, looking at her. "You are all right," he repeated.

She gave a single nod and whispered, "Thank you."

Before anything else could be said, sunlight streamed in as Roud pulled back the tent flap and knelt in the opening. "How is he?" he asked, inspecting Krista's hands that were being held by Garion.

"Just bruises and scrapes," Krista answered firmly.

The older man nodded. "Get them cleaned." Roud started to back out then paused, looking at Garion. He grinned. "The man comes out." He was gone.

"What was that about?" Garion said, stunned by the comment.

She shrugged. "What happened up there?"

"Roud was not going to let me go, in case of another accident."

"And you told him you were going."

Garion nodded, a grin spread across his face, replacing the anxiety. "Come on. Let's get your hands cleaned."

That evening around the campfire Krista sat between Garion and Marcus, as Marcus was once again apologizing for her rope breaking even though Krista and everyone else assured him that it was not his fault.

Brock moved up behind them and spoke up. "That is right. It was his own fault. He should have checked his rope first." Brock no longer bothered to hide his loathing for Krista.

"I did." Krista met his glare.

"Hah. If you ask me, you were careless, and then you endangered Prince Garion's life when he had to rescue you."

If it were not for Garion's hand closing on her arm, holding her back, Krista would've been on her feet and most likely on Brock.

Lord Cowley, observing from not far off, stepped forward. "I think it has been a long day. Everyone turn in. We head for home in the morning."

Brock looked to the Lord, then moved off with Krista's eyes following him until Garion squeezed her arm. She turned to him.

"Come on." He motioned.

Nodding, she stood. They were almost to the tent when he split her off from the others.

"You know," he started talking quietly, "after last night, I really do not like you confronting Brock like that. You could get beaten up again."

"Garion, I did check my rope. I do not know why it broke, but I was not careless. Also, I know the risks. I can't back down to Brock. If you were in my place, you couldn't either."

He stopped. "Kris, how far does this go?"

She waited only a brief second before answering. "As far as it has to. One day I will face Kuel. There is no other option, because I cannot sit back and let him kill you and your parents, and rule the people. I just cannot let that happen without trying to stop him." She stared back until she could no longer meet his eyes. She turned away, striding purposely to the tent.

Her back was toward him as he came in and settled down in his bedroll.

She knew his eyes were on her as were his thoughts. This was something Garion would have to come to grips with himself. It hadn't been an easy first day for him to be aware she was a woman. She could give him that, but she could not let it affect her. She was who and what she was, the Champion of Kallairion. She would have to face Kuel, put herself between one of the Mighty Ones and Garion. He would have to accept that, just as she had.

Pulling her blankets up around her shoulders, she tried to clear her mind, but fear seeped in, fear of clinging to the cliff, fear of falling, falling down, down. For her, the bottom didn't come. Laughter rumbled around her—echoing through the void into which she dropped. Kuel was out there—waiting.

Krista came awake with a jerk. She lay still, afraid the laughter would begin again right outside the tent, but the only thing she heard was a squirrel scurrying up a tree. She waited for a while longer, knowing that there would be no returning to sleep. Unable to stay in bed any longer, she quietly worked her way out of the tent. The sky was beginning to lighten, but she could still make out a few stars in the sky. She drew a deep breath of the chilly air, letting it wipe away the last tendrils of the disturbing dream. She rubbed her hands up and down her arms to ward off the cold.

It only took her a few minutes to bring the banked embers of the fire back to life. There was still no movement from any of the tents so she decided to take the opportunity to go to the stream and wash up. She walked along it quite a ways, enjoying the peace, before she settled on the bank. She washed quickly then lay back in the grass, ignoring the touch of dew, wondering what would happen now that Garion knew her secret. She hoped he could accept it because his friendship meant everything to her. There would be changes though, she realized.

The changes came sooner than she expected and mainly affected Garion. She entered the camp just as he stepped from the tent. He straightened, and his eyes met hers. In that look, Krista realized things were okay between them.

Garion had just started toward her when Roud stood and informed the group Garion would be in charge of the journey home. For the first time, the young man who would one day be king was given the responsibility to prove himself.

Over the next two days, Garion did well and the trip home remained uneventful. Garion was kept so busy that Krista figured he had little time to contemplate her. The evening after they returned, Krista went to practice by herself. She was going through blocking and attack routines when she spun around to find Garion watching her.

"I thought you were not coming," she greeted him.

"Sorry, I was tied up in a meeting."

Krista tried to figure out the odd expression that he wore and then made a guess. "Garion, if it makes you nervous, you do not have to practice with me. I understand. I also will understand if you want to have me replaced as your companion."

"Kris, that is not it at all. I have done a lot of thinking about you, and I have decided that the best place for you is where you are."

"Thank you." She swallowed. "I need your friendship."

Garion smiled, drawing his sword as he walked to face her.

"I need yours, too. There are going to be some changes though," he said as they moved around each other. Coming forward, he attacked only to be countered by her. "I am to spend less time in lessons and more time handling affairs of the kingdom."

"Congratulations," Krista said, coming around with a block.

"Thanks, but there is more. I am also to start doing drills with the palace guards, and there is to be a skills test. Those who pass will move up with me."

"What kind of a test?"

"There will be individual skills, then a final skills course. It will be very difficult. Everyone who decides to try will be judged by the way they handle it, not by age."

"You mean I will be allowed to try even though I am only supposed to be fifteen?"

He nodded. "Kris, how old are you—really?"

"I will be eighteen soon." She used his moment of surprise to attack, bringing the flat of her sword around to swat him on the rear as she moved past.

"Oww!" He spun to face her as she grinned back at him. "You," he drew the word out, "better be careful. That is not playing fair."

"You just have to keep your mind on what we are doing, not on other things," Krista said.

He smiled back. "All right, no more personal questions, but I am going to get even for that swat." Advancing, he forced her back, but she met his attacks, blocking each of them. They continued until they both yielded in exhaustion.

"Good practice." Garion walked around while he cooled off.

Looking over, he watched as she changed Kallairion back into a dagger and slid it into her boot. Shaking his head, he realized it would take him some time to get used to seeing that. Then, he felt a warm feeling that Krista no longer hid it from him. There was going to be a new level to their friendship.

Glancing over, she noticed his odd smile. "What?"

"Nothing," he walked toward her. "Just . . ." He tossed his sword aside. "I owe you this." He reached out and caught her before she had time to prepare.

Krista struggled as he brought her to the ground. Attempting to roll to the side to pull away, she was dragged back. Changing direction, she tried to squirm free. Garion caught her shoulders forcing her back flat on the ground, pinning her body with his. Slowly Krista ceased to fight.

"You still lose when it comes to wrestling." Garion could not keep back the wave of satisfaction rushing through him. Then, as he looked down at Kris, he again became aware of her as Krista.

Garion felt her work for breath. Yet, it was almost as if she was afraid to breathe. He looked into her eyes, amazed at the deep-blue tint. Suddenly, he realized he was drawing closer. Through her eyes, he saw a flash of uncertainty as if she too realized it.

Without warning, he rolled to the side, bringing her with him. As she cleared the ground, a resounding smack echoed as his hand hit her rear. Krista gasped and squirmed.

This time he let her go.

Krista stumbled to her feet, rubbing her bottom and glaring at him.

Garion broke into a laugh. “I said I would get even.”

Krista bit the edge of her lip to hold back the grin, but it was no use. She too joined in, lightening the tension between them.

That night, Garion lay in his bed thinking of the practice, thinking of Krista. When he had looked into her eyes, he hadn’t seen Kris. There was the tenderness and beauty of the young woman within. He had to admit to himself that he hadn’t wanted to slap her. He had wanted to kiss her, just to lower his lips those last couple of inches to hers. Maybe their friendship was indeed headed to a different level. He felt content at the thought.

Chapter Nine

Things seemed to settle down between Garion and Krista, though every once in a while Krista would catch Garion looking at her oddly. Usually it was in the practice yard when she was fighting with one of the other men. Their walks in the gardens continued, but he often asked her about her childhood and training. She knew he tried not to pry, but curiosity was there.

Garion became even more careful of her privacy. The one change he made that Krista greatly appreciated was for her to bathe in his private bath, giving her more time, and ending the chances of her being caught.

The test was announced when Lord Cowley joined Roud on the practice field about halfway through their drills. There would be two weeks of preparation for those who wished to try. The first areas they would be judged on were skills of combat and horsemanship. The final would be a skills course. The whole test would take a couple of weeks to complete. To give the young men a respite before the challenge, a ball was planned for that evening. They were released early to clean up for it.

Leaving the practice field, the conversation turned to the ball and young women. Krista fell silent during the boys' talk. Her mind drifted away to the upcoming test. Would she be able to make it?

Her supposed age was almost a year younger than the youngest that decided to try. She had already gained a reputation of being a good competitor and a fast learner. Despite her size, it was known she could do well against most of the others. She had to do well, at least well enough to be advanced, but just how much would it take?

Krista remained lost in thought all the way back to her room. She didn't even realize that Garion was behind her until he pushed her through her doorway. Startled, she turned to face him then stepped back from the anger that showed in his countenance.

"Do you enjoy that? Listening to the talk? What about the dancing? Is it exciting to you to fool the women as well? To know that they have no idea they're dancing with another woman. Do you really enjoy that?"

Shocked by his anger, she was too stunned to react. Then the door between their rooms slammed as he went through it.

For a moment, Krista just stood there, his words echoing in her mind. The pain of betrayal grew. It had never been as bad as she now felt. Why did Garion say those things? Crumpling to her bed, she cried. It was almost time for the ball when she finally stopped. Pulling in the feelings, she readied for the ball since she'd been commanded by Lord Cowley to attend.

Every ball she had attended had been miserable for her. This one was awful. Five times Lord Cowley or Sir Herald had brought a maiden to her to escort onto the dance floor. Several times she saw Garion watching her from where he was dancing. She couldn't meet his looks, and she couldn't help but cringe when she looked back at the maiden she was partnered with.

Garion's eyes fell on Kris the moment she walked in the door. It didn't take long to see how miserable she looked. He watched as she tried to stay out of the way, but Sir Herald brought a young girl over, and Krista was forced to dance. She held herself at a distance, moving awkwardly. Garion knew how unfair he had been to her. He could see how much she hated what was going on.

Excusing himself, he moved behind Krista, tapping her on her shoulder. She immediately stepped back to let someone cut in. Surprise filled her face when she looked at him, then her expression became guarded. Garion felt pain, knowing he'd caused that response.

"If you will excuse me, I am afraid I need your partner for a minute. Kris, will you follow me, please."

Krista silently followed him to a secluded area in the garden. Garion turned to her. "You looked like you needed help."

It was obvious that Krista had been ready for another lecture and could only whisper, "Thank you."

Garion tried for a smile, but became seriousness. "I owe you an apology. I guess I am still having trouble accepting this. Sorry. This must be hard for you." Even in the moonlight, he could see tears welling in her eyes.

"I do not like deceiving people." Her voice trembled.

Garion reached out, locking his arm around her shoulder.

She accepted the hug.

"I am sorry for what I said," he whispered. Garion felt her arms slide around him. He felt her tremble, as hot tears dampened his shirt. Once again she seemed so small, so vulnerable against him. Pulling her tighter, he tucked her under his chin. It wasn't long enough for him when she pushed back, wiping tears away in frustration with the back of her hand.

"We should return to the ball." She stepped to the pond to splash water on her face.

Garion waited behind her.

"You can go on without me." Krista kept her back to him.

"It is all right. I will wait."

"Please." The soft plea came.

Garion stayed still a moment before turning to leave. The ball was almost over before he saw Kris sneak back in, positioning herself out of the way. Krista was forced to dance the last dance but made for the door as soon as the music stopped.

Though many of the young people lingered, Garion made his way straight to his parents, saying good night before heading back to his room. Once inside, he knocked on Krista's door. He had almost decided she was not going to answer when the door finally opened a crack.

Krista's head tilted down, not meeting his look. "Garion, I would like to go to bed now." She started to close the door.

He moved forward, stopping the door with his hand. "Please, Krista, I would like to talk. We need to talk." He waited until she opened the door enough for him to step through.

Krista turned her back on him and moved away. On the bed lay her dress shirt and coat. On the floor by the wall were her wrappings, where he guessed she had thrown them. She was barefoot but still had on her breeches and an oversized nightshirt.

"Krista . . ."

"Garion, please go."

He stepped forward, resting his hands on her shoulders. When she tried to pull away, he moved with her.

"Please," Krista whispered.

Garion released her only to move in front of her. She tried to move around him. He shifted with her. Reaching out, he caught her shoulder. The hold was light, and she could have pulled away, but she stayed rooted in that spot.

"Krista, please stop the illusion and look at me." There was a softening about her though she didn't raise her head. Placing a hand under her chin, he lifted it. "Krista."

She caught a breath, looking up at him, pain etched in her face.

"I am sorry. I mean it. I am so sorry."

Again, she caught a breath before she tried to speak. "I do not like . . . I do not feel." For the second time that night, he slid his arms around her, pulling her to him. If he thought she felt small and vulnerable before, it was nothing to what she felt now as he could feel the curves of her body pressed against his. Her arms circled around him.

He stood in the middle of the room holding her. He'd hurt her. How could he have said those things? She'd given up her life for her duty. He had accused her of—well, he didn't understand it himself. It upset him when she fought with the others, then it upset him when she danced as a boy with the maidens.

Maybe what bothered him most was that he wished she could have danced with him. He wanted to walk with her out into the moonlight like many of the others who had special maidens. He wanted to slide his arms around her and gently kiss her.

Garion became all too aware of holding her. Her crying had stopped, but she still clung to him. His hands rubbed up and down her back. He ran his fingers through her hair. It was short but so soft. He touched his lips to the side of her head so briefly that he doubted she noticed. He tightened his hug and, as if she became aware of the intimacy of their stance, she pulled back.

Her cheeks were red with embarrassment.

Garion wondered if his matched. He felt very warm. "Are you all right?"

Krista nodded, walking to the door.

Garion took the hint and followed suit.

"Good night," Krista looked up through lowered lashes.

"Good night." He studied her features for a moment. This was the best look he had ever had of her as Krista. It was even more pleasing than by the lake. Her lashes were still damp from her tears and highlighted her eyes. Her smooth skin beckoned his hand to caress it. She had a beautiful mouth that curved up at the corners, giving her a sweet, soft appearance.

Tearing himself away, he reached behind him and opened the door.

Over the next two weeks, all the young men worked doubly hard preparing for the test. Evening practices with Garion became more challenging. Krista noticed his skill and strength increasing as he fought with the guards. Garion himself was amazed at her talent. He pressed her hard, but she could always match his blows.

Time passed quickly. They participated in competition after competition. Many evenings Krista felt ready to drop as she made her way to bed. She felt good about how she was doing, except for maybe hand-to-hand fighting. Still, she had made a fair showing there. In swordsmanship, she let a little more of her skills show and did very well.

The same was true in horsemanship, though she hadn't spent as much time on Shea's back as she had before coming there, it didn't take much practice to smooth out their rhythm again. They made an impressive pair with her ability to direct Shea without hands on the reins. Her shooting was as good as the day she had saved Garion from the birds. Even Roud complimented her afterward.

At last, it was the day of the final test to see the skills in use. The course was in a ravine not far from the castle. It had been set up with traps to avoid and targets to hit. The thick foliage and rough terrain added to the difficulty as each young man followed a laid-out trail. The score would be based on how well the individual performed.

The morning before the test, all gathered around the area after being given permission to make a ride through the course once. Krista stood talking with a group at the top of the ravine. No one particularly wanted to be the first to step into the course and possibly make a fool of themselves.

From behind, Brock approached. "You sound like a group of babes hanging on their mother's skirts. Pretty pathetic that even the prince's companion does not dare enter."

"We are waiting for Roud and the others to get here before we start. They might have further instructions for us." Krista realized Brock was trying to start something and decided that she wouldn't allow him to bother her, but before she could stop Marcus, he picked up the challenge.

"I will show you how to brave the ravine." Marcus swung onto his horse.

"Marcus," Krista reached to grab the reins as an uneasy feeling filled her. She was too late.

Marcus kicked the horse forward over the edge.

Krista watched helplessly as her friend's horse disappeared into the thick growth below. Behind them she heard a snicker. Krista spun around to face Brock.

"What is it?" She took a step forward.

"That oaf. I do not even know why he bothered." Brock sneered. "Even a weak runt like you can beat him. He should have given up long ago."

"Marcus is doing well." She defended her friend.

"He is laughable. He does not stand a chance."

A sinking feeling crept over her again, tinged with alarm. "Why?"

Brock glared back, tight lipped.

"What is it, Brock?" Krista eyed him suspiciously.

Once again it seemed that Brock was not going to answer her, then with a shrugged of his shoulders, he scoffed. "Just . . . I would guess he will not even make it a quarter of the way through."

"What do you mean, not make it? Why?" she demanded.

Behind her, a crash and an anguished cry rose from the ravine. Krista spun around with everyone else, searching for any signs of Marcus. "Marcus! Marcus!" she yelled. No answer came. She turned on Brock. "What have you done?"

"What do you mean?" Brock tried to deny, but his face paled slightly.

"You know what I mean? What have you done?" She stepped toward him, her hand falling onto the hilt of Kallairion.

"Nothing, I just added a few traps to make it more exciting. Anyone should be smart enough to avoid them."

"What kind of traps?" Her patience grew thin.

"Snares hooked to branches and rocks . . . some arrows." Brock shrugged his shoulders then pulled back to defend himself as Krista stepped forward. Instead of hitting him, Krista grabbed his horse's reins.

"That is my horse, you cannot do that."

She swung on the horse's back. "Shea is not ready to ride, and I would not take her down there with your surprises anyway. You had just better hope that Marcus is all right." She nudged the horse forward, knocking Brock out of the way.

At the edge of the ravine, Krista paused. "Sigmon, go get Garion. Tell him what happened. Everyone else stay here. Do not try to enter." With that, she urged the horse down the steep incline.

Chapter Ten

"Marcus!" Krista got no answer, but then a faint sound. Almost the instant the trees closed around her, she felt like she had entered a different world. Everything fell into shadows. A chill with an unmistakable eeriness pressed down. It didn't help that she knew there were hidden traps waiting for her, traps unlike the ones set for the contest, these would be dangerous, even deadly. Nervously, she fingered Kallairion.

Her eyes darted around as she moved forward. She hadn't gone far when a faint snap broke. Krista jerk back at the same time an arrow whizzed past her shoulder. She let out a sigh, moving on. To the side, she noticed rope. Following it, she found another crossbow; cocked, waiting to be triggered. Sliding Kallairion out, she carefully touched the rope, sending the arrow into a tree with a resounding thud.

"Marcus!"

"Kris." This time the answer came from closer.

"I am on my way," she shouted back, heading toward the sound of his voice.

She hadn't gone far when the trail she was following became blocked by downed trees and foliage. Sliding from the horse's back, she led the animal off the trail into the deeper growth. A twinge of alarm stopped her. Picking up a rock, she rolled it over the ground ahead her. Nothing happened.

Starting forward, she pulled back again, sensing danger. Taking another rock, she sent it rolling along the ground. It had gone only a couple of feet when a branch swung down out of a tree just in front of her. Krista barely managed to hold onto the horse as it shied back. She rubbed the animal's neck to calm it and then jumped when her name echoed from above.

"I am all right! I have almost reached him." Krista led the horse partway up the side-hill so she could bypass the blockage. Cresting a small rise, she saw Marcus. His shirt was covered with blood. A broken shaft of an arrow protruded from his side.

"Kris," he groaned at seeing her. He was alert but obviously in a great amount of pain.

Carefully, she worked her way forward. She reached him. Pulling off her vest, Krista sliced and tore it into strips. "Easy," she cautioned him. "Sorry. I know it hurts," Krista comforted when he groaned. "I will get you out of here."

Packing what material she could around the wound, she wrapped it in place to stall the blood. She had to keep the arrow from shifting and causing more damage. Krista knew it was the best she could do. She then started the task of getting him on the horse.

"Marcus, can you help me? I will never be able to lift you alone."

He gritted his teeth and nodded. It took a great deal of effort and most of the strength Marcus had to get him on the horse. He wobbled as he sat slumped forward on the horse's neck.

Krista mounted and wrapped an arm around the injured young man. Her other hand gripped the reins. The horse had barely moved when Krista found that she needed to use both hands to hold Marcus. She immediately wished she had Shea so she could use her knees to guide as Brock's horse didn't react to the same pressure.

From above, she heard Garion call her name.

"I have him!" She tried to make every word loud and clear. "He is badly injured. I am bringing him up now, but I cannot make it out the way I came in."

It took quite a bit of time to work around to what appeared to be a deer trail heading out. Alarm filled her. Krista pulled the horse back with all her might, nearly dumping them both off. She waited a moment. When nothing happened, she braced Marcus against her and reached out with Kallairion, slicing free a branch. It dropped, sending another arrow into the bushes.

"How many of those did he set?" Krista cursed, but Marcus didn't hear her as he had slipped into unconsciousness. Locking her arms around him, she fought to keep him on the horse. With a slight kick, the horse moved forward.

Krista figured she'd made it at least half the distance back. Her muscles felt strained from keeping Marcus on the horse. Taking a deep breath, she tried to calm the buzz of warning that ran through her. She stopped every few feet and studied the area, but she couldn't find any clue to the trouble. After the third stop and start, she was tempted to ignore the feeling when it literally blasted through her. She reacted immediately, but her control of the horse wasn't enough to keep it from taking the last step forward.

Krista caught just a glimpse of movement and automatically threw her arm up to protect Marcus. The breath was knocked from her, cutting off the outcry when the log slammed into her arm then glanced off her ribs. Krista felt herself being knocked from the horse. The back of her head hit the tree beside them as the frightened horse shied into it. Between hitting the tree and her hold on Marcus, who was slumped the opposite direction, somehow they both managed to stay in the saddle.

Broken branches and leaves rained down around her. The horse pranced nervously but, luckily, didn't dump them. In a brief moment it ended, and the only sound left was Krista's own gasps as she tried to breathe through the pain. Her body shook, and it was all she could do to keep from letting go of Marcus.

She knew right away that her left arm was broken. With the fire in her ribs, she didn't want to think if they were broken. She closed her eyes tight to keep from passing out and managed to catch a couple short breaths before urging the horse forward. Krista hoped there were no other traps waiting for her. If there were, she was in trouble. She didn't think she could handle another challenge.

Krista jerked, sending pain through her body as another arrow flew past just in front of her face. She held her breath, waiting for another as they moved on, but no more came. The sunlight broke through as the trees opened to the steep embankment. Garion and Roud slid down the hill toward her. Taking the reins, they led the horse up the slope.

Before Krista could say anything, several men lowered Marcus into a waiting wagon. With a nod of approval from Roud, the instructor hopped into the wagon, and it headed for the castle, leaving Krista sitting on the horse held by Garion. No one said a word as they watched the wagon take their friend and companion away.

Krista turned as it disappeared from view and caught sight of Brock standing to the side. Pain and anger intertwined, bursting out with strength she didn't have.

"You went too far this time." Her voice was low and tight. "That was meant for me."

Brock tried to look innocent. "I do not know what you mean. I was just trying to help by making it more difficult."

It was obvious he had rehearsed the response.

"Marcus better . . ." Krista tightened in pain.

Garion spun around and caught her as she slid from the animal.

A slight cry escaped her as he touched her arm and side. Her eyes closed as waves of pain threatened to overcome her consciousness.

Garion lowered her to the ground. He waited until she opened her eyes. "Where are you hurt?"

"Arm's . . . broken." She gasped. "Not sure . . . about ribs."

"We have to get you back to the castle."

"Garion, no."

Immediately, the light of realization donned in his eyes. There would be no way the physician could treat her without finding out she was a woman.

"You have to have help," he said softly, as his mind raced over options. Without stopping for an answer, he looked to Sigmon. "Find Lady Adele and have her come to my chambers! Tell her that Kris has a broken arm."

In way of answer Sigmon ran to his horse, leapt on, and rode toward the castle.

"Help me get Kris on my horse," Garion yelled.

Several of the boys stepped forward, holding her up while Garion mounted, then they boosted her up to him. With a quick thanks, he wrapped his arm securely around her and headed for the castle as fast as he dared.

He felt her tighten in pain several times but, surprisingly, she didn't say anything. For the first while, she squeezed his arm so tight that he would've admitted it hurt, but by the time they reached the palace, her hold was weak and lax.

Garion could see them moving Marcus from the wagon with a crowd swarming around to watch. A plan formed in his mind. He rode around the side to quietly enter through another door. With a gasp, Krista lost consciousness as he lowered her into his arms to carry her in. It wasn't hard to make it to his room unnoticed with most of the people watching them bring in Marcus.

Lady Adele was not at his room yet, so he proceeded to take off Krista's boots then stowed Kallairion under the pillows. He looked at the boy who he knew was actually a girl. He wished Adele would get there, but still jumped when there was a knock at the door. He opened it to Lady Adele and Sigmon, who carried a large leather satchel. Adele entered and Garion reached out to take the bag from Sigmon.

"Would you stand watch? I do not want anyone disturbing us."

Sigmon nodded. "Of course, Garion."

Garion closed the door and bolted it before moving through the inner room to the bedroom where Adele was already with Kris.

As he stepped in, she addressed him. "Garion, help me get his clothes off. I think we will have to cut the shirt away."

Garion froze. "I cannot."

Adele jerked her head up to look at him. "Garion, what's wrong? You have seen an injured man before. Now give me a hand."

Garion shook his head, staying back. "You will understand in a moment, but before you start, you have to give me your word. What you are going to find out here, you cannot reveal to another soul, not even my parents."

The lady looked at him, totally confused.

"Promise me," he stated.

Adele looked baffled and was about to question him, but seeing the sincerity in his, answered. "I give you my word."

Garion nodded. "It is very important, trust me. I will wait out here," he said, moving just through the doorway. He could hear the woman slice through the cloth.

"Well, the left arm is definitely broken." Then there was the sound of more cutting. "What . . . my gracious! Garion?"

Leaning his head back against the door, he fought the desire to hit something. "I am sorry, I cannot explain." Garion wasn't sure what to say. In a way, he felt that he had already betrayed Krista's secret, even though he knew that she had to have more help than he could give.

From the other room, Lady Adele commented. "Well, this is definitely no boy, and I would put her closer to seventeen, eighteen, than fifteen."

"Almost eighteen. As I said, I cannot explain. She will have to do that, but I am serious. You must not tell anyone she is a woman."

"Garion—" the lady started to object, but he cut her off.

"No one must know. Not even my parents."

There was silence while the woman took in the new knowledge. "I do not understand." She shook her heard. "How could she fool everyone? To look at her, her features are soft, fine. She is beautiful. How long have you known?" Adele asked.

"Not long."

"But Garion, why?"

"It is not for me to tell you."

Another long silence followed.

"You can come back in. She is covered."

Garion stepped into the room, his eyes going to the woman in his bed. The mask of a boy was gone. She looked as she did the nights at the lake and in her room. Her cheekbones were high and fine. Long, dark lashes were shielding her eyes. Her lips, opened slightly, seemed soft.

Lady Adele broke through his thoughts. "I have wrapped her lower ribs. I do not think any are broken but they may be. There is plenty of bruising. I think the wrapping on her chest saved her. I need your help with her arm."

He hesitated before taking Krista's arm as instructed. Krista jerked in pain a couple of times as they worked.

"She will be awake soon. Let's finish this before she does. Now, hold it still," Adele cautioned.

Garion's eyes followed Krista's arm to her bare shoulders, visible under the edge of the blanket, then looked away. Seeing that Adele had noticed, he turned red.

She just smiled. "Well, that answers one question about the relationship you two have."

"We are just friends," Garion answer quickly.

Adele's smile broadened.

A gasp drew both their attention to the bed.

"Easy there," Adele said, laying her hand on the young woman's shoulder to keep her still. Krista's eyelids fluttered open. She jerked involuntarily, then gasped as the movement brought additional pain. She tried to breathe amidst the discomfort. Her eyes focused on Adele with uncertainty then moved to Garion.

"It is all right, girl," Adele's comment pulled her attention back. In way of an answer, the lady gave her a warm, reassuring smile, brushing the hair back from her forehead. "You must lie still. You may have some cracked ribs. They are terribly bruised. Your left arm is broken. It is bad, but it will heal."

Krista swallowed. "What about Marcus?" She labored to get the question out.

"We have not heard yet. We just barely finished wrapping your arm," Garion answered.

Suddenly events seemed to come back to her, and Krista started to sit up. "I have to get out of here."

Immediately, Garion and Adele pushed her back into the soft pillows as dizziness flowed over her.

"You have to stay still," Adele commanded.

Garion followed up. "Do not worry. I will not let anyone else in here. I am sorry, but I had to have help for you."

Krista gave a slight nod. "I understand. Oh," she groaned. "I feel sick."

"It is the shock to your body," Adele said reaching over to wring water out of a rag then lay it across her forehead. "It is best you try to relax."

Krista closed her eyes, breathing as deeply as the wraps and pain would allow. After a moment she reopened them. "Lady Adele, please. It is important that it stay a secret that I am a woman." Krista's breathing became more rapid, causing more pain and dizziness. Immediately Garion cut her off, laying his hand to her lips.

"She is already promised. You can explain later."

Krista looked at him, calming. His fingers shifted to brush across her cheek. Krista closed her eyes with a sigh, succumbing to sleep.

Adele watched, saying nothing, as Garion seemed to study every fine feature of her face. His eyes drifted down her neck to her bare shoulders. It was then that Adele spoke up.

"Garion, who is she? Why is she pretending to be a boy?"

He shook his head, looking back at the lady. "I told you before, I cannot tell you. It is for Kris to decide to but, if she does not, you still cannot reveal that she is a woman. It must remain a secret."

"I do not understand, lad. What could be so important and how . . . she looks so much a woman now but, before, I would have sworn she was a boy." Lady Adele sighed. "I gave my word, I will hold to it."

Garion smiled. "Thank you." Before he could say anything else, there was a knock on the outer door. Garion looked in that direction then back at Krista. Pulling the blanket up further, he moved to the door. Opening it carefully, he was greeted by Roud and Lord Cowley.

"We heard that Kris was injured and found you had brought him here," Lord Cowley spoke. Garion was not sure quite what to do as the men entered.

Behind him, Lady Adele stepped from the bedroom, closing the door behind her.

"Please, keep it as quiet as possible. The lad is asleep." Moving across the room, she continued. "He has bruised ribs and a broken arm, nothing that will not heal, given a little time."

"How is Marcus?" Garion changed the subject.

"We do not know yet. He lost quite a bit of blood. He would have bled to death if Kris hadn't staunched the flow and brought him out when he did. Still, it may be some time before we know for sure," Roud answered.

"Is there anything we can do for Kris?" Lord Cowley asked.

"He just needs to be left alone to rest," Adele said. "Will you spread the word? No one is to come here. I do not want him disturbed."

Lord Cowley nodded.

Roud spoke up. "If you will excuse me, I have to go to the ravine and clear it out before anybody else is injured." He bowed to Adele.

"I should go talk with the young men. They will want to know what is happening." Lord Cowley also bowed and they left.

After locking the door behind them, Garion let out a sigh of relief. "Thank you, again," he said to Adele. "I was not quite sure how to handle them."

"I think it would be best to keep as many people as you can out. Just tell them the same thing, that he is asleep. We should also get a nightshirt to put on her the next time she wakes up. The bigger the better. We will have to cut the seam to get it on, but it would be best to cover her as much as possible."

After Garion found a suitable nightshirt, Lady Adele sliced up the side seam, and then sliced several strips free so there was a way to tie it on.

"Well, that should do. I am going to the kitchen to get something for her to eat. She will have to keep up her strength. I will get something for you, too. You missed lunch quite some time ago."

"Will you tell them that I do not plan to be down for supper, that I am going to stay here?" Garion requested.

"I am not sure what your parents will say to that, but I will see to it. You are right. One of us should be here at all times. Not only in case she wakes up, but to make sure no one gets in."

Garion walked Adele to the door and locked it behind her. Back in his room, he moved a chair beside the bed and settled down. Krista was sleeping. An occasional tightness came over her face from the pain her body was experiencing. Aggravation filled him. He didn't like the thought of her getting hurt.

Why did she have to be the one to go in after Marcus? Why didn't she wait until he got there? He laughed at himself. That would've been a fight. She wouldn't have let him go. She was his guardian, and he would've tried to stop her, to protect her. She wouldn't like his wanting to protect her, and she wouldn't have given into him, either.

In some ways, it would have been better if he had never found out that she was a female. Looking down at her, he was grateful that he had.

He laid his finger to her lips, then traced along her cheek, around to her chin, before letting his hand drop down to the soft smooth skin of her neck. It felt incredible, like touching the petals of a rose. He ran his finger along her collarbone and shoulder.

A small sigh escaped her. It startled him and he pulled his hand back, embarrassed and glad she was still asleep. What would she have thought if she had woken to his touch? But still the slight smile on her lips added to the warmth inside him.

Chapter Eleven

Garion was in the outer room talking with Adele when a groan from the bed brought them running. Krista lay, pale and fighting to catch her breath.

"Easy girl," Adele dabbed her face with the damp cloth. Slowly, Krista's breathing became steadier. "There now," Adele smiled encouraging. "I will not bother to ask you how you feel because it is quite obvious. Garion, will you step into the other room? While she's already in pain, I may as well slide the nightshirt on her.

From the outer room, Garion heard several gasps and weak outcries. Krista looked even paler against the pillow when he entered, but she also seemed more comfortable. Lady Adele was spooning broth to her.

When Adele slowed the spooning enough for her to talk, Krista started with, "Thank you."

Adele just smiled and placed another spoonful in her mouth.

Krista swallowed. "You do not have any questions about who I am?"

"Well, for the life of me, I cannot see why a pretty young maiden would go to such lengths to pretend to be a boy," Adele said bluntly.

Krista looked to Garion. "Is it safe?"

Garion nodded. "The door is locked. No one can overhear."

"You really do not have to tell me," Adele said seriously. "I already gave Garion my word that I will not reveal your secret."

"Actually, I would like to." It meant a lot to have a woman she could talk to, someone who would understand. It was wonderful having Garion know, but there were private things she still couldn't discuss with him, and she knew she could always go to Lady Adele. The older woman seemed to sense this and waited for the mystery to unfold.

Krista wasn't sure how to start, so settled for, "Lord Vallon was my father." She paused for the revelation to sink in.

The Lady was silent, the spoon held frozen in her hand. "That is impossible, Vallon's child died with his wife over sixteen years ago. My husband stood by him at the funeral. He never remarried."

As Krista tried to move to reach Kallairion, a small cry of pain escaped her.

Adele pushed her back in the pillow. "Be still."

Garion knelt beside her, touching her cheek.

"Hand . . . to me," Krista whispered, trying to catch her breath.

Garion worked his hand under her pillow and drew out the sword.

"Gracious, why did you put that under there?" Adele asked, but Garion just quietly placed the sword alongside Krista's good arm.

She fingered the hilt for a second then said, "Kallairion change."

Lady Adele pulled back as the sword shimmered. It shifted in shape and grew in size until it was the sword the woman recognized as Kallairion, although she hadn't seen it for years.

She looked at Krista, "But you are supposed to be dead."

"My nursemaid had taken me for a walk so that my mother could visit with some friends. It was their baby who died in my cradle when my mother was killed." As Krista paused to take a breath, a tear trickled down her cheek. "It was not until later that my father found out I was still alive. He decided I should remain dead for my safety." Again Krista paused, looking paler. The physical pain had opened a way for the emotional pain to affect her.

Garion again touched the side of her face giving her the needed tenderness. "Shh, I will tell her later while you rest."

Adele pushed back some of the obvious shock of the revelation to agree. With a slight nod, Krista's fingers touched Kallairion, and once more it changed, this time to the dagger. Without being asked, Garion took it, sliding it back under her pillow. Adele looked on in quiet amazement that Garion acknowledged with a nod of his head.

"It still amazes me every time I see it."

Adele poured a glass of water, holding it for Krista to drink. "Oh, you little dear." She smiled, putting the cup down. Adele placed her cheek on Krista's. "We will talk later." She placed a small kiss on her cheek. Straightening up, she slid a finger down through Krista's hair before following Garion from the room.

Alone in the room, Krista stared at the ceiling, trying not to think of the throbbing pain. Within, it felt good to have another person who knew her secret. Through the open door, she could hear Garion and Adele talking quietly. Gratefully, she listened to Garion tell her story. She just didn't feel up to it. Tears rolled down her face. Turning her head to the side, she willed herself to sleep.

Her rest hadn't been long when she woke up. The aching in her body was becoming difficult to handle. Every movement threatened her with dizziness and nausea. Adele went to great lengths to assure her that, by the next day, it would pass as her body accustomed itself to the shock it had endured.

Late in the evening, a knock startled the small group as they chatted, trying to keep Krista's mind off her discomfort. Garion answered the door, ready to send whoever it was away until it turned out to be his father, and the palace healer, Sir Allen, and his apprentice, Godfrey. Having no choice, he admitted the men.

"How is your companion?" his father asked. "I heard that he was injured quite severely saving Marcus."

"He is doing well. He is trying to rest," Garion answered, shifting in front of the men.

Hearing the men's voices, Lady Adele stepped out to greet them. Seeing her, Allen directed his question to her. "How seriously injured is he?"

"Kris broke his left arm. We set the bone with no problem and have it braced and wrapped. Now it just needs time to heal. His ribs were also bruised slightly but nothing to worry about. They just make him extremely uncomfortable. He should have bed rest for several days, I think."

The healer nodded accepting her word.

"Is the boy awake?" the king asked. "We would like to see him for a moment."

Adele and Garion exchanged glances with each other in silent communication about what to do, but before they could say a word, Godfrey headed to the room.

Garion moved to place himself in front of the group, ready to halt them if needed, but as he looked through the doorway at the bed, there lay the image of Kris, face pale and slightly tightened with pain but, in all appearances, a boy. Garion moved out of the way so that all could enter. Lady Adele took her place in the chair beside the bed before anyone else could settle there. She struggled to keep from staring at the difference in the person in the bed.

"Your Majesty," Krista greeted the king, grimacing as she changed position slightly.

"Be still now. We just came to check on you. It was a very brave thing you did today. You showed great courage."

"Thank you, Your Majesty. How is Marcus?"

The king looked toward the healer, who answered, "I am afraid it is still too early to know. He lost a great deal of blood. His wound is quite serious. He surely would have died if you had not reached him in time. As it is, we have done all we can. Now we must wait and hope that infection does not set in." The healer continued. "It looks as if we should leave you to rest. You are in good hands." Turning to Lady Adele, "If you need me, just send someone, though it looks as if all is well taken care of here."

With a short good-bye, the men left with Adele and Garion walking them to the door. Once it closed, they all let out sighs of relief. Adele leaned against the doorframe staring at the girl in the bed. Krista's eyes were closed as she tried to relax. The softness was back in her face, her features proclaiming her a woman.

"Truly amazing," Garion overheard Adele say to herself as she stepped back, allowing Krista to sleep.

Lady Adele returned to her chambers for the night. Garion settled on one of the couches in the outer room to sleep. His sleep was uneasy, with dreams of Krista getting hurt. A sudden crash burst him awake.

On his feet, it took him a second to realize where he was before heading to his bedroom. The faint glow from the fireplace gave enough light to show Krista sitting up, her good arm locked around in front of her, holding her other. She was trying to catch her breath and was obviously in a great amount of pain. On the floor, lay a broken cup.

Moving to the other side of the bed, he sat down, reaching out to her. Carefully sliding his arms around her, he laid her back onto the pillows. "There, it is all right. Lay still." He brought his hand up to brush back her hair, "Shh, now what happened?"

"I . . . sor . . . ry. Just . . . wanted a drink." She still labored to catch her breath.

"It is all right. You should have called."

"It is so stupid." The tears let loose.

Leaning to her, he wrapped his arm around her, letting her cry. Sliding his arm behind her neck, her shoulders felt small. He knew it wasn't comfortable for her to cry, but her body had to have a release. Tilting his head down, he kissed the side of her head. Slowly she stilled, finally just a few little shaky breaths sounded, and he pulled back from her. Sliding his hand up under her chin, he brushed away the tears on her cheeks.

"I will get you a drink," he said softly, rising from the bed. He stopped to pick up the broken pieces of the cup, then filled another with water and helped her drink. He could see the drowsiness in her as she finished. Garion had barely whispered, "sleep," when her eyes closed and she drifted off.

She was so incredibly fragile, why did this have to happen? He didn't want her getting hurt. His fingers tightened on the cup. The urge to throw it across the room was so strong, that only the knowledge that the smashing sound would wake her stilled his hand. She had no business fighting, and doing the other things she did. Garion shook his head, looking at her.

It was her decision, not his. He knew she wouldn't stop being Kris, nor stop doing what she felt she must do. Her being the champion of the sword was not as foolish as everyone would say, if they knew she was a woman. Krista was a true champion, giving all she had.

She was also a champion who cried in his arms. He touched the damp spot on his shirt, staring down at the sleeping young woman. Again the desire to kiss her ran through him. Pulling his mind from it, he drew the blanket up around her. Returning to the couch to sleep, this time his mind settled on the delightful thought of kissing her.

Krista woke in the morning with a sudden jerk of alarm. She wasn't sure what was wrong until she heard someone moving toward the room. She knew by the sound of the footsteps that it wasn't Adele and, within her, a voice told her it was not Garion, either. She caught her breath as Godfrey, the healer's apprentice, stepped into the room. By the fact that he showed no shock, she knew Kallairion must have covered her.

Without any greeting, he approached. "I am going to check and rewrap your arm."

"Why?" Krista gasped taking hold the blanket. *Where was Garion*?

"It should be done properly."

"Lady Adele has already seen to it," Krista objected.

"Lady Adele may not have done it right," he said bluntly.

"I am sure it is fine."

"You would not know if it was done right or not," he condescended.

"But Sir Allen did not seem to doubt—"

Godfrey cut her off. "Sir Allen would not have risked hurting the lady's feelings. Besides, he was tired from tending Marcus. I am sure he would want me to check you over," he insisted, reaching for the blanket.

"So, he did not send you?" Krista gripped the blanket tighter.

"I am sure he will later. Let go of the quilt."

"I am certain it is all right. Please, just let me rest?"

"Let go." He tried to jerk the quilt away. Krista gasped but retained her hold.

"Please go," Krista cried.

"What makes you think you can send me away? I am trying to help." Taking hold of her hand, he tried to force the blanket free.

"I do n . . . ot want your . . . help." Krista tightened with pain but didn't let go. Godfrey seemed to forget what he was doing. Placing on knee on the bed, he fought with her. Krista cried out, then Godfrey spun across the room landing in the middle of the floor.

"What do you think you are doing?" Garion's snapped, standing over him, ready to hit the apprentice.

"I . . . I, was just trying to tend." His voice broke, embarrassed at the circumstances. "I am sorry." He looked nearly as pale as Krista did in the bed.

"I think it would be best if you leave and just let Lady Adele take care of him," the prince said in a commanding voice.

The apprentice scrambled from the floor and stammered. "Yes, Your highness." Grabbing his satchel, he fled the room.

Garion locked the door before returning to Krista. Pain etched her face. She trembled, holding her arm tight to her like she had the night before.

"Are you all right?" Garion settled on the bed next to her.

She nodded. "It is really my fault. I got frightened about him trying to look at me. He would have found out . . ."

Garion nodded back. "I understand. I will talk to him later and apologize." His hand brushed her cheek. "I should not have left you alone, but I was called away by my father."

"Garion." His name escaped in a pleading whisper.

For the second time in just two days, he slid his arms around her, and she cried on him. He enjoyed the warmth of her breath on his neck. Once again, his lips touch her forehead. When she made no effort to break the hold, he thought of moving his lips down to hers, but quickly decided not to press her farther than she might be ready to handle. At least, she had come to him. That alone was a mighty start.

The knock on the outer door disturbed them, all too soon for Garion's liking. Going to open it, he found Lady Adele with the food for Krista. Garion excused himself to tend to his other duties.

After Lady Adele left, Krista tried to sleep for a while. Unfortunately, it didn't last long enough, and by noon, she was sick of lying in bed.

Bored without anything to do, she decided this was not for her. She needed to be active.

Angry with herself, she began to rise. It was foolishness getting hurt. What if something happened before she healed? What kind of champion was she? She would be useless in protecting the king and queen, or Garion.

Garion. She had cried in his arms, not just once. It felt wonderful being held by him, having him soothe her. But what he must think? Some champion she was, a girl who cries over everything. It was stupid, getting hurt.

With a swift movement, she shoved back the covers and swung her feet to the floor. Trying to suppress the outcry of pain, she forced herself to stand. Doubling over, she caught the edge of the table to keep herself from falling. Krista wobbled for a moment, but stayed upright. Straightening herself, she took a step and then managed a couple more before having to stop.

It took some time for her to reach the window, and when she finally did, she didn't look out but rested her face on the cool glass. Closing her eyes, she tried to breathe deeply. Tremors ran through her body. Again, she felt her anger rise. It was so stupid. She could hardly cross the room.

"Krista!" Garion startled her.

Her eyes jerked open, she bit back a cry and looked back over her shoulder at him.

"You should not be up," he declared as she took a couple of steps. Luckily, his long strides carried him across the floor in three brief seconds. She wobbled, starting to fall. Sliding his arm around her, Garion pulled her to his body for balance.

"This is stupid," she gasped, trying to push away. "I cannot stay in bed."

"Yes, you can. And that is where you are going to stay."

"How could I be foolish enough to let myself get hurt?"

Ignoring her, he slid an arm around her waist.

It didn't hurt, but she tried to make him let go. "I have to get up, I have. . ." She broke off, trying to catch her breath. The tears tried to rise within her, but this time she managed to force them down. She would not cry on him again.

Before she could object further, he lifted her off the floor, cradling her in his arms. "You are going back to bed," he said firmly, meeting her glare. "You can scowl at me all you want, but you are still getting back in that bed. And you are going to stay there, understand?"

"Garion—"

"No, you stay there. That is final."

Krista remained, silently fuming as he pulled the blanket over her.

Garion only smiled. She was too upset to think about the pain. "I have some work to do so I will be at my desk if you need me." He moved to the other room.

A short time later, Lady Adele came to check on her and spent the rest of the afternoon talking with her. Several times Garion let his attention turn to what they were saying. The first topic was him. Krista was complaining about how stubborn he could be.

During the afternoon, the conversation shifted to fighting, being a boy, growing up, and other things, allowing Krista to express some of her pent-up feelings. Garion tried not to invade her privacy, but it was hard for him not to want to listen. Especially, when what he heard gave him more insight into the feminine side of her that she didn't show to him.

That evening, when he returned from supper with his parents, she greeted him with a smile. He'd just settled into the chair beside her bed with hopes to talk about their relationship when a knock interrupted his uncomfortable start to the conversation. This time, it was both his mother and father.

Queen Anna was a slight woman, very pretty, but on the frail side. She gave all she had to support her husband, but everyone at the castle knew that inside she lived with a deep fear for her husband and son. It was a fear that threatened to overwhelm the little queen. It had begun with the death of her eldest son at the hands of Kuel and had escalated since the attack on Garion six years earlier. It had grown worse since the announcement of Lord Vallon's death.

"I am sorry to disturb you," the queen apologized, settling in the chair beside the bed. "I just want to commend you for your actions. It was a very brave thing that you did. I am pleased that my son has such a fine companion."

"Thank you, your majesty. You honor me far too much," Kris answered back.

"Oh, on the contrary, the story is buzzing through the whole castle. You are quite the man of bravery."

Krista made a slight grimace at the comment, knowing that the queen only meant to be encouraging.

The queen caught the twitch but presuming it was from pain, she continued. "We really should let you rest now so that you may recover soon."

The king gave another reassuring comment and they left.

After Garion escorted them to the door, he came back into the room and noticed Krista staring at the wall.

"Krista?" he questioned. "Are you all right?"

Not bothering to look back at him, she nodded. "It is just, sometimes, I wonder if I should tell them who I am. I think it would be good for your mother, maybe give her something to hold to."

Garion stretched out his hand, laying his finger on her chin. He turned her head to face him. "What you are doing is the best way. You know that. To let it be known would only endanger your life."

Krista nodded. "I know my main advantage will be surprise, but . . ." She sighed. "I would like to sleep now. Do you mind?" She turned away.

Reluctantly, Garion left the room. Leaning back against the wall, he felt his frustration rise again. He did not want Krista facing Kuel, especially for him. He was a man now. His father had even come to accept that fact lately, giving him responsibility rather than treating him as a boy. He had no desire to let someone else fight his battles, especially Krista.

That was not what he wanted of her. Lately, his deep thoughts had been more in the line of wanting to kiss her, to draw her up into his arms. He liked it when she cried against him, when his arms were around her. Pushing the thoughts back, he settled at his desk. That was not the relationship he and Krista had, unfortunately. Krista saw him as her friend and as the one she was bound to protect.

Chapter Twelve

Krista moved back to her own room while Garion was at morning practice. She even managed to get dressed. If forced she would have had to admit she was worn out by the time she finished but she felt more content.

When Garion returned, he frowned at the sight of her moving around.

She ignored his expression. "I am fine. Just stiff."

He arched a brow but didn't contradict her, instead going to his desk to work.

Krista spent the afternoon on studies, brought by one of the boys from Lord Cowley. She found that she actually welcomed having something to do since the boredom was getting to her. She no longer wanted to stay in her room. The moment Garion left to attend supper with his parents, she headed down to eat with the others. The walk had never felt so long. She had to stop and rest several times on the way.

Finally making it to the dining hall, she became the center of attention. Krista found in embarrassing being treated like an honored hero, especially when Sigmon served her. It wasn't long before being the center of attention became too much, and with her appetite not back to normal, she excused herself early to visit Marcus. Most visitors were not allowed, but when Sir Allen opened the door to her, he let her enter.

Marcus looked horribly pale but greeted her with a weak smile.

"I thought I would find you lazing around," Krista greeted him.

"Yeah, what a life. No work or practice." He met her tease.

"How do you feel?" Krista asked.

"Well, they have decided I am going to live. Thanks to you."

Krista brushed the remark aside.

"How is your arm? They told me you broke it getting me out. I do not remember much."

"It hurts, but you can understand that."

"Can I ever. I hurt so bad inside and the worst is the hunger pains. Sir Allen hardly lets me eat anything. That really hurts a man." Marcus grinned and Krista grinned back.

"I will try to sneak you something."

"Make it a double dessert."

Sir Allen chuckled from the side of the room and approached them. "It is time you should leave now," he said to her.

"I will visit you tomorrow," Krista promised, grimacing as she stood.

"You know, you really should not be up much either for a few more days," Sir Allen counseled her.

"I am heading back to my room now," Krista assured him, her strength about to give out. He nodded, seeing her to the door.

Turning into the second hall, she found Garion coming toward her. "I thought I might find you down here. You really should not be out." His face showed displeasure.

"I was just visiting Marcus."

"I know, but the decision about Brock was given out this afternoon. His father is taking him back home. Everyone knows what he did. I do not think he is taking the treatment of disgrace very well, and you are not in any shape to defend yourself if you happen to meet him in a hallway. Besides, you look tired."

"I will admit, I am hurting a little."

"A little? Come on, let's get you back to your room." Taking her by the elbow, he directed her down the hallway. As they passed the main hall, one of the men called out to Garion. Krista stood for a minute listening to them talk but not very intent on the conversation.

She could tell she'd been up too long. Pain was beginning to shoot through her side, leaving her trembling and dizzy.

"Garion, I am going to head back to my room," she interrupted.

"Here, I will walk with you. I can take care of this later."

"No, finish up. I will be all right," she assured him. "I am going straight back. See you later." She headed down the hall before he could object again.

Things had changed for Garion, she thought as she walked. Each week he handled more duties and had more meetings. He no longer was required to attend Sir Cowley's class, though he had to keep up with studies on his own. Now that he wasn't practicing with the younger boys, she wondered how much she'd see him.

The test . . . she'd forgotten. She never got to finish it. She had no idea what had happened. She hadn't thought to ask if it had been given to the others, or if they'd let her make it up. She'd done well on the other parts, but what if they wouldn't let her move up?

She turned the last corner to find Brock leaning up against the wall in front of her, arms folded across his chest. Dark tension boiled around him.

Krista froze. "What do you want, Brock?" After all the pain and troubles he had caused, she could not bring herself to be civil.

"Have you heard that I will be leaving in the morning?"

Krista nodded, eyeing him.

"I just wanted to say good-bye."

Krista watched him, skeptically. "Good-bye." She inclined her head slightly to him.

"I also wanted you to know that it is not over yet. I owe you."

"Brock, you caused this, not me. It is your own fault. It started before I even got here."

"Yeah, well everything was fine until then. You brought it out. You made it all look bad."

Krista stepped back, feeling Brock's uncontrollable anger building. It was as Garion had warned. She was in no shape to try to fight with him, and she couldn't even outrun him. Fear raced through her as he stepped forward.

Moving her hand to Kallairion, she doubted that it would help, since at the moment it was a dagger at her waist. She couldn't change it to a sword in front of Brock, and even if she did, she could hardly swing it. As a dagger, it wouldn't keep Brock at bay, not in the condition she was in. He'd just wait for a chance to knock it away.

Brock took another step toward her, then stopped. Krista could feel the presence of someone at her back. A wave of reassurance ran through her, confirmed by the look on Brock's face.

"What is going on?" Garion's voice sounded from over her shoulder.

"I just wanted to see if Kris was all right and apologize before I left." Brock didn't succeed in sounding convincing.

"Kris should be resting so, if you will just say good-bye, he can go in."

Brock stood quietly, his jaw locked. For a moment nothing seemed to move as the two men eyed each other. Garion was ready to meet Brock's challenge.

"Good-bye." Brock's voice was cold and hard.

Krista let out a breath she hadn't realized she was holding. Brock moved forward to pass her in the hall. Just as he drew beside her, his weight shifted. Krista saw his shoulder swing toward her, but there was nowhere to get out of the way. A slap echoed through the hallway as Garion's hand hit the wall. His arm wedged between Krista and Brock, forming an unbending barrier.

Leaning close, Garion's voice came like cold steel. "Do you not think you have caused enough pain?"

Krista caught her breath as she watched the two men tense. Time stood still until Brock took a step back and moved around them down the hall. His footsteps had died around the corner before Krista or Garion moved. Krista felt shaky as she released the breath.

"I wish you would have waited for me. I was afraid he would try something. What if I had not gotten here in time? Are you all right?"

"Yes," Krista said weakly.

Garion looked down at her.

Lifting her eyes, she met his gaze. Without warning, he lifted her off the ground. Cradling her in his arms, he stepped to the door. Krista started to object, but he cut her off.

"Quiet." Fumbling with the handle, he got the door open. Laying her on the bed, he continued with the commanding tone, "I want you to stay in this bed until Brock has left. Do you understand?" Without waiting for her reply, he was through the door to his chambers, and the door closed behind him.

Krista lay back, shocked by Garion's action but so grateful to be laying down she didn't even have time to think about it before sleep overcame her.

Garion leaned back against the wall. His adrenaline ran high from the confrontation with Brock, and then it had turned to Krista. Her soft answer brought out the need to protect her, the desire to hold her, and a yearning to kiss her.

It was some time before he turned to open the door behind him. On the bed just as he had left her, Krista lay sleeping. Kallairion was at work for he saw her as Kris, but in his mind he pictured the eyes that never seemed to change, the eyes of the young woman. Closing the door, he let her sleep.

It was only a few more days until Krista returned to her regular studies. Both Allen and Cowley agreed that her arm was nothing to keep her from that, though she was excused from practices in the yard. With Garion at practices in the mornings and attending other meetings and duties in the afternoon, she was left with a lot of free time. She started visiting Lady Adele. It felt wonderful to be treated and talked to like a woman for a short time even if was only behind the door of Adele's room.

Almost three weeks passed before Krista tried her first practice with Kallairion. By herself on the other side of the lake she tried her best to do her normal routine, minus using her left arm.

The practice was short and painful, but by the end of the week, it was closer to normal, though she still couldn't use her arm. It would be several more weeks until it would be healed enough to swing a sword. Krista consoled herself that at least it was out of the sling and, for the most part, no longer ached, just itched.

The decisions were made and it was announced that, because of her actions to save Marcus, Kris was allowed to move up with fifteen of the older young men as soon as she healed. Her schedule changed to practices in the morning with Garion and the guardsman. In the afternoons there were to be required studies and duties to help Prince Garion.

Marcus's wounds were slower to heal. Krista was already out on the practice field before he was completely out of bed. He didn't make the advancement, but with his normal, easy manner shrugged it off. Watching Krista at practice one day he even made the comment that he was glad he hadn't made it.

The workouts and training with the guards was not difficult for Krista. Most days she enjoyed the challenge of them, and she relished the fact that they got to practice with their own swords instead of the rough wooden ones. Roud remained their instructor, always watching over them with a careful eye. He was quick to break up, to reprove, but also to praise.

It was a perfect day to practice, not overly hot, but Krista couldn't keep her mind on what she was doing. She tried all the exercises Darm had taught her to clear her thoughts and concentrate, but nothing helped. Chad, who partnered her, beat her easily enough that Garion noticed from where he was. Roud, too, took notice and, at the end of practice, approached her.

"Is your arm bothering you today?" He gave her a way out.

Krista turned to him. "I am sorry, sir. I am having trouble concentrating."

"Is something wrong?"

"No, sir, it is not important," Krista replied.

"Well, if this had been a real fight, it would have been important. If you could not put it out of your mind and fought like that . . ." He let the sentence hang.

Krista nodded, accepting his chastisement.

As Roud left, Garion approached, "What is wrong?"

Unexpectedly, Krista felt angry and frustrated. "Nothing, I just need some time alone." Turning, she headed back to the castle, leaving him standing in shock. She hadn't taken twenty paces before the realization of how she treated Garion hit her, but she couldn't return and face him. She wanted to cry. Picking up her pace, she headed to Lady Adele's. Since she'd been back to practice, she had hardly visited the woman, but now she needed to talk with someone.

Krista was afraid Lady Adele wouldn't be in her room when she knocked, but to her relief a soft "Enter" greeted her. Opening the door, Krista froze. In the room was another of the ladies. Krista was about to excuse the interruption and leave, but Adele spoke first.

"Good, you are here. Just wait over there. Camille, I am afraid I will have to join you down in the hall shortly. I have something that needs to be attended to first."

Seeing the woman out the door, Lady Adele turned back to Krista, her voice picking up a tender tone. "Now what is wrong?"

"I am sorry. I did not mean to disturb you. I can come back later." Krista fumbled on the words.

"Nonsense." Taking her arm, Adele directed her to a small sofa. "Now tell me."

"I really do not know. It has just been bothering me. I . . . my birthday is in a few days." Adele waited while Krista paused for a moment. "I do not want to spend it as a boy. I feel like I am forgetting that part of me. I . . ." Tears escaped even as she tried to hold them back.

Adele's caring arm came around her. "Come," drawing her close, "I see no reason why should you not get to be a girl for just one day."

"But I . . ." Krista shook her head trying to object, but Adele had already made up her mind.

"Step behind the screen and take off those things." Adele pushed Krista in the direction of the screen before turning to a large trunk. "I have been saving this for years, though who knows why. There is no chance that I would ever fit in it again. It may be a little big for you. I do not think I was ever that slender, but it really should not take much to make it fit."

The woman continued to talk as she removed things from the trunk. "Here we are." Adele lifted what she was searching for, letting it unfold to reveal a deep blue dress. The laced front showed the white lace bodice. Tapered sleeves to the wrists were trimmed with the same delicate accent. It was simple but very beautiful.

"I told you to get those things off," Adele said, seeing Krista still standing there.

"I cannot."

"Yes, you can. Now, either you take your clothes off or I will remove them for you," Adele threatened her.

"It is beautiful," was all Krista could get out.

"And you will look lovely in it." Laying it over Krista's arm, she again pushed her toward the screen. This time Krista went, eyeing the dress. Adele smiled as she turned back to the trunk and removed several other things. "Here, you should have these to wear under it," she said, laying the garments over the screen.

Krista felt odd as she removed Kallairion, but with one look at the dress, she fumbled in excitement as she changed clothing. She'd never worn anything so beautiful. The dress was a little large but, stepping from behind the screen, she looked hopefully to the lady.

"Oh, that will be perfect on you." Moving to Krista, she started examining the dress. "It needs to come in just a little through here." Pulling it tighter on her sides, the woman eyed the front of it. "Yes, it will not take much at all. Here, look in the mirror." Holding the sides tight, Adele stood behind Krista as she looked in the mirror.

Krista couldn't believe what she was seeing. It was so amazing to see herself as a woman again. There really hadn't been much change in her body but as she reached up and ran her fingers over her short hair, her smile faded a little.

Adele picked up on her distress up immediately. "Do not worry, dear. I have something for that too." Picking up a lace scarf, Adele placed it carefully on Krista's head, draping the ends over her shoulders. "There, now no one will ever notice."

Reality struck her with a touch of panic. "No, this is not any good," she said, pulling the scarf off her head. Before Adele could stop her, she stepped behind the screen, already removing the dress.

"Krista, what is wrong?"

"What if someone saw me? I cannot risk that. It could ruin everything. I knew when I accepted this that I was leaving being a woman behind. It is just that at the ball the other day, I had to dance with the ladies. I let it bother me too much. I wished for just awhile that I could be . . ." Krista broke off. Coming from around the screen, she took a last fleeting look at the dress, stiffened her shoulders, and handed it to Adele.

"I better go. I am sorry to bother you." Moving to the door, Adele stopped her.

"Krista, are you sure there is not anything more?"

Krista turned back hesitantly. "What do you mean?"

"Do you have an interest in one of the men?"

Krista scoffed, "Of course not. Besides, they all think I am a boy."

"Garion knows you are not."

"We are friends. I am his companion, his guardian. That is all."

"Are you sure?" The woman fished for a reaction and it came.

"Of course! Garion could have any beautiful young lady he wanted. Why would he ever be interested in me?"

"As you just pointed out, you are friends, close friends. You are smart. You really are incredible in many ways," Adele pointed out.

"Yes, and none like a lady," Krista returned.

"You are pretty," Adele challenged.

Krista laughed. "I look like a boy."

"But as a girl, you are pretty."

"So pretty I might be appealing to a prince?" Krista scoffed and shook her head. "I had better go. I have studies."

Krista fled the room before anything else could be said, but Lady Adele had her answer. Krista had feelings for Garion, feelings she didn't want to admit. Feelings, that certainly seemed to confuse the young woman, but they were there and, at some time, they would have to be faced. Especially since, Adele was certain, Garion had feelings other than plain friendship for her. Adele looked down at the dress. For now, she could see to it that Krista would be given the couple of hours she needed to be herself, a woman.

That afternoon, as Adele altered the dress, she planned it all out. A simple request to Garion, and he agreed to get Krista freed from duties in three days. He was still concerned by her reaction on the field that day, but accepted Adele's refusal to explain.

Chapter Thirteen

Three days later, Krista worked hard in practice, using it to cover her inner feelings. Practice was almost at an end when Roud informed her that she was wanted in Lady Adele's chambers. For a moment, Krista considered not going, knowing that Lady Adele wanted to wish her a happy birthday. She'd already decided to let the day go by like any other day but, a few minutes later, Krista found herself in the Lady's room, seated on the sofa.

Adele handed her a plain wrapped package. "It should fit better now."

"I cannot accept this," Krista answered, not daring to take the package.

"Yes, you can. You have the afternoon free. You will ride out the castle gates until you find the most quiet, peaceful, secluded place you can find. There, you will put on the dress and spend the afternoon alone as a pretty young woman. There is plenty of food and everything has already been arranged so that you have no further duties for the rest of the day," Adele instructed.

Krista didn't move as she took the whole thing in. It sounded so wonderful to her. Adele was about to pinch her when Krista sprang forward, hugging her. "Thank you," Krista whispered in her ear.

Adele smiled back. "You are welcome, dear. Now go and enjoy yourself. Make sure you keep your hair covered," she added with a grin.

"I will." Krista laughed, giving her another hug. Controlling her excitement, she accepted the bags holding food and her dress. She slid out the door with one last smile back at Adele.

Garion was still in the yard when he saw Krista head toward the stable with two bags over her shoulder. Her face glowed with the happiest expression he'd seen in a week. Again, his curiosity rose. Working his way to the stable, he hid as she rode out. It took him only a minute, with the help of a stable boy, to have his horse saddled and ready to go. Leaving a message that he had an errand to attend to, he was headed out the gate. He was afraid he had already lost Krista in the village until he noticed her going up the hillside behind the castle. Urging his horse to a trot, he followed her.

Keeping back a distance, Garion relied on tracking her rather than keeping her in sight, catching only an occasional glimpse of her so that he knew he was on the right track. They traveled quite a distance. Ahead, he knew there was a small lake nestled at the mouth of a valley. Working his way through the rough terrain that surrounded it, he began to think of the last time he'd followed her. It, too, had been to a lake. She had gone swimming, and he found out that she was a woman, not a boy.

As the lake broke into view, he dismounted and led his horse forward. Several minutes later, he saw Shea tied to a tree, grazing in the tender grass. Krista was nowhere in sight. Shea looked up as he approached, but made no sound as he tied his horse. Garion moved a short way around the side of the lake but, seeing no tracks, he turned back.

He almost reached where the horses were when he caught the sound of singing, soft and sweet. He followed the song. Drawing nearer, he recognized the words, the love song they had memorized as a poem in Sir Cowley's lessons. Knowing that it must be Krista, he cut through the trees.

The way opened up to the lake but, instead of seeing Kris, a woman sat on a blanket on the grassy bank. Her back was to him. Her full, deep blue dress fanned out to the side of her, the tips of bare toes peeking out from under the hem.

He stopped, not sure what to do. Krista couldn't be meeting someone there, not a woman for sure. Had he gotten on the wrong trail, followed the wrong person? Shifting his weight, a twig snapped. The singing stopped as the figure spun around to face him.

The fear in her eyes broke into a gasp as she recognized him. "Garion!" Krista gazed at him from the frame of the lace scarf.

Garion could do nothing except let his gaze drift over her. The laced bodice only accentuated how small her waist was and gave curve to her breast. Always before her shape had been hidden by the baggy clothes she wore. He knew from seeing her shoulders that she was truly slender, but what was before him, he had only pictured in his imagination, and that hadn't done her justice. Climbing to her feet, Krista headed for the trees, breaking Garion's shock. With a swift movement, he caught her by the hand, pulling her back.

"Wait, where you going?"

Her breathing was rapid, obviously frightened. "No one was to see me."

"Krista, it is all right. It's just me." He held her back, not letting her pull away. "You really look beautiful."

She blushed, no longer trying to pull free.

"Where did you get this?" he asked, touching the lace on her shoulder.

"Lady Adele." Fire filled her eyes. "She told you. She set this up." Again she tried to pull away. "I must look silly, a boy in a dress."

Catching both her shoulders, Garion fought to pull her back. "Will you hold still before I have to take you down and sit on you?"

"Let me go." Krista fought, her voice going high.

Wrapping an arm round her waist, Garion lifted her off the ground and lowered her to the blanket. "Krista," he tried to get her attention, but received a resounding slap across his face. It was then that she stopped struggling and stared up at him.

Garion touched his cheek. "I am just glad you did not use your fist."

"Garion, I am sorry. You startled me."

"Are you ready to talk to me?" He settled back on the blanket beside her. "And I followed you. All Adele did was ask me to free you for the afternoon, nothing else."

"I am sorry."

"You already said that, and it is all right as long as you tell me what you are doing here and why the dress. Does it have to do with the other day?"

"I just needed to get a way for a little while, feel like a woman."

He could tell she wasn't saying it all. "And?" he questioned.

She looked down, straightening her dress. "It is my birthday."

He caught her hand. "Why did you not you tell me? You should have had the whole day."

"It is not the same date listed on my papers."

"But . . . all right. I still wish you would have told me so I could have gotten you a present." His smile brightened. "Do you mind if I join you?"

"No," Krista's voice dropped to a softer tone. "I have a lunch Lady Adele sent with me."

The food they shared was more than ample, though Garion didn't eat much. What he hungered for was in front of his eyes. He couldn't keep his attention from Krista. She was stunning.

After finishing the meal, he offered his arm very formally, leading her on a walk along the shore.

It was strange and wonderful for them both. Krista had never had the opportunity to be treated as a lady, and Garion thoroughly enjoyed her as the woman he had only dreamed of. She was unlike the women of the court, who always seemed full of false pretenses to him. Eventually, they made their way back to the blanket to eat a little more before walking to the water's edge, watching some birds on the lake.

Garion settled close to her. She turned back to say something and stammered as she looked into his eyes just inches from hers. He rested his hand on her waist. Her breath caught.

"Krista, you are eighteen today, are you not?"

Still looking into his eyes, all she could do was nod.

Garion looked as if he was about to say something else then closed his eyes tight, pulling back words of how amazing she was and a list of other things he knew would only embarrass her. He opened his eyes and met her confused look. Touching her cheek, he caressed it gently. She trembled but didn't pull away.

"And have never been kissed?" Not waiting for or needing an answer, he dropped his lips to hers before she could retreat. It was tender and soft. Moving his lips to her cheek, he kissed it lightly before settling back slightly.

She sat still, as if almost afraid to move. Her eyes were bright with a mixture of fear and excitement. Sliding his arms around her, this time he kissed her more firmly on her lips with a touch more passion. The kiss continued as he drew her tighter into his arms.

Settling her back, she clung to his shoulders, trembling, but she didn't try to break away. Neither moved, not sure what to do. Garion wanted to kiss her again but was afraid it would be more than she could handle. He could practically see the waves of emotions flooding and overwhelming her.

Still, he couldn't stop himself from leaning closer to kiss her again. The sound of far off voices cut through the silence. Krista eyes went wide as panic flared across her face. Before he could say anything, she bolted into the bushes. Garion knew that, when he saw her again, all images of the young woman would be gone.

Turning in frustration to the sound, Garion saw a couple of guards appear over the ridge a minute later.

"Your Highness, it is a surprise to see you here," one of the men greeted him.

Garion pulled in the anger of having the beautiful afternoon interrupted to answer, "I was just trying to get away for a while."

"You should not be here alone," the guard answered back.

"I am not, my companion is here." He heard Krista move from behind the bushes with Kallairion in her hand.

"We are sorry to interrupt," the other guard spoke up.

Not as sorry as I am, Garion thought but answered. "No problem. We have to head back now anyway."

"If you will let us water our horses, we will join you."

"Certainly," Garion answered. The guards finished off what food was left while the horses drank. Krista disappeared with the blanket for a minute before moving to tie it on her horse. Garion guessed that her dress was wrapped within it.

All the way back to the castle, she remained quiet. In the stable, she refused to meet his gaze, busying herself tending Shea. Even as they walked to their rooms she kept her eyes from him, darting through the door without a word.

Garion didn't try to get her to join him for dinner. He wasn't sure whether to confront her, or let her be. Several times he found himself at her door, but stopped before knocking. She needed time, maybe he did, too.

Lying back in his bed, he thought how wonderful it had been walking by the lake, sliding his arms around her, how her lips had felt against his. It was amazing how fast the afternoon had disappeared. He wondered what would've happened if they hadn't been disturbed.

He wanted to talk to Krista. He knew she was having trouble dealing with the kisses they had shared, but how long would it be before she would face him again. That thought made him nervous but, no matter how it affected their relationship, as long as she didn't totally push him away, he was glad it had happened. Glad that his interest in her was finally in the open.

Krista lay awake in the other room, her thoughts not all that different from Garion's, just leading her to a different conclusion. Garion had kissed her. It had been incredible. He'd been so tender. He was always kind to her, even as Kris, but there had been a different gentleness, a different closeness as they walked around the lake. It had been a lot like normal but very special in an unexplainable sort of way.

Of course, the kiss was just a birthday present. When he'd touched her cheek, well she didn't know what to think of that, and when he slid his arms around her waist, it had sent her heart racing with an intensity she had never known before. Flustered, Krista was not sure how to take everything that had happened. It truly couldn't mean anything for her. Krista had to be packed away in Lady Adele's trunk not to surface again.

With a groan, she wished Krista had never surfaced. She wished Garion had never kissed her. She wished the feelings inside her would go away. She blew out a breath. So much for wishing. Somehow, she needed to tamp them down, the foolish emotions coursing through her, but for now, they hung bare, and they hurt.

Longing for Garion to kiss her and hold her again, yet knowing that it was impossible, sent another wave of frustration through her. Why had she put on that dress? She'd left that part of her behind long ago. Garion's kiss was something she could never have again. She was his friend, his guardian, and the Champion of Kallairion. Focusing her mind on those words, she forced herself to sleep.

Garion was pleased when she greeted him on the practice field the next morning, though there was stiffness there. Facing each other when Roud paired them up, he flashed a playful grin, but she still stayed rigid.

As the practice moved on, though, Krista began to lighten up. She kept more of a distance between them as they fought than usual, but progressively joined him in normal teasing and conversation.

By that evening things had relaxed between them, almost back to normal. Garion didn't try to guess what Krista was thinking. He was just happy that she was talking. He'd give her time before he brought up anything personal again.

Training continued as usual. By the end of the week Krista had managed for the most part to get the kiss out of her mind, as Garion did not once mention it.

She was in Garion's room late one evening studying when there was a knock at the door. Cam burst in before she could open it.

"Good evening!" His smile was so big that it looked slightly foolish.

Garion looked at Krista and grinned. "Good evening. I have not seen you around much lately."

"What do you mean? I was at practice this morning," Cam paused then grinned again, shrugging his shoulders. "I have been a little busy."

"Busy," Krista nodded to Garion. Both tried to keep a straight face.

"What?" Cam noticed his friends' look.

Garion released his smile. "Nothing. You just look about to fly off the ground. I am guessing this is good news." Garion winked at Krista.

"She said, yes! I am getting married in a month," Cam burst.

Garion looked at Krista with an "I told you so" expression. "I knew I should have told her he snored before it was too late." Then he laughed, standing to congratulate his cousin. After a few minutes, Krista excused herself to return to her room saying she still had an assignment to complete, leaving the two men to talk.

Garion watched Krista leave, knowing that she was done with her work, realizing that, though Cam didn't know Kris was a girl, she didn't want to infringe on their conversation. Turning his attention back to Cam, they talked and laughed for an hour with Garion continuing to tease him.

Cam finally broke in, "When are you going to find a young maiden."

Pausing briefly, Garion answered. "In time, I am working on it."

"Oh, someone in mind? You have been holding out on me. Who is it?" Cam asked with curiosity.

"It is nothing yet, just an interest on my part. She does not even know anything about it." Garion reddened a little.

"You know, it works better if you let her know you are interested. Now, who is it?"

"This coming from a man with so much experience. No, really, it is not anything yet. She is not ready for me to make advances, so it is better if I back off and wait and see if there is something to the interest."

Cam grinned wickedly. "Now you have really got my interest. If you will not tell me, I will just have to ask Kris."

Garion sprang from his seat. "No! Please, do not mention it to Kris. I have not told anyone and do not want anyone to know right now. If word started getting around that I was interested in someone, everyone in the castle would go wild with speculation and rumors. Maidens would be vying to find out if it was them and pushing to make it so, and my parents would be determined to find out who it is and set the wedding date."

"Hey, all right. Do not worry, this is me. I will not say a word," Cam assured.

"To nobody, not even Kris," Garion stressed.

"Not even Kris, I promise. I am surprised though, I did not think you kept anything from him."

"Well, if you were not getting married in a couple weeks, I would not have mentioned it to you."

"Will you at least tell me what she is like?"

Garion thought for a minute. "She is incredible. I have never known anyone like her. She is smart, kind, she has so much honor, and is so giving. Not like any other maiden . . . she's kind of hard to describe, really."

"You did not tell me anything," Cam sighed, "but you do sound taken with her."

Garion shrugged and managed to change the subject.

The next night, Krista found a reason not to attend supper in the main hall. Garion guessed that she didn't want to be around when the formal announcement of Celeste and Cam's wedding was made. It confused him that she avoided it. He wasn't sure why it would bother her to be around a simple marriage announcement, but he was sure it did.

Krista was flooded with mixed feelings as she headed down to eat, but by the time she entered the commons the noise of chattering pulled her slightly out of it. When she noticed Marcus heading toward a table, extreme happiness filled her.

Marcus had changed a lot since the accident. He'd lost quite a bit of weight before he recovered. Now back to health, he was a young man in good shape. Krista had no interest in him, but it did make her happy to see him well.

"Hello. Are you new around here?" he kidded good-naturedly as she approached.

Krista met his grin, "You are looking fit."

"Thanks."

"Are you back in practices now?"

"Have been for almost three weeks. We just do not get to see you much anymore, especially since you have been dining in class. How is Garion? We have not seen him much lately, either."

"He is fine, just busy."

"With Cam getting married, any loves in Garion's life?"

"What do you mean?"

"Kris, is there any maiden of interest? You would know if anyone would."

"He has not mentioned anyone to me." Krista felt a little nervous. "Garion does not talk about the ladies with me."

"You are with him all the time. You cannot say you do not know."

"Honestly, I have no idea." After a little more prying, Marcus finally let it drop, but it left Krista with an uneasy feeling. Marcus excused himself saying he had a walk with a maiden planned. Krista wished him luck and headed back to her room.

She couldn't keep her mind on her studies, and then sleep wouldn't come. For some reason, it suddenly disturbed her to think of Garion with a woman. He truly had never mentioned anyone to her. At the balls, he danced continually, but she couldn't place anyone he seemed to favor. Her thoughts were still on Garion when exhaustion eventually forced her into sleep.

It wasn't until she arrived in the yard the next morning and found that Roud wasn't there to instruct them, that thoughts of Garion were pushed from her mind for a short while. The man in charge informed them that Roud had made a trip to his home, and started working them on their horsemanship.

Though Krista wasn't partnered with Garion, several times she found her gaze going to him. By mid-morning he, like many of the other men, had tossed his shirt aside. Krista tried to keep from glancing at him but, unable to stop. Her second look lingered until he caught her. After he caught her again, she felt foolish and kept her attention in check, but the damage had already been done.

All the other men had headed in for lunch when she finished brushing Shea. She guessed that Garion had gone as well because he had finished a lot earlier. The practice yard was quiet when she headed across it to put away the items she had used. She was surprised to find

Garion leaning against one of the racks. His arms were folded over his bare chest, his shirt draped over the rack where he'd thrown it.

Krista stopped, startled. "I thought you had left." She tried to read his odd expression.

"No, I was waiting for you. I knew you would have to come back here."

"All right, let me put these things away and we can head in." Moving to store the pad, she kept her gaze from him.

"Actually, I waited here because I thought it would be more private to talk."

"Is something wrong?" She finally turned toward him.

Stepping to her, he slid his hand up through his hair, moving it out of his eyes. For an instant, she thought how handsome he was. She quickly pushed the thought out of her mind, chiding herself. Those weren't the thoughts she needed to have about him, but as he stepped closer, she wished he would put on his shirt.

"I thought you could tell me?" His voice was smooth.

She could tell he was trying to imply something, but she wasn't sure what, so with all honesty, she answered innocently, "What do you mean?"

"You were watching me today." His directness caught her off guard. She didn't know how to answer. He waited but, when she didn't say anything, he asked, "I wondered what was wrong or what you were thinking."

"It was nothing, I had been talking to Marcus last night and he asked me . . ." Suddenly she felt uncomfortable about continuing. "It was nothing."

He took a step closer. "What?"

"It was nothing, really." She turned away, but it didn't stop him.

"I want to know what you and Marcus were talking about."

"Nothing."

A playful grin passed over Garion. In the same instant his hand shot out and grabbed her wrist, pulling her away from the racks into the middle of the field.

Her protest wasn't even out before he released her. "What are you doing?" she demanded.

"What was it?"

"Garion, honestly, nothing. He just commented how long it was since he had seen you and asked how you were doing." She took a couple steps back.

"And?" Garion moved around as he always did before he attacked.

"That is it."

As Garion came forward, Krista spun out of his way. His hand reached out to catch her but she deflected it, coming around to face him. He came in once more. Again she blocked then spun to meet his next attack, which came immediately.

Using his momentum, she sent him over her back. He rolled to his feet, then to the ground, back at her. Krista started to jump back, but her legs were caught. With a simple twist, he pulled her legs out from under her. Going down, she landed just beside him. Before she could get set, he was on her, pinning her to the ground.

"Now, what?" He was hardly winded, but Krista felt like she couldn't breathe.

"Garion."

He interlocked his fingers in hers on one hand and forced it above her head, placing more pressure on her.

"Let me go," she gasped.

"Then tell me what else you talked about?"

When she remained silent, he forced her other hand above her head. Krista tried to get her leg under her for leverage, but he kicked it out, wrapping his leg around hers.

She knew there was no way to get out. He pressed against her with all his weight. "All right," she gave in. "He was wondering about if you were serious about any of the ladies."

"What did you say?"

"That I did not know. You never talk to me about that." She tried to catch a breath.

"Why would you not tell me that before? And why were you watching me?" He didn't move to release her.

"I do not know!" Krista felt warm and flustered.

Picking up on it, Garion smiled.

Looking at her from just a few inches away, Krista felt as if he was looking right into her.

"If you were curious about whom I like, why not just ask?"

"Because that is just something I have not wanted to interfere with." The answer came honestly with distress.

"Maybe you should, or does that bother you?" He shifted his weight slightly.

Krista gasped.

"Is something wrong? Does this make you nervous?" he said with his lips brushing her ear.

"Garion, stop it!"

"Why?" He lowered his nose so that he touched her cheek before sliding it down to her ear. He kissed the side of her neck. He felt her shiver and another little gasp escaped her lips.

"Garion," she tried to force it into a protest. Trying to turn her head from him, she wasn't fast enough. His lips caught hers first. When he lifted his lips, it was only for a second. "Ga—" he cut her off, gently pressing his mouth to hers. She responded to his touch as he released her arms, caressing the side of her face. He felt her fingers run through his hair. The other hand rested on his chest as the kiss continued, growing more ardent.

Leaning back, he smiled. All images of Kris had disappeared, there was only Krista. Her eyes closed as he ran his finger along her cheek. Lowering his lips to her cheek, he kissed it tenderly before moving to her mouth once more.

For a moment, all protest was gone as she met his affection with her own. When her restraint returned, it was with fury. Pushing back, she twisted to the side, dumping him on the ground. She was on her feet, moving to the rack of wooden swords, before he realized what had happened. Her back was to him. He could still tell she was breathing hard.

Silently, he rose and moved behind her, "Krista."

Spinning to face him, fire lit her eyes, "Garion, what if someone saw?" Her breathing was irregular. He could tell she was trying to hold back tears.

"We need to talk."

"Garion, why did you do that? Why?"

"Because I think it needed to be done."

"What would people say? What would happen if someone saw us?" she repeated.

"Krista."

"Garion, how could you do that to me? I cannot have those feelings." She fought back the emotions sweeping over her.

"But you do." He stepped closer, challenging her.

She spun away from him defiantly. "No!"

"It is all right."

"No. It is not." She paced to the end of the rack. "They confuse me. I should not have them. I am the Guardian of the Sword, not some flirty maiden trying to find a husband."

Garion couldn't help but smile at her reference as he stepped forward, resting his hands on her shoulders. "I am not trying to confuse you. I just want you to know I have feelings for you. I do not know, maybe they confuse me too, but I know they are there, and I do not want to ignore them."

Krista took a deep breath. Turning back, she faced him. Looking up with a single tear on her cheek, "Garion, I cannot have feelings like that for you or any man. Any day I may have to face Kuel. I have to be prepared. I cannot become distracted from that."

Anger surged in Garion. He was trying to tell her he loved her, and she met him like— "So, I am distracting, making you a little uncomfortable. What is it? You can't handle being treated like a woman? You know that is what you are and what you will always be. You can dress differently, and you can fool the others, but you cannot change that fact. You cannot even ignore it, like you do your feelings. Every night when you take off your clothes, there is still a woman under there, and when you face Kuel, that woman will still be there."

Garion stopped appalled at what he was been saying. This had not gone the way he had wanted. He wanted to say he loved her. He wanted to hear she loved him. Instead, before him stood a woman crushed with uncertainty and hurt. He had flooded her with emotions she couldn't handle and topped it with pain.

"Krista." He wanted to say he was sorry, to say something, but nothing would come.

"I had better go." Before she had turned from him, the illusion of Kris was back. She broke into a run for the stable. He was still standing there when she came out on Shea, heading out the gate at a gallop.

When she didn't return for her lesson, Garion covered for her. That evening he didn't go down to practice with her, and she didn't bother to knock to tell him when she returned. Each remained silent in their own rooms, going over what had happened, both trying to come to grips with their feelings.

The silence continued through that week and into the next. They worked around each other and talked when necessary, but neither tried to break the barrier. No one seemed to notice the difference between them, or the fact that Krista didn't attend meals with the prince. There was too much going on with the people coming in for Cam's wedding, which was being held at the castle.

The preparations weren't exceptionally elaborate, but there were many people to accommodate. Krista felt extremely lucky. Being Garion's companion, her room was not bothered. Many of the others had to share rooms to make room for the guests.

With so many people around, Krista felt the need to head for the pond early for her evening practice to get away from them. To her relief, no one was on the far side of the pond, though they seemed to be everywhere else.

Alone, she started going through her routine. Garion was attending meetings, and she didn't think he would show. Besides, he hadn't been down since their fight, so it surprised her when she swung around and noticed him leaning against a tree, arms folded in front, with an approving smile.

"It still amazes me to watch you," he said, walking toward her, drawing his sword.

"I thought you would be busy," she said, ignoring the compliment.

"I needed a rest. When you were not in your room, I thought you might be here." He stood as if waiting for her invitation. "There are so many people, you can hardly move in the castle."

Krista nodded, taking a stance opposite him. Inside, it felt very good to be with him again, though it felt awkward too. "How are the meetings going?" she asked.

"Fine, but I have had four of my father's friends hint about taking their daughters on walks in the garden tonight. I do not think I am going to forgive Cam for this. They are all thinking of marriage, and I am the target."

"How many are you taking?" She couldn't help but tease at his distress.

"I do not know. How would it look if I took them all at once?" he joked back.

"A little conceited." She blocked his strike.

"Yeah, but it would get it over faster; and no one could draw any conclusion from it."

She laughed, a little of the old ease returning.

"Krista, do you ever think of getting married?" His question caught her by surprise. She tightened again and almost slipped. He pulled back and waited.

Finally, she found the words. "It is not likely, too much uncertainty."

"Uncertainty?" he asked.

"Well, it would not be wise until after I face . . ." She stopped, not saying his name.

Garion lowered his sword. One subject they never talked about was her facing Kuel. He had tried to bring it up on a couple of occasions, but she usually avoided it. This was the first time she'd ever brought it up.

"Does it frighten you?"

"Of course." She responded so casually, it shocked him.

"How can you handle it that way, like . . . nothing?"

"Garion, for six years I have known about it. You ask, does it frighten me? Yes, it does, but the thing I fear most is, if I fail, then you and your family will die. After that, all the people will fall under Kuel's rule. That frightens me the most. If I fail, I die, but it would be better off to be dead." Reaching up, she wrapped her finger around a short lock of hair.

"I do not want you to face him." The words came out before Garion could stop them.

"It is not your choice. It is not mine. It just has to be." Again the words came openly, but she turned her back to him to keep in the tears. "It just seems . . . the mighty ones went to all the effort to create Kallairion to even things up against Kuel. So why would they let it come to this, just a girl left to use it? It seems wrong. How am I supposed to succeed where my father and grandfather failed?"

Garion stepped behind her and placed his hands on her shoulders. He could feel the shudders coursing through her body. He squeezed gently in way of comfort. To his surprise, she leaned back against of him.

Garion felt his own breath tighten. This is what she faced every day. This is what he had opened up in her. It wasn't just his love that had frightened her. It was the other doubts that had risen. There was nothing for him to say. They just stood together for quite a while.

"Let's practice," she said to break the heaviness that had settled over them.

They pushed each other to the limit as they had never done before, all the pain, anger, and doubts coming out with each strike and block. At the end, both gulped in air for several minutes before Garion looked up and grinned.

"I do not think you have anything to worry about."

Krista met his look and forced her lips up into a smile.

The day of the wedding was hectic. Everyone was in best dress for the ceremony and ball. There were so many people that Krista thought it would be easy to stay back out of the way, hidden from the dance and festivities. Unfortunately, everywhere she went, one particular maiden, Lalain, always seemed to follow. She would've been somewhere between sixteen and seventeen years old, actually very pretty with dark hair and milky white skin. The dress she wore accentuated every bit of womanhood she had.

It made Krista very uncomfortable to have the girl watch her every movement. Before she had always been fortunate that none of the ladies had taken a real interest in her. This was something she wasn't ready to handle. It became even more uncomfortable when Lord Cowley stepped in insisting that Krista dance with her.

In distress, Krista moved around the floor with the young woman. Krista almost fled when Lalain ran her finger along her neck. Shrugging away only seemed to encourage her more.

It was to Krista's relief when the song ended. Making an excuse that she had to find the prince, Krista moved quickly away through the people to the other side of the room. Dodging in and out, she made it to the door. She practically ran down the steps, past couples talking in the moonlight. Almost before she realized where she was headed, Krista was on the other side of the lake where she normally practiced. Running her hands through her hair, she tilted her head back and let out a sigh.

"That bad?" Garion's voice made her jump. "Sorry, did not mean to startle you. I was already in the garden trying to find a moment's peace when I saw you headed this way. What is wrong?" He continued to talk as he moved closer.

Krista looked back, totally embarrassed. "There is a girl." She paused. "Every time I turn around, she is there. To make it worse, Lord Cowley made me dance with her."

Suddenly, Garion was beside her.

She felt the tears but refused to let them out. "I hate it," she said hollowly, looking up to him. "I do not feel comfortable trying to dance with another woman, to pretend to be interested."

Garion's hand rested on her shoulder, giving it a squeeze. "I cannot blame you. Why do you not go to your room? I will cover for you if anyone notices you missing. I will say I left some papers that I need to have finished by morning and asked you to take care of them. They are on my desk. You just need to total the counts on each item."

Krista was more than willing to accept. "Thank you."

He stared down at her. Without realizing, he moved closer. In the darkness it was easy to imagine her just as Krista. He smiled, "I only wish I could go, too. Believe me, I know what it feels like having a maiden in pursuit."

"How many?" Krista asked playfully, though she knew he was serious.

"Do not ask. I had better get back." He stepped back slightly. "You can head in."

With the exchange of good night, he turned. An odd feeling ran though Krista as she watched him walk away but she pushed it back, turning to head the long way around to Garion's room.

Krista hadn't made it halfway through the garden when the form of a girl moved into her path. She groaned inside when the light of one of the lanterns revealed Lalain. Krista tried to change directions, but Lalain called out to her. For a minute, she thought of running but knew that it would have been unacceptable. Letting loose an inward sigh, she turned to face the young woman.

"May I help you?" Krista asked with a bow.

"I was hoping you would escort me through the garden."

"I am sorry, but I must decline. The prince has asked me to take care of some papers for him," she said politely.

"I am sure the prince will not mind if you waited a while to do it, for certain reasons." Lalain stepped forward reaching out her hand to rest it on Krista's chest.

Immediately, Krista pulled back.

"My first duty is to Prince Garion."

"Do you not think I am attractive?" the woman put forth flirtatiously.

"You are very beautiful, but if you will excuse me." Krista turned, taking only a couple steps before she almost ran into Sigmon coming around a hedge with a young woman. To Krista surprise, Lalain stepped forward, taking her arm. Sigmon flashed Krista a grin and moved off the other way. Pulling back, Krista shook her arm free.

"I am sorry . . . if you will excuse me." She headed off rapidly before the woman had a chance to say anything else.

Once in her room, Krista leaned against the wall. Tears trickled down her cheeks in the darkness. Wiping them away, she headed through to Garion's room. At his desk, she forced her mind to concentrate on the papers. Unfortunately, it didn't take long until they were done.

Krista returned to her room only to pace back and forth in the small space. After a while she drew Kallairion and tried to go through her well-practiced routine, but when she almost sliced through her bed she gave up and dropped onto the inoffensive piece of furniture. She stared at the ceiling for some time before being able to fall asleep, but her sleep was not good. Several times she jerked awake from nightmares of a dark, haunting shape standing over Garion's still form.

The sun wasn't quite up when she got up, unable to force her eyes closed again. Pulling on her clothes, she headed out for a real practice, to burn away the tension.

Krista hadn't made it halfway down the hall when she was met by two guards. Greeting them, she went to step aside to let them pass but, instead, found herself shoved up against the wall.

"What . . .?" Before she could say anything else, one man pushed her head back against the stone wall with his elbow, gripping one arm while the other man started to undo her sword belt.

Krista reacted, thinking only that she couldn't let anyone take Kallairion from her. Kicking out, she caught the man undoing the belt in the shin. As the man stepped back, she threw a fist at the other guard, staggering him. They both came forward immediately. She didn't have the time or the room to draw Kallairion, but she met their attack with every skill she had learned from Roud and Darm.

Each time the men came in at her, she was there to block and counter, but the odds were against her. One guard's punch got past her defenses to hit home, catching her on the side of the head. Dazed, she felt hands grab her, shoving her face first into the wall.

She tried to fight through the haze that shrouded her mind but couldn't even form a protest as they took her sword belt. She slipped deeper into a stupor as unforgiving hands dragged her through the halls to the bottom of the castle.

Released, she fell forward, impacting with the cold stone floor. The clang of heavy metal reverberated into her heart.

Chapter Fourteen

Krista wasn't sure how long she lay there before her mind started to clear. A dank smell filled the room. The dungeon. It was seldom used, and she'd only been down there a couple times, but she had no doubt that was where she was.

Pushing up to her knees, she caught the wall and worked her way to her feet. Once the room stopped spinning, she headed for the door. As she guessed, it was locked. Panic filled her. Without Kallairion, the illusion would fail. If anyone came, she would look like a girl. She slumped against the wall.

Kallairion. It had been taken from her. What was happening? Why was she there? Nothing made sense. She had to get Kallairion back.

A sickening weight filled her. Flashes of the nightmare came back to her. Garion! Was he in danger? She checked the door, shaking it for any signs of weakness, and then she made her way around the room, looking for any possibility. It didn't take long until she stopped in the middle of the room. There was no way out. Again, she dropped to the cold, hard floor.

Garion wasn't surprised when he knocked on Krista's room and she didn't answer. After all, he was late getting up. It did surprise him a few minutes later when there was a knock on the door, and he opened it to Marcus.

The young man stepped in saying, "Is it true?"

Confused, Garion turned. "Is what true?"

"That Kris attacked a maiden last night? That he almost beat up two guards before they got him under control, and took him to the dungeon?"

Garion stared at him, realizing that he was totally serious. He headed out the door, not even stopping to say a word. Garion ran to the hall. Signs of the ball were all around. He slowed long enough to ask someone where his father was, and then raced across the floor. He pushed open the doors to the large library, where a meeting was already taking place. Lords and other men circled the room. All fell silent.

His father stood, "Garion!"

"Where is Kris?"

"He has been taken to the dungeon until everyone can be heard, and the punishment is decided upon," his father said calmly.

"Punishment for what?"

"Now, I know he is your friend, but I am afraid you will have to let us handle this," his father tried to calm him.

"Handle what?" Garion demanded. "What is this about attacking someone?"

"I am afraid that last night in the garden, your companion," he stressed the last two words, "tried to share his affections with one of the ladies. When she tried to refuse, he got a little physical. The maiden was not harmed seriously, but you understand that we cannot allow this to happen, especially by the prince's companion. When the guards went to detain him this morning, your companion decided to resist instead."

"What do you mean detain and resist?" Garion asked, trying to remain calm as the whole room watched in silence.

"The guards were sent to hold him and, when they tried to take his sword, he started a fight and tried to get away," the king answered.

Lord Hanford put in. "I think, leaving no question of his guilt."

Garion didn't try to hide the look of annoyance he gave the man. "So what happened?"

"He was knocked out and taken to the dungeon."

Garion tightened. Another man in the room followed with, "They should have done a little more than just knock him out."

Garion about burst, but managed to hold it in. He had to concentrate on helping Krista right then and not think of her being hit. Firmly, he said, "I am sure Kris is innocent. He would not do something like that."

"I am afraid you do not know your companion as well as you think," Hanford spoke up again.

"I trust Kris with my life."

"It was not you he was after," the man put back.

"Where is Kris's sword?" Garion decided that Kallairion was his next concern. Obviously, no one had noticed that Krista was a woman yet, but it would not take long if someone took a look at her without Kallairion in the area. Besides, he didn't know what would happen if someone else drew Kallairion without Kris around. Garion set his priorities: first, was to get Kallairion, second, make sure he was there when anyone went around Krista.

"It is here." His father motioned to the corner where Kallairion rested on a table.

"I would like to keep it with me," Garion announced.

His father looked surprised.

Again, Hanford objected. "He may try to return it and free him. After all, they are friends."

"I am also the prince. If I wanted to free him, I would not need his sword." Garion looked stern. "Kris will go free when he is proven innocent. I will hold his sword for him to prove my trust."

The king looked seriously at his son, then nodded. Garion walked over and picked up Kallairion, buckling it around his hips.

"We will meet back here in two hours to decide this," the king announced. The men in the room stood. Lord Hanford approached Garion.

"The guilt of your companion is not the question. That is known. The severity of the punishment is all that is left to be decided." The man walked off.

When only Garion and his father were left in the room, Garion felt his father's hand rest on his arm. "I am sorry, son. I know you and Kris are close. He has saved your life several times, and I admit I like the young man, but we cannot let this attack go unpunished. I am sorry."

"I know Kris did not do it. It is impossible," Garion stated.

"Garion, I am sorry. The girl admitted it was Kris, and they were seen together just before it happened."

"By whom?"

"Sigmon. And I believe he and Kris are friends, too. I think he could recognize him."

"Sigmon saw it happen?" Garion questioned.

"No, but he saw them together in the garden just before."

"Father, I would like to speak in defense of Kris this afternoon."

His father frowned. "That is not wise. It would say you support such behavior."

"I do not support the behavior, but I do support Kris."

"Garion."

"I intend to stand by Kris."

His father took a deep breath and let it out slowly. "Kris won't be allowed to the meeting until the judgment is passed so that he does not frighten the girl. If you wish to speak to him and present anything he wishes to say in his defense, I will agree to that."

"Thank you," Garion said gratefully to his father. "First, who was the young woman who made the claim?

"Lady Lalain."

"She is Hanford's daughter, no wonder he wants Kris."

"He is asking for stern measures. At the least, Kris will leave in disgrace. I will not go into the worst."

"You do not need to go into that. I will not let that happen," Garion said firmly. "Will you tell me what is said to have happened?"

The king told his son the whole story as it had been charged. The rest was to be heard later in the meeting.

Krista knew it had been only hours that she'd been in the dungeon, but it felt like days. She had already paced the room enough that she knew every groove. Still, nothing made sense. She sat on the floor, with her elbows on her knees, and her head resting on her arms.

No one had come, which in one way was a relief for no one would see her, but it didn't tell her what was really happening. Her only hope was that her imagination was worse than whatever the trouble was.

A clank at the door startled her to her feet. She pulled back into the shadows, then couldn't believe her relief at seeing Garion.

As she started forward, Garion lifted his hand in warning. Turning to the guard behind him, he said, "It is all right, leave us."

"But, Your Highness—"

"It is all right."

Garion stepped into the cell. Behind him the door shut and the guard secured it, but didn't move back far. Garion checked her over in one take. For an instant, he saw Krista, then the veil shrouded her, and it was Kris, a little roughed up, a slightly fat lip and a swollen, bruised cheek.

"Garion!" Krista kept herself from running forward. "They have taken . . ." She caught herself, but there was panic in her voice, "my sword."

"It is all right, I have it here." He motioned to his side.

As Krista's eyes rested on Kallairion, she breathed a sigh, looking up to him.

Garion continued, "Now tell me what happened?"

"I do not know. I came out of my room and headed down the hall. The next thing I knew, two guards shoved me up against the wall, and started to take my sword. I tried to get away but got hit. I remember being dragged here but not much else. Garion, what is going on?" she pleaded.

"You do not know? They did not tell you?"

Krista shook her head. "I was afraid something had happened to you."

"They did not tell you?" he repeated, unable to believe it, but continued without pause at the look on her face. "You have been charged with attacking Lady Lalain."

"What?" Krista almost went down with shock.

"Well, that answers that. Let me look at your cheek." He reached out.

"Ow." She pulled back, but he moved closer to look her face over, wiping her lip with his handkerchief.

He continued, "They say that last night during the dance you took Lalain for a walk in the garden and turned your attentions on her. When she refused, you tried to force her, but she got away. This morning, her father noticed her fat lip, kind of like yours, and bruises on her neck. She told him that you attacked her. He wants you beaten, disgraced, and sent away."

Krista had looked rough before, but now she paled, looking sick.

He waited a minute to give her time to digest what he'd said.

Krista tried to talk but lost the words, feeling helpless. She brought her hands to her head. This was not the time to break down. Krista felt Garion's hand on her arm.

"I know you did not do it. Was it Lady Lalain who you were talking about following you around?"

Krista looked up, surprised, she stammered, "Yes, why?"

"I just thought it might have been. She was seen with you several times that evening. Sigmon said he saw you together in the garden. That she was on your arm. I need to know everything that happened."

She nodded. "After we parted, I started toward your room. Lady Lalain caught up with me. She wanted me to take her for a walk in the garden. I told her I could not, that I had things to do for you. She tried to flirt with me. When I excused myself and turned to go, I ran into Sigmon with Kathryn. Lalain stepped up, taking my arm. I shook her away, then Sigmon was gone. I headed straight to your room, did the work, and went to bed."

"Where were you headed so early this morning?" he questioned.

"Out to practice." Krista shuffled, embarrassed. "I was upset she . . . she tried to slide her hand on my . . ." Krista stopped not able to continue.

Garion longed to hug her, but the guard was still there watching, so he settled for giving her arm a squeeze.

"Garion, what am I going to do?"

"Do not worry. I will see what I can do. They are meeting in a few minutes. I'm afraid you have to stay here until you are cleared. Can I get you anything?"

"No." Krista sounded, as well as looked, beaten. Her frustration showed. "You cannot say I am . . . but, then again, if I do not get . . .," Krista looked down at Kallairion, "back, you might not have to."

Garion understood. "Do not worry. I will not let that happen and I do not think I will have to. Kris, Lalain is Lord Hanford's daughter."

"So?"

"She is Brock's cousin."

Krista fell quiet, considering what he'd said. "You think?"

Garion nodded with an encouraging smile.

"What better way to disgrace you? I have to go, but I will be back." Again, he flashed an encouraging smile, and Krista moved back into the shadows.

Garion was sitting in the room with the other men when Lalain walked in with her father. He noticed the slightly swollen lip. Normally, his heart would have gone out to her like every other man's in the room did, but he couldn't feel sorry for her because she was in better condition than Krista. And, while she had people taking care of her, Krista sat alone in a cold dungeon, awaiting the outcome for something he knew she didn't do.

To begin, the king asked her gently to tell what happened.

The girl let out a couple of shaky sobs, acting nervous. "It began at the ball. I danced a couple dances with him. Kris seemed quite nice. Then I went to the garden for some fresh air. Kris appeared and asked me to take a walk with him. He led me out around the far side of the pond, saying he liked it over there because it was private, and that we would not be disturbed." She broke and made several more sobbing sounds. "While I was looking out over the water, he slid off his jacket and laid it over a branch.

"He took my hand and said why not sit on the grass and leaned forward and tried to kiss me. I told him I ought to get back. I tried to pull away. He laughed and said, 'You know, I am a hero and . . .'" she shifted her eyes to Garion before returning to stare at the ground, "'I am the prince's companion.' He grabbed me and dragged me down in the grass and kissed me roughly. He said the evening was young, and they had plenty to do. Then he undid the top lacings on his shirt."

Garion about came off his chair as she continued.

"He took my hand and pushed it into his shirt against his chest. It was awful. When I tried to push him away, he grabbed my neck and squeezed. I was frightened." The young woman put her hands over her face.

Her father came forward, laying a hand on her shoulder. "There, dear, it is all right. Just tell us the rest, and it will be over."

Stifling a sob, she wiped her eyes and looked up. "He kissed me again. I slapped him and pushed him away and ran. I ran all the way to my room." The girl lowered her head again.

Her father came toward Garion. "I demand that action be taken against this young man immediately. No matter who is his friend." He cast a look at Garion. "He should not be allowed to get away with this!"

A murmur of agreement ran though the room. Quite a few eyes found their way to the prince.

Even the king watched his son for a moment before he stood. "I think we should have Kris brought here, so we can discuss his punishment. I am truly sorry, dear," he said to Lalain, "that your stay here was marred by such an event."

When he finished, Garion stood. Everyone in the room watched him carefully, surprised when he started. "I, too, would like to give my apologies. I had great doubts at the possible guilt of my companion until I heard your story. When you said how awful it was to touch his chest, well, I knew it was the truth. I do feel so sorry. I am probably the only one at the castle who knows that the reason Kris never removes his shirt in public is because, as a child, he was burnt by a fire, and his chest is horridly scared. I saw it once. It about made me sick."

Lalain looked up, dabbing her eyes. "It was horrible. He made me touch it, feel it. It was so hard and rough," she stammered. Garion nodded, turning from her, he paused then turned back.

"Lady Lalain, why are you lying? Who put you up to this?"

Immediately her father started to react, but Garion faced him down. "Quiet."

"Garion, what is this?" The king stood.

"Kris does not have any scars on his chest. Ask Lady Adele, she tended him. The reason Kris never takes off his shirt is because it is so smooth, he is embarrassed. His growth is not like the other men." That was the truth, he thought. "It is, shall we say, baby soft."

The king stood, not sure what to do, then turned to the young woman. "Well, what do you have to say?"

Lalain broke down in real tears.

"Lalain?" Her father looked questioning, "Why?"

"I . . . did not want . . ." The girl couldn't answer.

The whole room was silent, shocked. No one knew what to do as the girl sobbed in an honest release of tears.

Garion again came forward. "Did Brock put you up to this?"

"Brock?" her father said, surprised, but Lalain looked at Garion and nodded.

"I was told to flirt with Kris, have him take me for a walk in the gardens. Brock was waiting on the edge. He said Kris owed him, and he was going to pay, but Kris wouldn't come with me. When I told Brock that Kris had gone in to do something for you, Brock was furious. He slapped me and grabbed me by the neck. He threw me down. I was so frightened. I was not sure what he would do. Then he came up with this plan. I'm sorry. I did not want to go along with it, but I was afraid of what he would do if I refused."

When the girl finished, the king addressed them. "It seems that we almost committed a great injustice here. Lord Hanford, why do you not take your daughter back to her room?"

Lalain stood and stopped by Garion. "How did you know it was Brock?"

"I knew Kris would not attack you, but I believed that you were honestly scared. It was too much of a coincidence that you were Brock's cousin. He has hated Kris since Kris first arrived."

"I am sorry," the young woman said through tears. "I really did not want to."

After the two left, somewhere in the room someone spoke up. "Why did he resist the guards then? It made him look guilty?"

Garion turned back. "He had no idea what was going on. The guards didn't say anything, just threw him against the wall and started to take his sword. It is a family heirloom and very special to Kris. In fact, if you will excuse me, I would like to return it to him and see to his release personally."

"Of course, immediately," his father said. "We owe him quite an apology."

Chapter Fifteen

Krista was leaning against the stone wall in the shadows when the sound of Garion's boots drew her attention. Jumping to her feet, she pulled back farther, though still trying to see through the bars. *At least Garion is smiling*, she thought. As soon as the guard swung the door open, Garion held out Kallairion.

"You might like to have this back."

"Garion?"

"It has been cleared up. I will explain everything in my chambers." Stepping aside, he motioned for her to move out ahead of him.

Curious and relieved, Krista accepted the sword. Outside the door, she immediately relaxed.

Garion took her by the elbow, leading her down the hall.

Krista glanced nervously back at the guard. "You are not going to be in trouble for this are you?" she whispered to him.

"No, you have been cleared. Lalain admitted that Brock was behind everything."

"You were right."

Garion nodded. "Brock wanted her to lure you out into the gardens. He was waiting to ambush you. When you would not go with Lalain, he beat her up and then decided to blame it on you. Lalain is so afraid of him that she went along."

"Then, how did you get her to admit it?"

"We are almost to my room. I will tell you there."

Krista watched him as he walked silently beside her. She wanted to know what had happened, but she really didn't care, as long as it was over. She shuddered, thinking of being in the dungeon. Garion caught the action.

"Are you all right?" he whispered.

"Yes, I just would not list it as one of my most pleasant experiences. Would you mind if I had a bath? For some reason, I feel a real need for one."

He let out a laugh that seemed a little forced to her. "I will see to it."

Stopping just long enough to order up water, it wasn't more than another minute until they reached his chambers. As Garion closed the door, he locked it.

Krista turned back puzzled. "Garion, is everything all right? I thought you said I was cleared."

"You have been. I just did not want anyone to walk in." He stepped to her, sliding his arms around her.

With thankfulness, she accepted the hug. His touch felt so good and reassuring, but Krista quickly drew back. She had turned too much to his embraces lately. They were causing way too many feelings for her to handle. So, since she was in control of herself, she didn't want to press it.

"I am all right," she said softly.

"Yes, but I am not," Garion returned. Bringing his mouth to hers, he kissed her passionately. When he stopped long enough to look at her, the illusion of Kris had disappeared. In his arms was Krista, eyes still closed, and breathing heavily. Starting with the bruise on her cheek, he traced it with his lips. She met his fervor with her own. This time, when it ended, she laid her head on his chest, clinging to him for support, but he had no intention of letting her go. Time passed but neither tried to move, neither said a word, until there was a knock on the door. For a second, they didn't move, then Krista made a dash from his arms to her room.

Garion opened the door to allow the water to be brought in for the bath. Moving to his desk, he feigned work until they had left.

Krista slipped quietly from her room to the bath. Garion stayed at his desk, not getting anything done. She stayed in for a long time. As soon as Garion heard the latch click, he was on his feet.

Her hair was wet. She had on a clean shirt and breeches, but was barefoot. She crossed the floor, head down, not meeting his look until he stepped in front of her. Krista looked up quickly. The blush of her cheeks was so rosy that Garion hardly noticed the bruise. Sidestepping around him, she ducked through her door.

A few minutes later, she knocked and entered his room with her hair combed, boots on, and Kallairion at her side. She looked more comfortable, but the illusion was still gone, and she was still Krista. Garion wondered if she realized it.

"Will you explain everything now?" she asked softly as she fluttered around the room.

Garion couldn't help watching her closely as he did. He too moved around the room, purposely drawing near to her.

"She said you had opened your shirt and made her touch your skin. Garion looked close. "It was obvious, that if you had she would have known," he smiled, "certain things. So I went along with it, telling her I was sorry, that it must have been awful because you were burned as a child and are horribly scarred."

Immediately, Krista reacted. "Garion, what if someone wants to see my scars?"

"I told them Lady Adele could verify the truth, but I am not finished. When Lalain agreed, said how awful they were, I asked why she was lying. I said that your chest is smooth and that is why you never show it; that you are embarrassed because it's not like the other men."

He reached out and caught her in his arms in one motion, pulling her to him. "Now for my reward for quick thinking." Once again, he kissed her.

As he released her, she broke away from him. "Garion, please, you have to stop doing that."

"I was just trying to get your mind off what happened . . . hopefully, to something much more pleasant." He gave her a weak grin. "Do not worry. I will not kiss you again." Then it was like he was trying to hold back words, but they wouldn't stay. "It is just that I had to get it out. It has not been a smooth day since I heard you were knocked out," the words vibrated with emotion as he said them, "and put in the dungeon."

This time it was Garion who couldn't meet her look. Krista stepped to him. Reaching out, she laid her hand on his arm. He looked up to her warm smile and couldn't help returning it. Krista's arms slid around him, and she gave him a hug.

"Let's get something to eat. I have not had anything all day," she said into his ear.

"Come to think of it, neither have I," he said, letting her go. "I am starved."

Krista was cleared, given a formal apology, and the incident was forgotten, although she felt a change in the castle. Though most of the men still seemed to accept her, she felt as if some had odd feelings toward her. To make matters worse, the biggest change was from Roud. When he took back over their training on his return, nothing Krista did seem to please him.

He insisted that Krista go over drills repeatedly while he let others slide by. Once she made the mistake of questioning him about it. He dismissed everyone and gave her a lecture that, as Garion's companion, she had to be better trained and prepared than any of the others. Then he made her go through more skills and assigned her several additional duties, saying she was getting lax.

The extra duties didn't stop. Krista found herself cleaning the stables. At the silversmith's she had to stoke the fires and any other thing Roud could think of for her to do. In a short time, her arms felt so heavy she could hardly lift her sword. Krista soon found she saw Garion very little. And, by the time she did Roud's chores and Garion's duties for her, she had no time to do her assignment for Lord Cowley who, in turn, lectured her on getting behind.

After a month, Krista found she couldn't even get to eat for, invariably, as soon as she sat down, she fell asleep because she was spending half the night trying to do her assignments. Krista started to take what food she could with her as she ran between duties. Then one morning she slept in and was late making it to the practice field.

Garion wasn't there because of a meeting with his father. Roud's lecture and criticism took place in front of the whole group.

Krista felt like crying as Roud said she should be removed as Garion's companion since she was obviously too weak and too lazy to ever hope to serve him well. The whole practice he humiliated her. She was fighting with one of the men, Roud stuck out a staff and tripped her. Krista went down hard. She looked up at Roud, who stood over her, looking down with a great deal of displeasure.

"When you can manage to stand up, you might as well give up and head to the stables. You would make a much better stable boy."

Krista groaned inside, making her way to her feet. To Krista's relief, just then Roud was called away. Several of the men, younger and older alike, gathered around her.

"What did you do to get in so much trouble with him?" Sigmon asked.

"I do not know." Krista could hardly answer.

Luckily, Roud didn't return before they were done for lunch. Numbly, Krista stood in line to eat. When she saw the food, she felt sick. Settling at a table, she lowered her head to her hand. She wanted to cry right there in the commons. She wanted to yell, to scream at the world that she could not take anymore, but she didn't have the strength do even do that.

She caught the tears as they threatened to spill free. Trying to keep them in as she rose and made her way through the halls to Lady Adele's room. She knocked on the door, but no one answered. Krista leaned against it, still fighting the tears. She thought of going to her room, but someone would find her there. She needed someone who would understand. It seemed to take forever as she made her way to the dining hall.

Garion was sitting by his parents. At the sight of him, the tears came up again, but she caught and forced them down. She wanted to go to him, to have him hold her. Everything was confusing when he held her, but it was so very wonderful. For over a month, he hadn't tried to kiss her or press the issue of them being anything but friends. It was better that it stayed that way.

Lady Adele was near the far end. Making her way around the side of the room trying to go unnoticed, Krista came up on the woman.

A slight touch on her arm and Adele looked back at her. To Krista's relief, without a word from her, Adele turned and excused herself.

Adele hurried her along the hall, still not saying anything. As soon as they were through the door into Adele's room, the Kris illusion faded.

"What is it, dear?" Adele hardly got the words out before Krista broke down in the woman's arms.

"Oh, Adele, I cannot do it. I am so tired. I cannot do anything right in practice. The blisters on my hands hurt so bad I can hardly write. I am behind in all my work." With each word, her tears flowed harder. "I just cannot do it. It is no good."

Adele held her, letting the sorrow fall. It took quite some time for the tears to subside. When they did, what little strength Krista had was spent.

Adele leaned back to look at her.

"You are exhausted." Adele touched her cheek, brushing back a lock of hair. "The first thing is to get you out of those clothes and cleaned up a little, so you can get some sleep. Taking her by the elbow, Adele led her into the bedchamber. Pouring some water into a wash-bowl, Adele directed, "Start taking off those things while I find you something to wear."

Krista was too tired to do anything but obey. By the time she had removed her outer clothes, Adele was standing by her with a nightgown. Krista stepped behind the dressing screen, stepping out a minute later in the gown, feeling truly feminine again for only the second time since she had arrived. Lady Adele had already turned back the covers on the bed. Coming over to Krista, the older woman slid her arm around her.

"All right now, into bed with you."

Krista stepped forward then froze. "I cannot, I have studies. I am already behind," she rambled, trying to pull away.

"We will take care of that later. For now, you need rest." The woman guided her along gently.

"But I cannot take your bed."

"Nonsense. No more. Get into that bed." Adele pushed her down. Krista again started to object, but her body took over, and she was asleep almost before she had lain all the way down.

Adele smiled as she pulled the blanket up around the young woman, then she became serious. Taking some balm, she rubbed it into Krista's hands, who hardly stirred. Leaving the room, she went out into the hallway. Catching the first person she saw, Adele sent them to find the prince, and ask if he could stop by her chambers.

It was not long until there was a knock on her door. Opening it, Adele let him in, motioning to him to be quiet.

"You wanted to see me," Garion asked curiously. "Is there something wrong?"

"I would say so. What has been going on?"

"What do you mean?"

"With Krista?" she questioned him.

"I have no idea. I have hardly seen her for the last while, why? Is there something wrong with her?" His concern now showed through.

"She is asleep right now in the other room, totally worn out. She broke down in tears, because she is so tired she can hardly move or eat. It is not good for a young woman to be like that."

"She has not mentioned any troubles to me. Since all the lords were here, there have been a lot of things that my father has wanted to go over with me, so I have spent most of my time with him. I have only been attending sword practice two to three times a week, and she has not been paired with me lately." He thought on. "The other night she was doing studies in my room and fell asleep. When I carried her into her bed, she did not even stir."

"Well, Garion, someone has been working that girl until she absolutely dropped. Her hands are blistered and swollen."

Garion looked to the doorway leading into the bedroom. "Let me do some checking to see if anything out of the ordinary has been going on. I will get her cleared from all duties today."

"You had better make it several days. It may take her that long to get her strength back," Adele added.

Garion looked back at the lady, surprised. "She is that sick?"

"I think she pushed her body much too far. As I said before, she is a young woman, no matter how she dresses. Her body has to be treated that way. It has to be given the time and care it needs."

Again, Garion's eyes drifted to the door. "May I go in and see her?"

"Just do not wake her, though, I sincerely doubt that would be possible."

Quietly he pushed open the door, making his way to the bed. Krista was snuggled down into the pillow—delicate and pale. One hand was partially uncovered. He lifted back the quilt to see it. Blisters had broken and bled, then blistered again. Her whole palm was inflamed. He winced, knowing how they must hurt to move. He thought of trying to hold a sword in them and have it come in contact with another sword. Quickly, he covered them.

Touching his finger ever so softly to her cheek, he caressed it and then touched his finger to her lips. Turning abruptly, he found Adele watching at the door. Once out of the room, he said firmly, "I will find out what is going on."

Chapter Sixteen

Garion was gone several hours before he returned, knocking softly. "Is she still asleep?" he asked once the door was closed. Adele nodded, leading him to the sofa.

"Well, the most interesting thing I found out was that it is Roud who has been giving her all the extra work, in practice and out. He has been lecturing her about not being good enough to defend me. Everyone guessed he is just trying to build up Kris's strength, but no one has ever seen him use this method before. Everyone thinks he is being unfair, but no one dares say anything about it."

Garion continued. "It has been said now, though. I told him I did not like Kris's treatment. He insisted it was for my good. I informed him it is not doing me or Kris any good having him end up sick. Kris has three days off and from now on, will be partnered with me in practice, and I told him that he is not to give Kris any extra duties. I stressed that Kris has enough of his own besides what I give him. You cannot believe what he has been having her do."

They sat and talked a while longer before Adele asked outright the question she had been obviously wondering since she'd watched him though the open door.

"Garion, what is happening between you and Krista? The way you touched her cheek . . . it is not the first time I have seen you do it . . . and that was not a touch of plain friendship."

Garion stood and walked across the room, starring out the window in silence a full minute before he spoke. "I have feelings for her, more than just friendship. Since Cam and Celeste got married, it is worse. I want what Cam has. I want to make Krista my bride but . . ." he stopped.

"How do you get your guardian to give up her sword?" Adele finished for him, and he nodded.

"We had a fight one night when I told her I did not want her dying for me. She said it is not my choice, or her choice to make. It is just the way it is. Adele, I feel she loves me too."

"I am quite certain she does, but she has been given a duty that has had to come before every other thing in her life. Her love for you, if anything, makes it more important to her not to fail."

"So, I am to sit back and let her fight a battle with a being that cannot be beaten, one which will likely kill her? What about my love for her?" His frustration burst through. "Do you know the reason that I told Roud that she was to be partnered with me in skills? It is not that I am afraid the others are too rough on her, it is that I cannot stand to see them fighting with her. At the last practice I attended, one of the men took her down. I wanted to go pull him off . . ." Garion cut off. "I am having a lot of trouble handling this. I am trying. For weeks I have not kissed her, but the urges have not stopped. If anything, they come more often. What am I supposed to do?" he asked.

"So you have kissed her?"

He nodded.

"And did Krista respond?" When the first hint of a smile appeared on his lips, Adele didn't wait for him to answer. "That is good." She too smiled, and then turned serious again. "Garion, I do not have an answer for you. I am afraid that you and Krista will have to work this out for yourselves, though, I would say now is not the time. Right now she is weak and probably quite vulnerable. I would say be gentle and understanding with her. Do not try to pressure her into any decision she would not be able to make." Garion looked downcast, so she added, "That does not mean you cannot show her a little of your love."

He gave her a weak smile. Turning to the window, he stared out. Adele picked up her needlework, and the room fell quiet. They stayed that way some time before Krista pushed open the door and stepped into the room, making hardly a sound. She didn't see Garion standing behind her, still at the window.

Adele noticed her and put down her needlework. "You are up. I will have something brought for you to eat."

"No, thank you." Her voice was soft and weak. "I have to go. I am already late. If Roud finds out, he will double my assignments."

"No, he will not. I have cleared you for the day." Garion stepped up behind her.

Krista spun, the motion making her dizzy. She almost fell, but Garion reached out and caught her.

"Garion," she gasped, realizing she was wearing just the nightgown Adele had given her. She pulled back, wrapping her arms in front of her.

From behind her, Adele put a hand on her shoulder. "It is all right, dear. You are decent enough, though I will get you a dressing gown." Adele stepped into the other room. Krista still backed a couple more steps away.

Garion tried not to stare, but even his quick glimpse revealed how much Krista was a woman under the soft flowy material. Then Adele was back, holding out a dressing gown for her.

"Slide this on, dear."

With the gown on, Krista looked at Garion, "Why—"

Adele cut her off. "I sent for him."

"But—"

This time Garion cut Krista off. "You should have come to me first, so I could have helped. I had no idea you were being worked and treated like that."

"I have to do—"

Again, he cut her off. "No one could stand up to what you have been trying to do." He shifted to using Adele's words. "You are a young woman, and your body needs to be treated as such." Stepping to her, he took her hand carefully. "You should have come to me," he ended softly. On her own accord, Krista slid into his arms, laying her head on his chest. He held her, saying nothing.

Adele stepped from the room to get something for her to eat, leaving them alone.

"Why did not you tell me?" Garion asked after a while.

She leaned back and looked up but didn't take her arms from around him. "I have to be able to handle my own duties."

"But those were not your duties. Do you have to try so hard to prove yourself that you work yourself to death?"

"Garion."

"No, Krista. You pushed yourself past endurance. If you will not take care of yourself for any reason other than that you're not any good to me if you are as sick and weak as you are now, so be it. You must take care of yourself. If you are being overworked, tell me. Take care of yourself, please, for me."

Krista nodded.

Gently, Garion brought her into a very loving hug.

Krista felt all too glad to accept. It was wonderful being in his arms.

Adele stepped into the room with the food, and Garion released her. Krista felt like they were both trying to force feed her. Though she ate with hunger, it did not take much to fill her. With her hunger appeased, she again grew very sleepy. Without even mentioning it, Adele ushered her off to bed. Once more, Krista had hardly lain down when she was back to sleep.

It was almost sunset when she awoke again. Garion had gone to supper with his parents, but Adele was there to make sure no one disturbed her. Krista dressed and sat on the couch while Adele reapplied the balm. They were talking when a knock interrupted them.

"You are up." Garion greeted as Adele let him in the door.

"I feel much better," Krista said in the way of an answer.

Adele sat down beside her, continuing to wrap her hands.

"You have to keep your hands clean and rub the balm into them three or four times a day. Either Garion can help you, or you can come to me and I will do it."

Krista nodded and Adele continued. "All right, why do you not go down and have a light dinner?"

"I will see to it," Garion said from where he'd been waiting.

Krista leaned forward, giving Lady Adele a big hug. "Thank you," she whispered in her ear.

Adele smiled warmly, brushing back a lock of her hair. "You get a lot of rest, now."

Walking down the hall, Garion remained quiet. Krista cast her eyes up at him. His jaw was set so that it gave him a very serious expression.

"Garion?" Krista questioned.

He dropped his eyes to her, forcing a smile. "Yes?"

"You are upset."

"I would rather wait and talk about it back in my room," he said tightly. "But let's get you something to eat first." That ended the discussion all the way through the commons back to their rooms, where, just before they reached doors, he took her elbow and steered her into his room. Inside, he moved her to the couch, settling so they could face each other.

"Roud approached my father about having you changed as my companion." The words came out.

Krista's mouth opened, but she couldn't form any words. Her eyes searched his face. Her voice trembled, "But . . ."

"You are not going to be changed. My father said you have proven yourself time and again. Though Roud argued that you were too small, and it is evident that you are not going to gain much in size. He said you would always be weak and lack stamina. That it was proven with you becoming ill today."

Krista's breathing quickened.

He reached out, taking her bandaged hands. "I am sorry to tell you this now, but I knew you would rather know."

Krista nodded. "I just do not understand. Roud has never seemed to doubt me, nor has he treated me like this before.

"Roud has never treated anyone like he is treating you, but it does not matter. You will continue as my companion."

Krista gave him a waning smile.

He continued. "While we are talking seriously, there are some things I have to say. Please listen. There are feelings running between us."

He saw her start to react but cut her off, holding up his hand. "No, Krista, they are there. I, too, find them confusing, but I also know that holding you is the most wonderful thing I have ever felt. I could not figure out why you did not come to me with what was happening, then I realized, this afternoon while I was thinking of holding you, that is the reason. You were afraid to tell me because you would end up in my arms, just like you did, and you are trying to keep a distance from me. Am I right?"

The silence drew out until she finally answered. "Yes." Krista bit the edge of her lip.

Running his fingers up through his hair, he sighed. "I do not want that distance between us."

She started to object, but he cut her off.

"Wait, I understand the difficulties of a relationship other than friends between us, and I am trying to abide by that for now, but I never want there to be a hesitation to coming to me. I am your friend first, no matter what happens," he ended firmly.

"All right," it came out almost a whisper. She leaned forward, giving him a hug, to which he grinned playfully.

"It does not mean I am going to avoid the other contact between us. Kissing you is too enjoyable."

Krista blushed, unsure what to say.

Garion laughed, easing the tension, "Now off to bed with you."

"I have slept all day," she objected.

"All right, but do not stay up long."

She nodded. Drawing out the assignments that had been left for her, she settled down while Garion worked on other tasks. It really wasn't long until she found herself getting sleepy, and at her first yawn, Garion sent her off to bed.

There she lay awake, and for the first time, could think clearly of how Roud had been treating her. It was so uncharacteristic of him. She had always admired his fairness. He seemed different lately. She couldn't help wonder if something was wrong at his home. It was when he returned from there that he started acting strange. Krista couldn't come up with the answer and decided not to worry about it any longer as she drifted off to sleep.

It took several days, with Garion constantly watching over her, for Krista to feel better. The warmth of being in his arms hadn't faded for her and, from some of the looks she'd seen him give her, she knew it hadn't for him, either. Though no contact was made between them other than was normal with their everyday activities, a closeness remained.

Maybe it was the warmth she was feeling which made her feel so uncomfortable when Lord Richem came to visit with his daughter, Carolee. Carolee was very beautiful with long thick brown hair that hung in curls around her shoulders. To top it off, she was very sweet, gentle, and kind.

Garion had asked Krista to attend supper with him. There she found herself with Carolee between her and Garion. She sat quietly to the side as the conversation ran all around her. It was after dinner, though, that she felt totally awkward when the king asked aloud to Garion, "Why do you not dismiss your companion and take Carolee for a walk in the gardens?"

Garion looked down the table at her. Krista felt totally out of place as Garion didn't say anything. All eyes seemed to fall on her. She wanted to rush from the room.

"If you will excuse me, I do have some duties to attend to," Krista said softly.

"I will see you later," Garion answered back.

Krista tilted her head and left the table.

Garion watched Krista leave. He didn't like what had happened. Several times during the night, his gaze had found its way to her. She sat quietly, not trying to enter any of the conversations. Krista also hadn't touched much of her meal, and after her being ill such a short time before, he didn't like that. Mostly, her behavior puzzled him.

Krista was not usually that quiet. Then he couldn't help but smile. She was jealous. The one who had insisted there could be no relationship between them, and that he should find someone else, was jealous.

For a moment, Garion felt like going after her to tell her not to worry. Though Carolee was very beautiful, he had no interest in her. Then he decided against it. Maybe a little jealousy would be good for her. Maybe Krista would have to face a few things about her feelings for him.

As everyone in the room divided to go their own ways, he was a little uncomfortable being left to the walk in the garden with Carolee. He didn't want to deceive her, but he had to be polite. Offering her his arm, he led the way to the gardens. Light conversation drifted as they made their way around the trimmed bushes and sweet-smelling flowers.

It was he who was taken by surprise when Carolee dropped his arm and turned to face him. "Your Highness, I feel I must be honest with you. I, I know my father hopes that you will take an interest in me but, to be honest, I already have someone I am in love with. He hopes to ask for my hand in marriage soon. I thought you should know right away."

Garion smiled in relief at the revelation. "Thank you for your honesty. I have been trying to figure out how to approach this very subject myself."

"I was not aware you have a lady," Carolee said.

"I do not exactly. There is someone I am interested in, though. I will ask you please not mention this to anyone. I am having enough trouble without all the pushing that would happen if there was word of an interest."

"I understand, Your Highness. I give my word," Carolee promised.

"Since we are sharing such secrets, please will you call me Garion? I do prefer it."

Carolee tilted her head toward him, "Garion."

He smiled. "Maybe you could help me."

"How may I be of assistance?" she asked as they began to walk.

"The young woman I am interested in tries not to let her feelings out. I am sure they are there because they slip from time to time. How do I go about bringing them out?"

"May I ask who the lady is?" Carolee questioned.

"I am sorry, but that is something I am not ready to divulge."

"Well, it would help if I knew something about her, but have you tried to talk about it openly? I would say most women like an honest approach."

"I have tried. It ended up in a fight, definitely not how I wanted it to go. She is strong-willed and refuses any relationship between us. So how do I win her over?"

"You are sure she has feelings for you?"

He nodded. “Yes. In fact, I’m sure she is jealous tonight because I am with you.”

“It sounds a little unusual.”

“If you knew the whole story it would sound more than a little. But tell me, what do you think are the risks of trying to use her jealousy to force out her feelings?”

She hesitated. “It could cause more problems than good.”

“You do not think it is possible it could get her to admit her feelings?”

“It is possible, but I honestly would not try it unless you are sure no other way will work,” she answered truthfully and waited as he thought a moment.

“It has been a struggle for quite some time. I really cannot think of any other way. Would you be willing to help me for a few days?”

Carolee nodded. “What is it you have in mind?”

“I want to keep it very simple, just walking in the garden, attending meals together, and I will escort you to the ball in two nights.”

“Do you want me to say anything to anyone?”

“No, that will not be necessary. I will do all that. You can say just simply we’re friends. I am having enough problems in my relationship. I do not want anything to get back to your intended and cause problems for you.”

“Thank you, I appreciate that.” She smiled. “You know you are . . . Garion, a woman likes to be treated tenderly, with kindness, knowing that a man truly cares for her.”

“I know, but this one tends to run from that. Things have to be extremely bad before she will come to me. When she does, though, it is the most incredible thing in the world to take her into my arms.”

“It sounds like she is fortunate.”

“She is very special, and I can understand her hesitation, but I just don’t want the division between us.”

They continued to talk and plan out how things would be, and then Garion escorted her to her room. Returning to his own, he knocked on the door between his and Krista’s room. It took a minute before Krista opened the door, her head slightly down.

When she didn't say anything, he spoke up. "I just wanted to say good night and to let you know that I might be late for practice in the morning. I am having breakfast with Carolee."

"You had a nice evening?" Krista asked softly, still not meeting his gaze.

He beamed, "Yes, very. In fact, signs are that things are going as I hoped." He eyed her carefully. "Tomorrow afternoon I may take her for a ride. Would you be free to attend us?"

Krista's head came up. "You really do not want me along, do you?"

"Of course, I want you to make sure that we will not be disturbed. Besides, only knowing each other for such a short time, we should be escorted. It would be improper. What if people thought I tried to kiss her?"

He caught the small breath Krista took before she nodded.

"Well, good night," he said, turning from her abruptly, leaving her to close the door. He felt guilty as he heard the latch click. He was playing with her feelings and wondered again if it was wise. He wanted Krista to admit she loved him, but maybe this wasn't the way. Unfortunately, he knew she wouldn't admit it any other way due to her uncompromising sense of duty.

The next morning, Garion wasn't too late for practice. Krista was torn between being uncomfortable and relieved when he got there. Roud still tended to be hard on her, though doing it so no one else would notice. It was mainly little cutting remarks to make her doubt herself, and today she definitely didn't need that.

She'd spent a restless night with unsure feelings. It had been just over a week before that Garion had held her in his arms. His warm glances had caused feelings to rise within her. Now he seemed to be focused on another woman. There was no way Krista could compete with her, which was even more foolish, since she shouldn't think of competing for him. He was supposed to be finding someone to love and marry, so why did it hurt so much that he might possibly have found that someone?

In swords, their workout went pretty much as normal. In hand to hand, he seemed to come at her with more determination. Krista fought harder than ever to stay out of his grip.

When he won, it was by taking Krista down. He seemed to deliberately force her under his body. His lips brushed her neck. It was not a kiss, but the warmth of his breath on her neck caused her to tremble. Letting her up, she couldn't meet his gaze as she tried to catch her breath and bring her feelings under control.

As if the morning wasn't bad enough, the afternoon was worse. The ride took them to the lake where Krista had gone on her birthday. She followed just far enough behind them that she couldn't hear their conversation. She then sat on the hillside as Garion walked Carolee along the shore. Inside, Krista's emotions ran this way and that. Their stay at the lake hadn't been long, and fortunately, Garion let Krista bow out of attending supper in the main hall that night.

Garion returned early, knocking on her door. "Would you come in and help me with some work?" he asked. She followed him inside, settling down by him to help. An odd quietness settled over the room while they worked.

Garion finally couldn't take it. "Krista, is there something wrong?" He hoped she would admit that she was upset.

"No." She bit the edge of her lip.

"Are you sure? Something seems to be bothering you."

"No, really, I'm fine."

"Is it about the ball tomorrow night? I know you do not like to go to them, but I am afraid you will have to attend."

"Could you not excuse me?" She hadn't even thought about the ball before but, right then, it sounded dreadful.

"I am sorry. Actually, I think it will be quite enjoyable."

"Garion, do you need me any longer?" The words came with such a forlorn feeling that Garion about broke. He wanted to take her in his arms and tell her just to say she loved him.

Instead, he shook his head and softly answered, "No."

She walked to the door, turning. "Good night," She disappeared inside.

Garion grabbed a pillow, squeezing it in his hand. He threw it across the room. Why did she keep things in so? Why did she have to refuse him? Maybe this wasn't fair of him, but somehow, someway, he'd get her to face the fact that there was more love than just plain friendship between them.

He sank back into his chair. He didn't want to hurt her. After a moment of thought, he stood and went to her door. His hand hung for a breath before he brought it down on the door.

At first there was nothing but silence. Krista was still wearing her breaches with her oversized nightshirt when she opened it.

"We have to talk." He blurted out and turned away, walking back into his room. Hesitantly, she followed then stood still as he moved quietly around the room. Finally stopping, he turned to face her. "I cannot do this to you."

Confusion filled her face as he continued. "It is hurting you, and I do not want to hurt you. I am not interested in Carolee at all. In fact, Carolee is practically engaged."

"I do not understand," Krista whispered.

"I wanted to make you jealous, to get you to admit that you loved me." He saw her pull back and stepped toward her. "I cannot do it this way. I want to hear it so bad, but I do not want it to be forced. Krista, please. End the illusion."

She didn't change.

"Please." The change was so subtle that there didn't seem to be a difference but, suddenly, she looked very feminine. Automatically he took another step toward her, arms out.

She pulled away. "It was a trick to make me jealous," she whispered. "How could you?" She could feel the tears rise. Out of sheer anger, she wouldn't let them loose.

"I thought that maybe if you thought, well, if Carolee and I were becoming involved, then maybe you would let out how you feel."

Growing very defensive, she reacted. "What do you mean, how I feel? What you do is your own affair. You can see all the women you want. It means nothing to me."

"You can say that, but I know better."

"Well, maybe you have got it all wrong."

"I have held you in my arms. I was on one end of the kisses we shared. You cannot tell me that there is not something between us."

"There is not."

"You cannot keep lying to yourself."

"I am not." She held herself rigid. "I have no such feelings. Why would you think I would get jealous? I have no interest in you other than as your guardian."

"Then why do you get so warm when I hold you? You admitted that it confuses you."

"I was just going through a hard time. You are the only one who knows I'm a woman."

"And it did not mean anything when I kissed you?"

"No." She shook her head defiantly.

"And if I reached out right now and kissed you, it would mean nothing?" he challenged.

"Of course not. I am your guardian, plain and simple."

"Really?"

Grabbing her wrist, he pulled her forward, wrapping his arms around her before she could resist. He pressed his lips firmly to hers, not letting her break away. He continued, easing her body into his.

She fought to push away. When he released her, she moved across the room, fighting to keep herself under control. "How dare you? You have no right! I am the Guardian of the Sword and nothing else to you."

"That is a lie, because I happen to love you. You mean more to me than the guardian."

"No! I cannot ever love you. You do not love me. You just need to spend time with the other ladies, and you will see."

"And if you would spend time as a woman, you would see. It is about time you were who you really are, a woman not a man." The words came out with more force than he intended. Immediately he tried to take it back. "I did not mean it like—"

"No, Garion. I am what I am, the Guardian of Kallairion. Every day and every night that does not change, and it will not change. Whenever you, your father, or your mother are in danger, I will be there. That is my life, my duty. That is who I am. Now, if you will excuse me." She headed for the door.

"Krista!"

"No, Garion. It is Kris! Krista can never be here." She closed the door firmly, both metaphorically and literally.

Garion ran his fingers up through his hair. He had done it this time. He had pushed too hard trying to bring out her love, but succeeded only in pushing all of Krista away. A deep, aching sickness welled up within him. He wondered if she would ever let the feminine side of her show through again.

Would he ever again hold her in his arms?

"Krista, please, I love you," he whispered into the still room.

Chapter Seventeen

Behind the door, the tears did not fall. Krista pushed them all away. The hurt, the pain, the love, all were Krista's, and she could not exist anymore. She should never have surfaced in the first place. It was all her fault. It was about time she got her thoughts back to where they should be.

Slowly drawing Kallairion, Krista laid it on her bed. Taking a breath, her fingers barely touched Kallairion, and the sword shimmered into its large, mighty broadsword.

Dropping to her knees, her head came down on folded arms. "Oh, why, why me? How can I hope to stand against Kuel? If he were here, he would laugh, the girl champion." Alone in the darkness of her room, she knelt by her bed until sleep finally came and, with it, unrest of a different type.

Night was nearly over when she awoke. Through her mind only one thing remained from her sleep. Or was it sleep at all? All she knew was that she had to leave the castle. To where she didn't know, but she had to leave now, before morning when answers would have to be given.

Her muscles protested as she pulled herself off the floor, but she didn't let it slow her. Pausing only long enough to light a candle, she quickly redressed, then gathered what she would need, keeping it light. The last thing was changing Kallairion into her sword.

Picking it up, she stopped, looking at the blade. "Where are you taking me?" she whispered.

A feeling of assurance came over her that she was doing the right thing. Strapping Kallairion to her waist, Krista blew out the candle. At the door, she stopped, looking back at the door that led to Garion's chambers.

Walking back to it, she took hold of the handle. It turned. He hadn't locked it. Inside, long shadows were cast across the room but Krista didn't pause, heading to the open door to Garion's bedroom.

Never before had she entered his room while he was sleeping. Drawing near him, she caught her breath. He shifted in restless sleep. She wondered what he was dreaming about, if it was her and the fight they'd had. She bit her lip. What a bad time to leave. He had said he loved her.

In a whisper so soft that it hardly broke the air, she couldn't keep her words back, though he wouldn't hear them. "I wish I could have your love and give you mine in return." Taking a shaky breath, she went back to the outer room and his desk and took out a paper.

Garion,
I wish I could explain, but I cannot. I have to go.
I cannot tell you where, why, or even when I will be back.
I want you to know I am not leaving because of what
happened last night. This is something I have to do.

Kris

Krista left the note lying in the center of the desk and made her way out of the castle, careful not to get caught by anyone who might be up. There was a brief stop in the kitchen for food, then to the stable. She had Shea saddled before she thought about how to make it past the entry guards. With no other options, she put her faith in Kallairion.

Quietly leading Shea to the gate, she tried to stay in the shadows but once at the gate, they were in the open. There was no way to go through without someone taking notice of her but, as she walked past the guards, they seemed oblivious to her, as if she wasn't there.

She climbed on Shea, keeping their pace at a walk until they were clear of the village, then she urged the horse faster. By sunrise, they were well away from the castle. Krista pushed on, keeping the pace to a gallop, before finally breaking to a walk, with short rests scattered throughout the day. It was almost nightfall when she stopped. She brushed down Shea before eating just a little. She fell asleep the moment she dropped exhausted on her bedroll.

The next morning, their trek continued at first light. As she did the day before, Krista wondered what lay ahead. Inside her, the urgency seemed to grow, though there were no answers. The trail remained familiar through the mountains of Han. The morning of the next day, she passed the lake where Garion had discovered that she was a woman. She longed to stop and swim but settled for just washing before moving on.

Before she reached the cliffs they had climbed, her trail changed. It took her in the other direction, dropping into another valley. She had just started up the slope on the other side when an eerie feeling hit, sending an uncontrollable shiver through her.

She pulled Shea to a stop long enough to steel herself before urging the horse forward again. It wasn't far until the trees opened to show the mouth of a cave.

Kallairion tingled at her side. Apprehension, mixed with fear, filled her, but she dismounted. She stood, fixed on the gaping black hole and she stroked Shea's neck, as much for her own comfort as for that of the skittish animal.

"Well, it seems as if this is the place," she said in a hushed tone to herself.

Krista moved with caution into the cave's mouth. It was only a few feet until the light was swallowed up, and she was enveloped in the darkness. She pulled back. Something told her that she really didn't want to go in there, but something else told her she must.

At least, she could set a few of her own terms. Returning to Shea, she opened her pack, took out some food. She ate while wrapping the top of a stick for a torch. Krista busied herself tending Shea, to put off entering the cave.

Finally, it was the only thing left to do.

Lighting the torch, she again carefully made her way into the opening. Her skin crawled. She pressed on farther, studying every inch illuminated by the light, then tried to peer deeper into the darkness. The temperature cooled immediately, but it was nothing like the cold she felt inside.

Pausing, she scratched a mark on the wall so she would have a trail out. She couldn't help but wish to return to the opening. She didn't know, couldn't imagine, what could have been so important to bring her from Arlanda, away from the royal family? They were her duty.

One certainty burned in her, she had to trust Kallairion. It would not have brought her here if it was not important.

Kicking a loose rock, she jumped at the sound. Her hand pressed to her chest as she fought to still her rushing heart. "This is foolishness. I am scaring myself. If only this creepy feeling would go away." Around the next corner, the tunnel closed off. Only when Krista made it to the very end, did she see a crack in the floor.

"Oh." She looked in hesitantly. At the same moment, she felt a strong urge to head down through the opening. The climb was not difficult, even holding the torch. It was not too cramped, and there were plenty of foot and handholds, but she was glad when the tunnel leveled once more. She wished there was some way to know how far she had gone. It felt like quite a distance. Her eyes grew accustomed to the dim light, but nothing eased the eeriness.

Krista continued marking the walls. She moved around two more bends before the way opened into a large cavern filled with water. Krista could never have imagined anything so incredible. The torchlight glistened across the glass-smooth surface. From the ceiling, light caught huge spikes that looked like frozen icicles extending down in a myriad of colors. By the shore, other spikes jutted upward to meet the ceiling. Drawn to them, Krista ran her fingers over the rippled stone spears.

A noise echoed across the cavern but, when Krista spun to meet it, nothing was there. Still, it kept her attention from the beauties of the room. She paused for a minute to get a bearing on which direction to follow. Making her way to the side of the lake, she worked her way along a narrow ledge. About a third of the way around the edge, the path disappeared under the inky water.

Steadying herself, she cautiously stepped forward, feeling for the footing that the surface wouldn't reveal. Each step was carefully tested before she moved on. The water grew deeper, reaching her calves, but remained below the top of her boots. The next few steps it got shallower. Still, she didn't walk easily, afraid that it might drop out from under her, plunging her into the ominous black depths.

There was no sigh of relief for Krista as she came out of the water because the tunnel dropped again into a narrow slit of passage. Her fear grew. She didn't want to go farther, casting a glance back across the lake. Only the knowledge that Kallairion led her kept her going on. A tremor of alarm struck her.

Working the grip of Kallairion in one hand, the torch held high in the other, she walked on, expecting at any time to be jumped by a creature lurking in the darkness.

A creature did not leap out as the flickering light crested over the body lying on the floor, but a gasp escaped Krista loud enough to echo through the stone corridor.

The familiarity of the form made her sick. The stillness held her back, but the need to know overcame and drove her forward. With a quick survey of the shadows, she took a step forward, kneeling by the crumpled shape of a man. With Kallairion still in her hand, she grasped the shoulder, pushing the body over.

Instantly, she turned away, her body threatening to be sick. Drawing back, she studied the well-known scarred face.

"No." The cry broke from her as tears trickled down her cheeks. All was clear, the reason for being drawn here, everything of late. Everything was answered in Roud's body lying in the depths of the cavern. Even with the coolness to preserve it, it was easy to tell he had been dead for weeks. And if Roud was here, then the man at the castle was . . . Kuel, waiting, playing out his game, and Garion would be his prey.

A loud ringing burst through her mind from Kallairion, sending her scrambling to her feet. Krista spun around into a defensive stance, but nothing was there.

In the distance, a rumble sounded, growing, and closing in around her. The mountain shook at her discovery, jolting her into action. Krista ran down the tunnel, having to use the walls to keep her balance. Clinging to the torch and Kallairion, she knew that the loss of either could mean her life.

At the opening to the underground lake, Krista didn't slow to test her footing. Splashing, she ran through the water. From the ceiling beautiful spikes broke loose, crashing down around her in a deadly shower. One came close, drenching her with a spray of water.

Krista stumbled, falling to her knees. The torch flew from her hands, landing on the small lip she'd walked across earlier, threatening to go out. Trying to regain her feet, she was jerked away before she could reach the torch. From under the water, a thick, scaly coil slid its way up her leg, around her waist, dragging her into deeper water.

Krista swung out with Kallairion but only contacted the bottom. The squeezing around her middle forced the air from of her lungs. Her fight for breath only yielded water. With her free hand, she groped at whatever was holding her while she continued to hack with Kallairion. Whatever it was seemed to not react with pain, for each blow seemed to have no effect.

Krista felt her struggling lessen as her life drained away. The roaring in her ears drowned out the sounds of the rumbling and falling rocks. Willing herself to keep swinging Kallairion, she struck again and again. She couldn't tell if the pressure slackened, but she was no longer under the water. There was air! Another blow, and she pulled free.

Staggering her way to the ledge, she dropped to the ground, wanting nothing more than air and light. Again the ringing came. She rolled to the side. A large spear of a rock missed her only by a foot. Splinters showered her body, some piercing her skin. Lurching to her feet, she grabbed the torch, pleading that it wouldn't go out.

The whole mountain groaned, coming apart to destroy her. Krista stumbled on as fast as the shifting floor allowed. There was no stopping or the whole earth would close around her. Reaching the crack, she began to climb, only to be showered by rocks and knocked back. There was so much dust in the air that the torch hardly cut through it, but she clung to it with hope.

Pulling upward, the roar seemed to press down on her. She realized that the crack was closing in. With each inch she made forward, it narrowed on her. She wasn't going to make it. She was going to die here with her secret, leaving Kuel back at Arlanda playing his final mad game, toying with them as he had done her, breaking her down, making her doubt herself. Was he doing that to Garion right now, breaking him before he destroyed him?

Pushing herself up, she dug her way into the crevice, forcing herself up as rocks showered down. Before her, the crevice opened into the tunnel. Gripping the edge to pull herself over with everything collapsing around, a rock crashed down on her shoulder.

"No!" Krista screamed as the torch fell from her grasp into the darkness below. "No!" she cried again, starting to slide down after it.

Clawing at the rock, she found a handhold, stopping the motion. Exhaustion screamed through her body but there was no time to rest. Groping in the dark, she pulled herself back up an inch at a time until at the top, she rolled over the edge.

Coughing from the dirt in the air, she tried to take a breath. The whoosh and rumbling beneath her made her almost glad she couldn't see. It was enough to know that there was no more crack. But without light, she didn't know how to find her way out? "Kallairion!" she cried loud enough that the cry echoed above the thunder. In her hand, the sword began to glow, comforting her at once and willing her to go on.

Staggering to her feet, she fell, then tried again, making her way forward. Above her, a section of the roof gave way. Krista wished for a shield then, it was there, though unseen. Rocks tumbled over her, not one impacting. She didn't understand how, she just knew that it was Kallairion's doing. She'd never been told about this ability but, at in this moment, she didn't care. She forced herself to a run on under the dome of soft golden light. She ached to stop. Her body couldn't take any more, but to stop would be death for everyone.

Rounding a bend, a shaft of light blared like a beacon, cutting though the darkness, but it seemed like it was an eternity away from her. The ground quaked under her feet. She stumbled and fell, going down. Dust choked the air from her. Clinging to the wall, she pulled herself up. The floor shifted with each step. She staggered on using the wall to keep herself upright until she finally broke into the light.

Shea pranced nervously before her. Dust bellowed out behind. With a final roll, the earth gave up its challenge, sending Krista tumbling to the ground. Trying to rise, she fell back down, remaining still as unconsciousness claimed her.

Chapter Eighteen

Garion awoke with the same uneasy feeling he had gone to sleep with. He wished he'd never told Krista. He should've played it out and let her jealousy get the better of her. Maybe it would've been different then, instead of her pulling away from him totally.

Walking through his room, he didn't notice the cold on his bare feet. He dropped into a chair, running his fingers back through his hair. Leaning forward, he rested his elbows on the desk, head in his hands.

For a moment, he stayed like that, rubbing his eyes. He then caught sight of familiar handwriting. Grabbing the paper, he read.

Garion,
I wish I could explain, but I cannot. I have to go.
I cannot tell you where, why, or even when I will be back.
I want you to know I am not leaving because of what
happened last night. This is something I have to do.

Kris

He stared at the paper, unable to move for a moment, then he lurched to his feet and crossed the room. Slamming open Krista's door, he found the room empty.

She was gone.

She hadn't taken all of her belongings but it was plain that she had left. Rushing to his room, he grabbed his clothes. Pulling them on, he ran through the castle to the stable. Shea wasn't there. A quick word with the stable boy revealed that the horse was gone when he'd arrived early that morning.

Slowly, he made his way back to his chambers. Why? Why did she have to leave? Why had he pressed her? He remained in his room with feelings of guilt and great loss.

Finally, making his way to the yard to practice, he made the excuse that Kris had a personal problem to attend to and would be gone for a while. Garion wished he knew for how long, and Roud's comment that he was better off without Kris always around didn't help.

That night Garion excused himself from attending the ball, saying he didn't feel well. It was impossible for him to attend, knowing what he had planned and what it had caused.

He lay back in his bed, hands pushed into his hair. All thoughts were on Krista. Where was she? Was she safe? Was she thinking of him? Was her hurt as bad as his? He prayed not. He prayed for her return, on any terms she wanted, just as long as she was back.

The days passed slowly. After the third day of her absence, worry took up his every thought. What if something had happened to her and she was alone? He hadn't felt this helpless since Kuel had come after him.

He tried to comfort himself. After all, she was far from helpless, and she had Kallairion with her, but the image of her father after the fight haunted him.

Lady Adele was the only person he confided in. She tried to comfort him that Krista wouldn't leave because of their fight. She tried to convince him it had to be something else to take her away from her duty, but it was of little comfort. Krista was gone. Their parting had been awful, and he wanted her back.

Krista's eyes fluttered against the light. When they finally focused, Shea and the whole forest were gone. The sun radiated through the window adding warmth to her body. The room smelled of sweet flowers. It was all strange to her.

The stone walls were formidable, but it was not the castle. The room was plain but had a warm, comfortable feeling. Moving slightly to look around brought with it a stab of pain and the feel of silky blankets against her skin. A damp cloth was laid across her forehead.

"Lie still," the soft voice said from behind.

Krista looked up to catch the movement of an older woman, walking toward a middle-aged woman with brown hair. "Go and tell Halayne that she is awake," the soft voice came again. At once the other woman turned and left the room quietly.

The woman turned as Krista moved and gasped. "Now be still, dear. You were quite battered but everything will be fine." The soft voice of the woman fit with her gray hair and gentle features. A few wrinkles framed her kind smile.

"Where am I?" Krista's throat felt dry, making it hard to get the words out.

"Our valley is called Laire. You are quite safe," the woman said reassuringly, bringing a cup to Krista's lips.

"Sisters of Laire." Krista's voice was still hoarse and weak.

"So you have heard of us."

Krista made a faint nod. "What happened? How did I get here?" Krista felt totally confused. Her head hurt to think.

"As for what happened, you will have to answer that. As for how you got here—"

Krista heard the door open. Looking to the side, she saw another woman enter.

"We found you lying outside the cave in the next valley over and brought you here," the woman finished.

"That was yesterday." The woman who had just entered spoke, "We were getting quite concerned, Guardian."

Immediately Krista reacted, trying to sit up, but both women were there holding her back. "Calm now."

Krista gasped, as her body ached. "You know who I am?"

"Certainly, dear, Kallairion has been here before. It was one of our sisters who was given the task to present it to your great-great-grandfather." The woman reached out and brushed Krista's hair back from her face.

"And now you are the Chosen of the Chosen. The final battle may be at hand, but we will talk about that later, when you have eaten and regained your strength. You were not hurt seriously, but it will take a couple of days for your strength to return. There will be food here shortly, and then we shall see about you getting up and moving around."

"Where is Kallairion?"

The woman smiled. "Right here." She motioned behind her. "It has never been out of your presence."

Krista shifted until she could see Kallairion resting on a pillow on the dresser. A sigh of relief escaped her as she settled back onto her own pillows.

There was a knock, and the woman who had left the room earlier stepped in with a tray.

As she was assisted in sitting up, Krista became aware she had been changed and was wearing a simple linen bed shirt. All else was forgotten at the sight of the food. With her hunger appeased slightly, she began to talk. "I do not even know your names to thank you."

The woman, who Krista decided was the leader, smiled and spoke. "I am Halayne. This is Adra," she said, motioning to the older woman tending to her. "And Tammen, who brought in the food."

"Thank you," Krista said, between bites.

"You are most welcome. We are honored to be of assistance to you. I must also ask what your name is since we cannot keep addressing you as Guardian."

"Oh, sorry, I am Kris. I mean Krista."

Somewhere off in the distance Krista heard a rumble and the grounds shook slightly causing her to jump.

"It is all right, dear." Adra laid a hand on her arm.

"The mountain is still grumbling after its failure to trap you," Halayne added.

Krista bolted upright, trying to get out of bed again. The women reached to hold her back.

"I have to go. Roud's dead. Kuel, he will kill them." Her breathing became unsteady as the past day's events raced back to her.

"Easy, child, you have to rest first."

"No! Kuel will kill them. I have to stop him." She fought to get up.

"And you will have the chance. But first you need a few days to recuperate and prepare," Halayne soothed. "Kallairion would never let you come if they were in danger. It will let you know when it is time to return."

Krista thought on the words and calmed. Lying back, she closed her eyes and nodded.

"Why do you not rest for a while longer? Later Tammen can show you around. She will introduce you to the women who will help you practice. They are quite skillful and are waiting to be at your disposal whenever you wish. Just do not push yourself too hard at first. It will be better to give your body a chance to heal." Halayne stood. "I have to attend to some details. We will talk more later."

The women left Krista lying back in her pillows. She didn't like the thought of Kuel back at the castle, but Halayne was right. Kallairion would not have brought her here if there were immediate danger. And she was not in any shape to face him now. If she hoped to win, she would have to be at her top strength and skill.

Looking at Kallairion, she drew her feet from under the covers and stood. For an instant, she felt shaky, though it passed quickly with each step she took to Kallairion. Halayne was right again. Her body ached in many places, but it would heal quickly.

As she touched Kallairion, its reassurance flowed into her, easing her fears for the safety of Garion and the king and queen. Garion. She had tried to keep her mind from him, but it was no use, she wished to see him. It wasn't only to make sure he was truly all right. It was . . . she closed her eyes to imagine him . . . to have him hold her, reassure her.

The time she would face Kuel was at hand. It was past being a possibility now. It was reality.

"Garion, I am frightened," she whispered aloud. She felt Kallairion's comforting influence, but still longed for Garion's strong arms around her. She would risk all the confusion she felt for the warmth of his love.

Why hadn't she put her stubbornness aside and told him she loved him? He was right. She had been afraid. Would she ever get the chance now? That became her personal reason to defeat Kuel, so she could have the chance to tell Garion she loved him, but would he really want her? That, she decided, she wouldn't worry about now.

Sliding her finger down Kallairion's blade, it soothed her again, almost wiping away all thought. She didn't even remember lying down and going to back to sleep, but several hours passed before she awoke again.

Clothes had been left on the table for her, a soft linen shirt and breeches. The fit was tight but comfortable, made for ease of movement. Even before she strapped Kallairion on which tightened the shirt to her waist, the clothes showed the shape of the woman within. She was sitting on the bed, pulling on her boots, when the door opened.

Tammen stopped at the opening. "I was right, that you would want to be up. I will show you around, if you are ready."

"Yes, thank you." Krista finished tugging on her boots and stood.

The structures of Laire were old but extremely well cared for. Tammen explained all the details as they walked. The buildings were set in a square with a large courtyard in the middle. On one end was a large garden where several women were working. Tammen said that, at the moment, twenty-seven women were at Laire. Only nineteen were there permanently. The others were there for their own reasons. Wherever they went, Krista was greeted with warmth and openness.

From the courtyard, they moved to the halls, then to the study that was filled with bounteous books, through the kitchen and laundry. They ended, at last, at the stable. Krista's heart jumped at the sight of Shea. Wrapping her arms around the horse's neck, Krista clung to the animal, as Shea nudged her with her nose.

"Would you like to go back to the courtyard?" Tammen asked after a time. "You can have a light practice before supper, then another afterwards?"

Since Shea had obviously been well tended, Krista nodded.

In the courtyard, Tammen introduced Krista to three women who were waiting for them. Quickly, she explained that they were the most skilled fighters there and perhaps in the land. They would help her practice any time she wished. The first, Alise, was not quite as tall as Krista but heavier. Her brown eyes gave her a soft, doe-look, but they were sharp and alert. The second woman was tall and thin and wiry. Her name was Jana and her actions were almost cat-like quick.

Elsa, the third woman, was the tallest woman Krista had ever seen. She was not overly large, as her size fit her height. But this wasn't why Krista found herself staring. What drew attention was her absolute beauty. The woman was truly stunning, especially when Elsa greeted her with a smile.

It was Jana who stayed for Krista's first practice, which was more like a light exercise before supper. Returning to the courtyard after eating, Krista found Elsa waiting.

"I am at your disposal, Guardian," Elsa greeted as Krista neared.

"Oh, thank you. But I think I need to wait awhile first. I ate too much."

As the woman smiled, Krista realized she was at least ten years older than herself.

"As you wish, Guardian. We can sit and talk if you would like."

"I would like that very much, but please, call me Krista." Krista hesitated only a second before she asked, "Elsa, what brings you to Laire? If you do not mind my asking?"

"Not at all. I, myself, was drawn here. I am not from your kingdom, and before you ask, no, everyone from my land is not this tall."

Krista smiled because that was the first question that popped into her head.

"I was always tall. To make my story short, it seemed that men always wanted to possess me, like a showpiece to be seen with. The women never accepted me very well, my height and well . . ." She blushed.

"You are beautiful," Krista answered for her.

Sheepishly, Elsa nodded. "Anyway, finally I met a man who was different from the others. Theo was even taller than I, but he was shy, and so sweet and gentle. Over time, we fell in love and finally got married. Shortly afterward, he was killed. Not long after that, I left. I could not stay for missing him. I was not sure where I was going. I had such pain. Finally, I ended up here. That was about two years ago. The memories still hurt, but at least, I am happy again."

Krista nodded.

"You have a love," Elsa observed.

"I . . . kind of. There is a man that I love."

"He does not love you?"

"Actually, I believe he does. He says he does. It is just not that easy."

"Because you are the Guardian. Does he know?"

"Yes, but it is not that alone. He is . . . he is Prince Garion."

Elsa was quiet, obviously not knowing what to say.

"I do not know what to do, but until I face Kuel, there is no reason to worry about it. Let's start practicing." She stood.

Elsa nodded and joined her.

The next day, Krista met with the women to practice, sometimes one at a time, sometimes more. By evening, she faced all three at once. Each shared their skills and knowledge with her, and, with each practice, the soreness left her muscles, and Krista felt her strength returning.

For four days the regimen continued. Krista practiced, trained, rested, and ate. And in that short time, her skills became more refined than she had ever dared hope.

Each evening she walked through the courtyard thinking of Garion before returning to her room to drop off to sleep. On the evening of the fifth day, Tammen waited for Krista to finish her routine, then informed her that Halayne wanted to speak with her in the library.

The woman sat at the desk as Krista entered.

"Good evening, Krista, how is practice going?"

"I am afraid that I am as ready as I will ever be."

The woman smiled back understandingly. "That is good, we will leave in the morning."

"We? You will be going with me?"

"Of course. A group of eight of us will be your escort. As I said before, you are the Chosen of the Chosen. It will be easy for us to see you to Arlanda without any interference. Even Kuel will not hinder your entrance, since you will be surrounded by us, cloaked, and not saying a word. If he even suspects you are there to reveal his identity, he will not be concerned, since he believes there is no one who can stand against him. You will be free to unveil him when you decide the time is right."

Krista shuddered within. Somehow, Halayne picked up on it. "I know this is a heavy burden for one so young."

"I have known about it most of my life," Krista said firmly.

"Of course."

"I owe you such thanks for all your assistance. I hate to make you go to such trouble."

"There is no trouble. It is our duty to help you as much as it is your duty to face Kuel. Now get a good night's sleep. We will prepare everything for you."

Once in her room, Krista had a hard time going to sleep. Garion! In the morning, she would be returning home. Arlanda was her home now. She wanted to return, even if it meant facing Kuel.

Fears of failing filled her, forcing her to her knees. Tears did not fall as she made her resolution not to be defeated. The words Garion had once said to her in the garden came back, reassuring her. He had faith in her, and she must have faith in herself.

Morning dawned bright. Krista arrived at the stables with Halayne and Tammen to find Jana, Elsa, Alise, and three others waiting with the horses ready to leave. Shea was not among them, but before Krista could ask, Halayne spoke up. "It is best that no one figures out who you are. If you arrived on your horse, it could ruin everything."

"Of course," Krista chided herself. The nervousness running through her was not letting her think clearly, but Halayne had thought of everything.

From the side, another woman stepped forward, holding out a bundle. Halayne took it, allowing it to unfold. She held the long cloak out for Krista. Laying it on her shoulders, Halayne came around and tied it under her chin. It barely skimmed the ground.

Something about it felt immensely comforting. Krista fingered the material. It was plain, much like the breeches and shirt they had given her to wear and, like her clothes, bleached white, whereas the rest of the women were clothed and cloaked in plain brownish and rust colors.

Krista took the reins of the horse provided to her, and they all mounted. The other horses surrounded her, two in the lead, two behind, and two positioned on each side, and they were off. There were only a few out to wave goodbye. It felt strange to be traveling this way. Hardly anyone said a word. What lay ahead left everyone in a reflective mood that she couldn't help but feel. If she failed, no one was likely to return. Her gaze drifted over the trees.

Everything was so beautiful and peaceful. Krista set her fears free to drift away on the light breeze and enjoyed the ride. What lay ahead would still be there when she arrived. It would do her no good to worry about it beforehand. She fingered Kallairion under her robe. All was well, it assured her. She lost herself in the pleasure of the ride.

Three days seemed to disappear. They made frequent stops in which Krista would duel with Jana, Alise, or Elsa, to keep her loosened up and ready. After a quick bite to eat, they would continue on. In the mornings and evenings, the other women took care of the tasks for camp while Krista drilled. Halayne was watchful, making sure that she ate well and rested. Several times Halayne made way to talk with Krista, counseling and reassuring her. But most of the trip they remained quiet, what lay ahead looming heavily on everyone.

With the mid-morning sun of the fourth day warming the riders, Halayne signaled for one final stop. "Arlanda is not far ahead now. We will reach there before lunch."

They all dismounted, but this time, Krista's practice did not start. Quietly, the other women led the horses away from Halayne and Krista.

Once they were alone, Halayne addressed her. "Your destiny is near at hand, Guardian." Looking directly at Krista, she continued. "Remember, you are not the Guardian by mistake. You were not chosen in error. You have met every challenge set before you. This is just another.

Krista hugged the woman. "I am frightened." She let the words escape her lips.

"And you should be. Do you not think that your father, your grandfather, or his father were not frightened? That is to be expected. You would be foolish not to be, just do not let the fear overcome you. Use it to strengthen and alert you. And, remember, you pick the time to confront Kuel. Do it when you feel it is right. But a warning—keep yourself covered and hidden from now on. Do not say a word until you are ready to make your stand. Hopefully, he will not have time to figure out who you are."

She paused and then continued. "When we first arrive, we will ask for a place to rest. As the word of our arrival will no doubt have reached the castle before we get there, I am sure they will have rooms waiting for us. No one will think anything if we choose to remain in our chambers tonight, but the decision will be up to you."

Krista nodded and found herself receiving another hug. Halayne turned and walked back to the group. Left alone, Krista took a steadying breath. She was almost home, almost back to Garion. Her heart leapt with excitement before the thought of facing Kuel slipped back in.

"I can do this. I will do this," she said to herself. Raising her hood, Krista pulled the cloak around her so that it covered her completely. With another deep breath, she joined the others and mounted her horse. The circle was formed once more around her.

Krista had not felt so odd or uncomfortable entering the castle gate since her first arrival, except that the first time no one took any notice of her. This time, the streets of the village were lined with people trying to see. The crowd hummed with hushed whispers of speculation.

It surprised her that nothing seemed to have changed since she left, until she realized how silly it was to think there would be any changes. She'd only been gone a fortnight. Then, from under her hood, Krista caught sight of Garion on the main steps with his parents. He looked well but sad. Something inside her shattered. She wanted to slide from her horse and run to him.

Pulling her eyes away, she searched the crowd. She didn't have to look far to find what she wanted. The image of Roud stood not far away, arms folded across his body. He watched with an amused look.

A shudder ran through her. Her eyes saw her instructor, a man she trusted and respected, but within, she knew different. Picturing the still body lying in the cold depths of the cave, she forced herself to remember this was not the man she knew. It was not a man at all, not a true man. He was evil, there to corrupt, to enslave, and to destroy them. It was her responsibility to stop him.

Bringing the horses to a stop at the front steps, the women dismounted, forming a protective circle around Krista so that no one could get close to her. Halayne stepped forward to greet the king as he came down the steps. The king bowed.

Krista didn't pay attention to the rest of the formalities as Garion had also moved down the steps into the line of vision she had under the hood. With Elsa's tall body shadowing her, Krista peered around at the prince.

He listened attentively to his father and Halayne. His eyes drifted over the group with interest mostly centered in Krista's direction. She pulled back slightly so he couldn't catch a glimpse, but it was not necessary for the cloak did its job, covering her completely. Turning her attention finally to the king and Halayne, she found that the conversation was ending. Sir Herald stepped forward to direct them to their chambers.

A few minutes later, Krista settled on the bed in the room she was directed to. Everything felt as shadowed as she had been under the cloak. An eerie unease seemed to linger around corners, unseen by the eye but sapping the life from the air itself.

It was all a dream, it had to be. None of this could be true. She tipped her head up to face the ceiling. Tears filled her eyes until they spilled down her cheeks.

Lying on the bed, she cried. The time had come. It wasn't a dream. All was about to be decided. She would denounce Kuel. Face him in battle. A battle she was as prepared for as she could be. Yet, a battle that she wondered if she could in any way possibly win.

She hated to admit it, but inside she knew it was true. She tried to chasten herself. That was not the attitude to go into a fight with. It had been one of the first lessons that Darm had taught her, to have faith in herself. Just never get so confident that you think you can't lose, for then you will make mistakes.

At her side, Kallairion pulsed, breaking through her fears. Pushing up, she wiped away the tears with the back of her hand. Lifting the robe, she drew Kallairion, laying it on the bed. It shimmered and changed. She fingered every detail of the greatsword. "How?" Was all she could get out, and the tears of self-doubt came again.

She didn't know how much time passed while Kallairion held her mind and soothed her soul. There had been no words, just the warm feeling and its strange tingle. Krista wondered if she must've slept for a while because, when she looked around, it was almost dark. With a shimmer, Kallairion changed, and Krista slid it back into its scabbard.

With her movement in the room, the door opened, and Halayne announced supper was waiting. Explaining they had decided to eat in the room, and the food had been delivered. Krista noticed that the food appeared to have been prepared with extra special care. Everything was cooked to perfection and was amazingly delicious. The conversation in their chambers was kept light; mostly talking about the wonders of the castle, the food, and how they'd never been treated so well.

Getting her fill, Krista excused herself. Lifting the hood of her cloak, she moved to the balcony, pausing a moment before stepping out. The sky was streaked with the flaming hues of the setting sun, but it lost her attention as soon as she noticed a solitary individual moving through the garden.

Loneliness hung over Garion's movements. She knew he was missing supper and wondered what had brought him to the gardens. Was it the sadness she had noticed on his face earlier? Was it the same sadness that had taken her for walks in the sisters' garden? Could he be missing her? Stepping to the rail, she leaned forward, stretched out, wishing she could go to him, but it was not yet time.

Garion paused. Turning, he looked up at the balcony. From that distance, there was no chance of him recognizing her, but she pulled back into the shadows as he took a couple steps in her direction.

He stopped, looking up to her. Krista couldn't take it any longer. Turning, she went inside.

Chapter Nineteen

To Krista's surprise she went to sleep as soon as she stretched out on the bed and slept peacefully the whole night through. She woke early with doubts no longer clouding her mind. Today was the day. She would confront Kuel, then all would be decided and done. Either she would win, or she would die.

She dressed with great care, making sure that nothing fit too tightly, restricting her movements, or was so loose as to be in her way. She ate lightly of what was left from the night before. With Kallairion, she went through the old drill Darm had taught her long ago, warming her muscles. Then she sat quietly in her room contemplating her moves while waiting for the others to get ready for breakfast. She had prepared and was as ready as possible.

People crowded the great hall when the group of ladies entered. Krista was hoping it would be empty but knew that everyone was curious about the group of women and wanted to be around if anything was said.

From under her cloak, again her eyes rested on Kuel. He stood back out of the rays of light. *A beast waiting in the shadow,* the thought ran through Krista's mind. Her attention moved to the royal family, as the Sisters of Laire all curtsied in unison.

After the assurance from Halayne that their stay had been most pleasant, the king announced breakfast was ready to be served. Krista's eyes found their way to Garion. This time, she couldn't take them away as his locked on her. Even as everyone moved to be seated, the two remained fixed in place. The whole room hushed, watching the pair. Halayne started to move toward her but stopped as Garion stepped forward.

The ache within Garion soothed with each step he took, drawing him nearer to the cloaked woman. Facing each other, he stopped.

Still in silence, she took a single step forward, bringing her less than a foot away from him. Lifting a cloaked arm, she reached out and touched his cheek, a caress that ended when her fingers neared his lips. He turned his head slightly to kiss them.

A gasp spread through the room. Everyone waited for what would happen next. Garion raised his hands to the hood of the cloak, carefully lifting and lowering it to reveal the young woman it concealed. The short brown hair, if anything, accentuated her high cheekbones and large, beautiful blue eyes.

"Krista." Her name escaped his lips as a whisper, but the room was so quiet it could be heard throughout.

"Garion." Though her answer wasn't much louder, it brought an avalanche of gasps.

"I was beginning to think you would never come back. I am so sorry. I did not mean to hurt you."

A smile crested her lips. Love burned in her eyes for a minute before it shifted to a look of seriousness. "I told you I would always be here when you were in danger. Besides, that is not why I left. I was being foolish when I got upset, but that does not matter now."

"I do not understand. Why did you leave, and why did you return like . . . this?" He extended his arm toward the group of women, not quite sure how to say it.

Reaching out, she took his hands. "Garion, Roud's dead." Her voice was soft, full of feeling.

"What?" The revelation hit home. For the first time, his eyes broke from her, moving not far away to where the form of Roud stood, then back to her.

"I saw his body," a tear broke free and trickled down her cheek, "In a cave in the mountains of Han."

Garion's eyes closed, with a single nod, he opened them.

"Garion, what is going on here?" his father questioned from behind. "Who is this? And what is she saying? Roud is dead? Roud's right here."

Krista let go of Garion's hands, looking to the king. "Your Majesty," she bowed slightly. "That is not Roud. It is Kuel."

At the name, a gasp ran through the crowd. The queen grasped the king's arm, dropping to her seat, going deathly pale.

The king took his wife's hand to comfort her. "Young woman, that is far from—"

"Father," Garion cut him off forcefully before he turned his attention back to Krista.

She started to reach out to touch his cheek again as if it was involuntary, then her hand stopped in midair. "I am sorry. I do . . ." The words "love you" caught in her throat. Now was not the time.

Turning abruptly, she took several steps in Kuel's direction. "The game is over." She lifted her voice, addressing the being. "Roud is dead." Around him, the people pulled slowly back, not truly sure if they believed, but the possibility making them wary.

Roud's hand came up. His fingers moved along the underside of his chin in thought, then stopped, his face breaking into a cruel smile. His laughter broke out, echoing through the room. "You, Chosen, have always been annoying, ruining my fun. But no matter, I was getting a little bored. It is time this ended."

His voice turned cold. His laughter echoed around the room in thunder once more. Suddenly, it stopped. "That knowledge shall do you no good, because you, our melancholy prince, will be the first to die. Then your parents and all will be mine."

The whishing sound of a guard's swords being drawn cut the air, but Kuel took no heed, laughing again. "You cannot really expect to stop me," he roared. "No one can stop me."

From the side, one of the guards stepped forward, only to be thrown back with a swift blow of Kuel's arm, though he didn't touch the man. The guard fell with a groan. Several people grabbed him, pulling him to safety as everyone pressed back against the walls, watching Kuel move to the center of the floor.

"Who would challenge me?" He looked around the room drawing his sword, daring all to step forward. "Come, Prince. Meet your death and the start of my reign."

Krista saw Garion flex and start to step forward but across the room, Marcus's voice called out.

"I will challenge you."

Kuel turned to him. "You! You would be no challenge," the being mocked.

Krista was thankful for the distraction. With a quick breath to steel herself, she took several paces forward, raising her hand to undo the cloak. Kuel turned back toward her as she let the cloak drop from her shoulders to the ground revealing her slender, young form dressed in shirt and breeches, the sword fastened around her waist.

"Then I, as the prince's companion and guardian, accept the challenge." Sliding Kallairion free, she took her stance between Kuel and Garion.

Kuel, like everyone else in the room, looked over her form. Every curve announced that she was a woman.

"Kris, no!" Garion commanded, taking a step toward her.

"Garion, stay back."

"I cannot let you—" he started to object.

"Garion, this is my fight, my duty, we both knew that one day it would come."

He reached out to her. "But . . ."

Kuel broke through. "Oh, how delightful. The prince's companion has been a girl all this time. I never guessed. If I had known, I would have played you differently when I tried to break you. You were quite difficult, but can you honestly expect to stand against me?"

"I can. And I will." Krista raised her chin, meeting him with determination.

He laughed again. "Then come, girl. I must say you are amusing."

Moving to the center of the floor, they circled each other, swords held ready. Kuel taunted, trying to bring her in. Krista held back, waiting, watching for his attack. When it came, it was a shower of blows, one coming right after the other. Each strike Krista was there to meet and return her own. When the hail stopped, Kuel stepped back, surprise shown on his face.

"I always knew you were good, but how good, you never let it be known, did you?"

Before she could answer, he came forward again. Krista blocked, struck out, blocked, and blocked again, watching for an opening. She went in only to meet his sword. For a fraction of an instant, she was pulled off balance, only bringing her sword around in time to deflect the blow. Still not steady, the force of the impact knocked her over. Krista rolled with the fall ending up down on one knee, ready for Kuel's next strike.

"Nice. I must say, I am impressed. Beauty. Courage. Fight." He accentuated each word. "I think I will not kill you." He walked around her, looking her up and down with an appraising gaze.

Carefully she stood. Her sword facing him at all times, ready for his next move.

"Yes, I will not kill you. You will bow before me, as my bride." Kuel's face pulled into a twisted smile waiting for a reaction, lifting his eyes to Garion who was now positioned over her shoulder.

Behind her, she heard Garion move. "Garion, stop! He is just playing with us," she called, pointing Kallairion at Kuel.

"Oh, but I am serious. Besides, you might as well let him come. With the wave of my hand, I could destroy you, and the prince's life would be mine. Do you really wish to throw away your life for nothing?"

"I do not intend to throw my life away. I do intend to stop you."

Kuel's laughter again started low, rolling into a loud rumble. It stopped the same instant his free hand reached toward Garion. Kallairion rang with a warning in her hands. The air around Kuel's hand began to glow like a ball of lightening, then the glow stretched out.

"Kallairion," Krista called. From the sword, the golden glow appeared, intersecting Kuel's glow with a burst of power that rocked the room as they met. The force sent both Kuel and Krista to the ground. The people huddled back shielding their eyes from the flash.

Kuel shook his head, stunned, as he rose, now glaring at Krista. "Impossible!" he growled as she made it to her feet. "Kallairion is gone. All the champions are dead."

Krista took advantage of his hesitation to move. "Are they or have you made a mistake? Next time you kill an innocent baby, you'd better make sure you kill the right one." She came forward, attacking with fury and pent-up feelings.

She drove him back. He struggled to meet her blows. Bringing Kallairion around in a crescent, she slashed across his left arm. With a roar, the whole castle rumbled, sending several people to the floor. He swung at Krista, but she brought Kallairion around to block. The force caused her to stumble back. Under her feet, the ground shifted, knocking her to the floor.

Kuel pulled himself up straight. "You will die, Champion, as will they." He flicked his hand toward the royal couple. "You have learned to shield, but how many can you shield at once? The king and queen." From Kuel's hand, a ball of power shot out toward the royal couple, only to burst short.

At Krista's command, Kallairion's shield blocked it.

"Your prince!" Kuel yelled. The burst came again, forcing Krista to shift the shield to Garion. "Or yourself!"

The blast came so suddenly, she hardly got the shield to form as energy impacted with her, sending her rolling across the ground. She had no time to recover as Kallairion's warning rang. With her will, she sent the shield back toward the king and queen.

Through the hall, screams of the women echoed as the next burst headed at Krista. Rolling to the side, she dodged, managing to keep from being hit directly, but the force of the power tumbled her across the hard floor. Kallairion skidded free as she came to a halt face down.

Krista stirred, trying to pull herself up, but nothing in her body wanted to work. She fought to catch her breath. Her head rang. She tried to clear her mind. She hurt. With a slight gasp, Krista forced her head up enough to focus on Kuel walking toward her. She pushed herself up only to fall back to the cold stone floor. Kuel was so intent on her that he didn't notice Garion as he moved toward Kallairion.

"Kuel," Garion shouted, posed ready to fight with Kallairion in his hand. Kuel faced him with amusement, anticipation filling his face again.

"So our prince does have fight, but it will do you no good. Kallairion will not heed your commands. You cannot wield it. Still, it will be more pleasurable to kill you this way."

Striking out, Garion brought Kallairion up to block as Kuel brought his sword down on him. The swords locked together as the two men fought for the advantage. "For my love of Krista, I will not let you kill her." Garion pushed back with all his might, sending the being stumbling back a couple of steps.

Kuel eyed him carefully as they each took their stance. Kuel made a small, testing strike, which Garion swatted away. "You have grown a great deal since I last faced you. Do you remember it still? You tried to stand against me then also." Kuel let out a low laugh. "This is just as feeble. You have no hope and no true champion to save you."

Kuel came forward in a wave of blows. Garion met them all but couldn't gain the upper hand. Krista's sword felt light in his hands. He wished with all his might it was larger. With a shimmer, Kallairion changed, growing heavier. Kuel noticed the change and pulled back.

"No, it is not possible! You have no right!" He struck out.

Garion was there with the block, bringing Kallairion out, down and around, cutting deep into Kuel's side. No blood came, but Kuel roared and the ground rumbled. Garion stumbled back but immediately lunged forward. Kallairion sliced down at Kuel only to meet metal. Both bodies groaned with the impact, forcing each other back.

The two circled in battle. Coming together, they locked again. Kuel struck his elbow out, catching Garion in the throat, and knocked him back across the floor, fighting to catch his breath. With anger, Kuel formed energy in his hand ready to cast it at Garion who was pulling himself from the ground.

Krista dove for Garion. The instant she touched him, a dome of golden light formed around them. As Kuel's blast hit, the whole room disappeared. No longer were people crowded around. There was nothing, not even a building, tree or rock that they could see—just them and Kuel.

Kuel looked around, disturbed but not shocked. Krista found herself clinging to Garion's arm as he stood. "Where are we?" he whispered in her ear, one hand on Kallairion, the other massaging his neck.

She shook her head slightly. "I do not know. I was wishing I was some place where it was just him and me, with no one else to get hurt."

"It looks like Kallairion agreed, but I get to remain part of it."

She caught his brief look before her attention went back to Kuel. Her hand slid down Garion's arm to take Kallairion. Garion tried to pull his hand free, but she caught it.

"Garion, this is my duty. Everything has come to this."

Kuel attacked, using their distraction to his advantage. Kallairion's warning hit Krista first, and her shield caught the blow of his sword. The pain the blow held seemed to sear through her. Garion's free arm went around her, holding her up while she sliced through the next bolt of energy with Kallairion. Energy burst back against Kuel.

Kuel howled in pain. All his strength seemed to blow back against them, knocking them to the ground, forcing them apart. Power snapped and crackled through the air. Stunned, Krista's body shook with waves of energy that sought to overcome her consciousness, leaving her helpless as she watched Garion stagger to his feet, Kallairion in his hand, making his way toward Kuel.

Sluggishly Kuel faced him and stretched out his hand, but no glow came, only a shriek of agony. With fury, Kuel charged Garion, swinging blow after blow. Garion staggered under their power and fought to meet each strike. Kuel brought the blade down, sliding it across Kallairion. It deflected to the side and sliced through the prince's shirt into his arm.

In pain, Garion brought the sword down across Kuel's abdomen. Both staggered back. Garion struggled to change Kallairion to his good hand. Kuel straightened, then took a step forward, hatred shadowing his face.

In horror, a scream erupted from Krista as Kuel's hand glowed, gaining in intensity. Garion had no chance to block or dodge the blast that sent him flying back. Hitting the ground, he remained still.

"It is done!" Kuel yelled into the air, only to be drowned out by Krista's cry.

"No!" She came off the ground and scooped up Kallairion before Kuel could turn to meet her. For every strike he blocked, another came. Fury, pain, heartbreak flamed in each swing.

His sword came around, driving her back, but she wouldn't relent. His blade came down slicing a cut down her leg. Blood soaked her breeches. She gasped, her heart pounded, causing a ringing in her head.

Bringing Kallairion around, she swung it back across his body, then she fell forward, driving Kallairion into the beast with all the strength and weight she had. All around the ground rumbled, throwing her off balance into Kuel, then he was gone. She crashed to the ground.

All was still.

For a moment, she could do no more than gulp breaths of air, waiting for the pounding in her head to cease. Using Kallairion to push herself off the ground, she staggered to Garion, dropping beside him. Trembling, she reached out to touch his face. There was no movement in him, not even the gentle breath that showed life.

"No!" The tears broke, flooding from her as she crumpled to his body, her own body racked with sobs. Lifting her head, she screamed into the empty space. "No! It is not fair! It cannot end like this!"

Around her the air shimmered, colors swirled, gathering into shapes so bright she couldn't bring herself to look, but she knew she was surrounded by some kind of beings.

"It is over, Guardian, you have done well." The soothing sweet voice flowed all around her.

"I failed. He is dead," she forced out through tears. "You have taken everything from me. I have done all that was asked. You cannot take him. Not now that it is all over." She dropped her head to the lifeless body.

"Guardian." Again the musical, gentle voice reached out to her.

"No!" she screamed back. "If anyone is to die, it is me. My duty is done, his has still . . ." The tears came harder. "I do not want to live without him."

"Then you are willing to give your life to him? The decision must be yours." The soothing voice cut through her. Krista's tears stopped as the words burned in her. Lifting her head, she looked up, squinting at the being in front of her.

Drawing in a shaky breath, she stumbled over the words. "He can live?"

"Kuel broke the rules set for him in killing the prince with his power rather than by the sword. You may heal him, if that is your heart's desire, but are you willing to give your life to him?"

"Yes." The words came out soft but sure.

"Take Kallairion in your hand and lay it on his chest, with your other hand pressed to his heart. Now, will him to live, just as you have given Kallairion your other desires, but give it with your whole heart. You must not break your touch with him, no matter what the pain."

Krista only nodded before closing her eyes. Within her, she thought of Garion, her love for him, his love for her, his arms around her, the warmth it brought. The warmth began to burn through her, searing her hands. She didn't need to open her eyes to know that Kallairion glowed. She longed to take her hand from the sword as the pain burned deeper.

The cut on her leg itched. She felt the tissue and the skin pull back together. She tried to ignore it and think only of Garion. Krista gasped at the pain, shuddering as his soothing touch floated through her. She no longer had strength to continue but the pain and burning were gone. She dropped her head to Garion's chest, exhausted. Tears trickled free as she felt his chest rise and fall under her head.

She had no idea how much time passed before she felt a hand touch her cheek, caressing it softly, wiping away the tears. The other arm tightened around her. Krista lifted her head just enough to meet Garion's gaze. His lips tilted up into a gentle smile. Relaxing back, she wanted nothing more than to die in his arms.

"No, Guardian, you may not die in his arms." The voice sounded around her, restating her thoughts. Garion pulled himself up into a sitting position, keeping her cuddled tight against him. The voice continued. "Your reward has been granted. The prince is healed."

Krista's arms slid around him, hugging him. She let go, bringing her head up. "I'm ready." She swallowed, trying to be brave.

"Then stand facing each other, holding Kallairion in your hands together. Its duty is done. It is time for Kallairion to return home."

Garion helped Krista rise. He seemed less confused than she as he faced her. His hand came up touching his fingers to her cheek, sliding them across to her lips. He stopped, smiling as she kissed them. Lowering his hand over hers, they held Kallairion between them. A tingling ran through Krista. She knew it was Kallairion's goodbye. In a shimmer, it was gone. Left in its place was a thin golden cord, lying across their hands.

"Now, it is time for the prince's reward for his efforts." One of the beings stepped forward. Krista was frozen in place as it reached out. Another tingle caught her breath and ran through her as the being placed her hand in Garion's. Taking the cord, it carefully wrapped the ends around her wrist. Crossing their hands, it wrapped the ends around Garion's. "I bind you together, never to be separated in life or death. She is yours, young prince. You have both done well. Make each other happy."

Krista suddenly felt even more confused. "I do not understand. I thought I was . . ."

"To die? No, Guardian, you have already given enough to set right what was wrong."

"But you asked for my life."

"Yes, to be given to him, not for him. Prince Garion's heart's desire was to have you for his wife. Since it is your life, you had to agree. We could not grant his wish if you were opposed, even though we knew in your heart you loved him. See, it was that love that allowed you to work together to defeat Kuel. Thank you again."

Weary and confused, Krista tried to make sense of what he was saying. "Do you mean all along, it was to come to this? All before me fought in vain?"

"No, Krista, each had the same ability. We cannot control free will. That is why even Kuel had the right to choose the path of evil. And, though we gave Kallairion to help defeat him, it was up to each person to use that ability. You have done well, Krista. Enjoy your love and your life. One last thing . . . look." The being stretched out its hand. There amidst them were glowing images of themselves standing together that seemed to reach out forever. "That is how your lives will be, going on forever, bound for eternity by your love."

Krista looked to Garion. He met her with a grin. "Will you now admit that you love me?"

Taking a breath, she slowly nodded, "I do love you."

"Finally." He bent forward, meeting her lips. Their whole bodies tingled as the kiss continued. Around them, the air shimmered. When it faded, they were back in the great hall, but for a moment, they took no notice.

The crowd watched in silence as the pair appeared, glowing in the middle of the room. No one knew what to do, what to say. They were still in shock from watching them disappear in a shimmer of light with Kuel a moment before. Now, they were back, locked in an embrace, with no sign of Kuel.

Parting, Krista and Garion looked around. Krista's eyes returned to Garion. "It is over." She could hardly believe it was true, but here she stood with Garion in the middle of the hall. No Kallairion, no Kuel.

If it weren't for the fact that she felt so weak and battered, she would have fled from the crowd even if it meant leaving the warmth of Garion's arms. Somehow, Garion seemed to sense her uneasiness. Wrapping his arms around her, he brought her tighter to him and tucked her under his chin.

"Garion?" His father's voice drew his attention.

Lifting his head slightly from Krista, with a nod Garion announced, "It is over. Kuel is dead."

Gasps and murmurs ran through the crowd.

"How?" was all his father managed to say.

"It is a long story, and I will tell you everything after I get Krista lying down to rest." He could feel her now sagging weakly against him.

"Krista . . . is Kris, your companion?"

"Yes, and Lord Vallon's daughter, the Champion of Kallairion."

Again, gasps and murmurs filled the room.

"Kallairion?" questioned his father.

"Taken back now that Kuel is gone. Please, just let me take Krista to my room to rest, and I will return and tell you everything. Lady Adele, will you stay with her?"

The woman came forward, reaching out fondly to brush back Krista's hair. "To your room?" She looked at him.

He met her grin with one of his own. "You do not expect me to take my wife anyplace else, do you?"

"Wife!" Shock burst from everyone in the room.

Garion smiled, having fun with the reaction. "Sealed by the Mighty Ones." He raised their wrists for everyone to see the golden thread still wrapped around them.

Krista stared at the thread. She shifted back from him then clung to his arms as dizziness swept over her.

"Enough." He drew his hand free to slide behind her knees. "Up you go." He lifted her up into his arms.

"You cannot carry me all the way to your room," Krista objected.

"I only died, which was actually quite restful, not like what conquering Kuel and healing me took out of you."

"Died!" the queen burst out.

"Garion!" Krista's chided. "Stop!"

He looked down, grinning at her. "You are right, it is a long story. We both could use some rest and time before it is all told. For now, it is enough to say you are my wife, and I love you."

Her smile warmed with great pleasure. "And I love you!" Sliding her arms up around his neck, she tilted his head down to receive her kiss. She let out a shaky sigh as she laid her head on his shoulder.

"What is it?" His voice came softly, rubbing away the tear on her cheek with his own cheek.

"I never thought it would ever be possible to be in your arms, to truly be yours. I do love you."

Before anything else could be said, Garion drew her up, kissing her. Everyone in the hushed room was forgotten. For Krista, being the Champion of Kallairion was no more. The only thing she wanted now was to be Garion's wife and his love forever.

About the Author

Alysia grew up in a small town, loving the outdoors, sports, and reading. She has always been a storyteller and started writing her own stories while she was in high school. She writes with a touch of intrigue, because she believes that the world needs more heroes, love, and adventure. She is not out to change the world with her writing, but she is hoping to touch lives and make someone's day a little better.

Alysia married an honorable man, and together they had five children. She is now a widow collecting grandchildren. She loves traveling and has had the opportunity of visiting many intriguing places that continue to provide ideas for her stories.

Scan to visit

alysiasknight.com